THE LOVE OF A LIBERTINE

THE DUKE'S BY-BLOWS BOOK 1

JESS MICHAELS

For everyone who ever feels like they made a mistake that couldn't be forgiven. And to Michael, who always forgives mine.

PROLOGUE

Spring 1811

R unning away from home in order to marry in secret had been a decision Elizabeth Margolis doubted from nearly the first moment she escaped into the night. But now, huddled before the fire in the tiny cottage, clenching and unclenching her fists before the flames, she dared to let herself believe it was a mistake.

It wasn't that she didn't care for Aaron Walters. She *did*, with every fiber of her being. She loved him, or at least she thought she did. She didn't have much experience with such things. She'd been taught by a tutor, and her small circle of friends was as sheltered as she was. But she read a lot of books and the feelings those books described when it came to love were certainly something close to what she felt.

And she had to love him now. She *had* to. After all, she had given herself completely to him the night before, when they stopped for the second time along the long road to Gretna Green and the marriage that awaited them there.

"You're being silly," she chastised herself softly.

"Silly about what, my love?"

She pivoted to find Aaron standing in the doorway of the small adjoining dressing room where he had been readying himself for bed. She shifted at the sight of him, his shirt undone and revealing his flat stomach, with his hair mussed. He was a handsome man, there was no denying that. And when she looked at him, some of her doubts faded.

They *would* be happy.

"My nerves," she explained with as bright a smile as she could manage. "I only wish we could have made it across the border tonight and to Gretna Green at last. I'm tired of this madcap escape."

"So anxious to be my wife," he drawled as he entered the main room of the cottage and reached out to touch her face with just his fingertips.

She forced herself to stay right where she was and allow that caress. She wasn't quite accustomed to being touched so intimately and knew she needed to learn. Aaron didn't like it when she hesitated, and she so wanted to make him happy.

"I am," she said, hoping that saying those words would make the feeling clearer. "My only regret is that my brother isn't here. That we had to deceive him."

Walters' face fell and his hand dropped away from her as he scowled. "We've been over and over this, Lizzie," he said, his tone a bit sharper than it had been. "I grow tired of repeating it. The Duke of Brighthollow is a snob."

"No!" Lizzie burst out. "Hugh is stern, yes, but he isn't—"

Aaron ignored her and spoke louder. "He would *never* accept a common man such as myself to be linked to you forever. This is the only way we can be wed. And he will forgive you, will he not? He loves you *so much*, or so you tell me every day."

She worried her lip at his suddenly hard tone. She'd upset him and she didn't like that. So she moved toward him, hoping to placate him. His eyes lit up as she did so, tracking her movements with what felt like an almost predatory light.

"I know you're right," she whispered. "Hugh can be protective, but once he sees how happy we are together, he will forgive the method of our union."

She hoped that was true. She did adore her older brother, as serious as he could be. After her parents' untimely deaths, he had all but raised her and was more father than sibling. She missed him and his kind, steady counsel desperately.

Aaron interrupted her thoughts by reaching out to catch her hand. He drew her forward a few more halting steps, then touched it to his bare chest. Her hands shook as she wound them around his neck, and he drew her closer as he looked down at her.

"I don't think we should talk about your dear brother anymore, my love," he drawled. "I have far more pleasant activities to occupy our time before tomorrow, when our marriage will be complete."

She smiled, though the expression felt false. "Will it be like last night?" she whispered. "P-Painful?"

His brow wrinkled. "Every woman experiences pain the first time, Lizzie. Something about God's punishment for the apple or some nonsense. But it will get better as you accept it more. One day you may even come to like what we share. Crave it."

She worried her lip again. She did like the parts that led up to the claiming. The kissing was very nice. Some of the touching felt good. But the act itself? She couldn't imagine she would ever long for that the way he said she would. But perhaps if she had more practice…

He smiled at her and she relaxed a little, lifting up on her tiptoes to seek a kiss. He lowered his head, but before he could touch his lips to hers, there was a great crash at the door.

Lizzie couldn't hold back a scream as she clung tighter to Aaron. They watched as the wood splintered and the lock broke, allowing her brother to tumble into the room. She stared at Hugh, unable to speak as he straightened to his full height and ran a hand through his curly, light brown hair. He stared straight back at her, standing in Aaron's arms, her sins laid out for him to see. She dropped her stare in shame and humiliation.

Aaron, though, seemed less concerned by her brother's unexpected arrival. He stared directly at Hugh and smiled. "Brighthollow, we did not expect you. Come to witness our wedding, have you?"

Lizzie caught her breath at his dismissive, jovial tone. It certainly didn't fit the circumstances and she tightened her grip on his arm to try to send him that message.

"Hugh," she whispered, blinking at the tears that flooded her vision.

Hugh's face had been bright with anger — no not anger. Rage. But she watched him take a few breaths, master his control. And then he extended his hand and said, "Lizzie, come."

His voice was so gentle. The same voice that had soothed her hurts and celebrated her successes over the years. The voice that always made her feel safe and loved. She leaned toward him and felt Aaron's fingers dig hard into her arm. Hard enough to hurt. She stared down at his fingers and let out a shuddering sigh. She pulled from his grip and went to her brother. He took her hand and gently pulled her behind him. Her hands shook as she clung to his.

"She is sixteen," Hugh said, his voice strained with upset.

Aaron arched a brow and shrugged one shoulder. "It hardly matters now."

Lizzie cringed at the coldness of her intended's tone. He was very angry, it seemed, at the interruption. And she supposed she ought to be upset, as well. Only she was so relieved to see her brother.

Hugh sucked in a deep breath through his nose. "Lizzie, go outside. I'll join you in a moment."

"No!" She tightened her grip on his hand as panic swelled in her. She needed to protect Aaron from Hugh's outrage. To take responsibility for her own part in this terrible mistake. It was too late to go back on it, at any rate, considering what she'd already done. She had

4

to do everything in her power to make peace between these two men who would soon be family. "Please, please, no, Hugh. Please don't. We—we care for each other."

Hugh jerked his gaze down at her and when he met her gaze, she saw home and peace. Tears gathered in her eyes, and one slid down her cheek.

He shook his head as he wiped it away gently. "He does *not* care for you," he whispered.

She flinched because when her brother said those words, they felt...true. Certainly when she glanced at Aaron, with his arms folded and a smirk on his handsome face, she didn't feel that he cared for her. It was like some balloon had burst, or a mask had fallen and now she questioned herself and all she had believed.

"One way or another, I get what I wanted, don't I?" Aaron said, his tone smug and mocking.

She stared at him, unblinking, trying to find the man she had told herself she loved. The man who had wooed her and convinced her to escape with him. He wasn't there.

"What—what do you mean by that, Aaron?"

He looked past Hugh to her. "My dear, I would have married you, and engaged in all those pleasures you and I had just begun to explore."

Heat flooded her cheeks at his crude revelation of their wicked activities. Hugh was a smart man, he had to have guessed what she'd done, but there was no need to flaunt it in his face.

And it generated a reaction. Hugh let out a grunt and lunged for Aaron. Lizzie clung to his arm with all her might, digging in her heels to keep him from pummeling Aaron to a pulp.

"But as you can see, Brighthollow will never allow it," Aaron continued with a shrug.

"I will not," Hugh said through clenched teeth.

Aaron tilted his head and held her stare. "So you remember that when you look at him. *He* took your future from you, not me."

Lizzie recoiled. Aaron wasn't trying to reason with her brother,

5

or declare his devotion. He was just trying to hurt Hugh. Worse, he was trying to make her hate her brother. Not that she ever could or would.

"Don't you *dare* act like a gentleman thwarted by my cruelty. You are only interested in my sister's inheritance," Hugh spat.

Those words landed in the room with a resounding thud. She stared at Aaron, waiting for him to deny the charge. Waiting for him to say anything that told her he truly cared for her. But he didn't, and the truth of everything began to rot its way into her chest, throughout her body, into every bit of her. She found herself curling inward, trying to make herself smaller, trying to escape what now felt so obvious.

"It *is* a very nice inheritance," Aaron said at last. "But I won't need it now."

"A-Aaron," Lizzie whispered and wished her tone weren't so broken, so vulnerable.

"What do you mean you won't need it?" Hugh asked, his voice shaking, this time with more than just anger. He sounded...afraid.

"My driver, the woman who owns this home, my friends... everyone knows that we snuck away under your very nose." Aaron sneered at Hugh. "And that we have been alone for several nights."

"But—" Lizzie began as nausea rose up inside of her, threatening to deposit onto the cheap carpet what little she'd eaten that day.

"Hush now, Lizzie, your brother and I are negotiating," Aaron said, never looking at her, never seeing how the sharpness and dismissiveness of his actions and words cut to her very spirit. Not looking because it was becoming evident he didn't *care*. "You don't want all this to be unleashed into Society, do you? This thing that will ruin all her chances at a future?"

Hugh released Lizzie's hand. He did not move forward, he didn't move at all. He just held the stare of a man she'd thought *was* her future and said, "I will kill you."

Aaron seemed unmoved by the threat. He just smiled. "Do it, go ahead. If you do, it will only make this scandal all the larger and drag down your entire legacy…along with her."

Lizzie lifted her hands to cover her mouth. God, Aaron was right. If what she'd done came out, if her ruin was public knowledge, it *would* affect Hugh's future as well. Her beloved brother, who had spent years carefully building his reputation, would lose it all because she had been such a little fool.

"What do you want?" Hugh asked, his voice choked.

"For you to do what any loving brother would do in this situation. You will pay me handsomely to cover up your sister's foolish, youthful mistake."

Lizzie staggered forward, her hands shaking even as she tried to manage the trembling. Her body tingling with all the consequences and lies and fears that now burst in her one after the other. This man, Aaron Walters, had done that to her. Callously. Because she was such a fool, such an easy target.

"How could you?" she whispered. "How?"

Aaron looked her up and down, his face devoid of any emotion he'd ever created to manipulate her. He shrugged. "You wouldn't understand. You've always had everything you ever wanted."

"Get out," Hugh said, his hand shaking as he pointed toward the door behind them.

Aaron grinned at her brother. "I'll go to your solicitor's in London in…shall we say two days? I will assume my very generous payment will be waiting for me there. Good evening, Your Grace," he said as he strode past them. At the door, he paused and turned back. "Oh, and Lizzie?"

She had been staring at the floor, tears streaming down her cheeks. She lifted her gaze toward this man she didn't know. This man who had played her like her favorite pianoforte. "Yes?"

"It's been a pleasure," he said, and walked out, laughing the whole way.

The moment he'd gone and shut the door behind himself, Lizzie tipped forward, dropping to her knees on the floor beside the bed.

She buried her head in her hands and began to weep, even though she hated herself for it. She didn't deserve to cry after what she'd done, but she couldn't stop. She'd thought there was a future for her out there. A happy life with the man who had just crushed her.

And all the while it had been nothing but a cruel illusion.

Hugh rushed to her, dropping down beside her and gathering her into his arms. She felt him rocking her and it brought her back to so many nights he had held her when she was a little girl, troubled by nightmares. But did she truly deserve that after what she'd brought down on their family? On their name?

"I'm sorry," she finally hiccupped against his shirt. "I shouldn't have thought he could truly love me. I was such a fool!"

Hugh slid a finger beneath her chin and tilted her face toward his. She saw all his kindness and gentleness and love for her, just as it had always been. He didn't hesitate. He didn't judge. He just looked sad on her behalf as he sighed, "No. Sweetest Lizzie, if you believed he cared for you and he took advantage, it is he who is the fool, not you." He cleared his throat. "But I do wonder why you thought you could not tell me about him."

She squeezed her eyes shut. "He encouraged me to sneak out. Said he'd tried to talk to you and that you were uncertain based on his lack of title."

"You thought I would be so cruel as to separate you from someone you truly loved, even if I believed he had your best interests at heart?" he asked gently.

She worried her lip at the question. "You are…protective. I know you wish for me to be safe. To be settled well. Oh, and now I've ruined everything," she said, putting her head back into her hands and returning to the sobs. "And after you've taken care of me for so long."

He wrapped his arms more tightly around her and smoothed a hand over her hair. "You've ruined nothing. I adore you, and being your older brother and your guardian has been one of the greatest joys of my life. Even if I have made a muck of it, it seems."

His kind words permeated the pain and slowly her sobs subsided. She rested her head on his chest and let out her breath in a long sigh. "You haven't made a muck of it. I thought he loved me. But he didn't. So what will happen now?"

Hugh hesitated a moment before he said, "I will pay him a handsome sum."

She flinched. Her brother might have the funds to do so—she knew he was well off and managed his estates as impeccably as he did anything else. But why should he suffer for what she'd done?

"Take it from my inheritance," she suggested as she pushed from his arms and used the edge of the bed to get back to her feet.

"I shall do no such thing. I have more than enough money. Once he is paid, we will...move on. If you think you can do that."

Her answer was no. She couldn't move on. What she'd done, who she'd trusted...that would haunt her for the rest of her days. She knew that. She could never forget it. But she lifted her chin slightly, so that Hugh wouldn't feel her regret.

"Yes," she lied.

She turned away and quickly fixed her hair, her cheeks hot once more as she thought of what she'd done with Aaron. With what Hugh must have guessed she had done. It was all so humiliating.

"I will do my best, Hugh," she said, forcing herself to look at him. "And I promise I will never do anything ever again that will force you into such a situation. I will look for respectability. I shall never seek out love. I promise."

With that, she turned toward the door and moved outside. It was only Hugh's horse waiting there, and she walked up to the beast and rested her head on his flank.

"I've ruined everything, Wren," she whispered, and the horse whinnied as if he agreed.

She pulled away and stared up at the stars in the cold sky above. Once upon a time she'd wished on those stars, for frivolous things and silly things and deeper things like love. But now she had to put those wishes away. Now she had to be more careful. More aware. More cynical.

The world was a dangerous place and she could never fall prey to a rogue again. She could never, ever again let herself be so seduced by a false promise of love or adventure. It was staid responsibility for her for the rest of her days.

As empty as that sounded, it was what she deserved in the end.

CHAPTER 1

July 1815

Morgan Banfield smelled his surroundings before he could manage to find the gumption to look at them. Piss, shit, vomit, fear…it all permeated the air around him and his stomach turned at the pungent odor of decay. The sounds pierced his throbbing head next. Screaming in the distance. A constant scream, not intermittent. Banging closer up, but not so close as to make him feel endangered.

He had a feeling he knew exactly where he was, but he didn't want to look. If he didn't look, perhaps he could just ignore the truth. That was a fun way to live. He was good at it.

He opened one eye and looked around. Cold stone walls. A flat, straw stuffed mattress on the floor that was stained with God knew what. And, of course, the steel bars that blocked his or any other man's escape from this hellhole.

Prison. Newgate, he guessed, based on the vague recollection of where he had been last night. Donville Masquerade, at first, looking for someplace to warm his cock. Once that had been dispatched with, he played cards. But he'd been sober there. At first.

Why had he started drinking?

It rushed back to him and he winced as he recalled who he'd seen at the game. A former friend he'd wronged. Gareth Covington. He'd been thrown off his game and he'd lost over and over. *That* was when he'd started drinking. Drank enough that he was asked to leave because he was causing a scene.

Morgan shook his head. He was very good at causing a scene. He'd moved on, he thought, to a different hell. One that wasn't quite so discerning as Donville. That was where things got very blurry. More cards, he thought. More drink. Shouting, he thought. Had Covington followed him?

He must have. Morgan vaguely remembered that angry face in the crowd. Had it escalated? It must have. He worked his jaw gently and winced. He'd gotten punched, it seemed. He lifted a hand to tap his face and found his left eye was also sore when he grazed it.

When he drank and gambled, it was a bad combination. Had he continued to lose? Probably. He usually did in that state. And if he couldn't pay…if that had led to a fight…well, depending on the man he'd swindled, that was a *very* good way to end up in gaol.

He flopped onto his back and dropped his arm over his eyes with a groan. "Shit."

"Indeed. Shit. You're certainly in it now," came a voice from the other side of the bars. It was a voice Morgan knew well. He didn't want to look at the man who owned it. And yet there was not really a choice.

He lowered his arm to find his half-brother, Robert Smithton, the Duke of Roseford, staring at him from outside the cell. He was dressed impeccably, just as he always was, not a hair on his head out of place. His expression was unreadable, though Morgan could tell he was irritated by the way his arms were folded tight across his chest.

"You look like shit, too," Roseford added, and there was a hint of a smile that tilted one side of his lips.

Morgan slowly sat up and tried not to react to the searing pain that burned through his skull and into every joint in his body. God's teeth, how much had he drunk?

"How did you know?" Morgan grunted. His mouth was so dry it was difficult to speak. "*I* didn't even know I was here."

That elicited a chuckle from Roseford. It was well known that Robert had lived a wild life, himself, for a very long time. Not recently, of course. Not since his marriage. "Do you actually need to guess?"

Morgan let out a long sigh. "Selina?" he asked.

Roseford inclined his head in the affirmative. Morgan slowly got up, hating the roil of his stomach as he steadied himself on the wall. Selina Oliver was another half-sibling shared by the two. They all had the same bastard of a father, along with God knew how many others. And while his relationship with Roseford was...strained and uncomfortable at times, his bond with Selina was much stronger. Perhaps because they were so much alike.

"I suppose she *was* there," he admitted.

"Yes, at Donville Masquerade," Roseford mused with a troubled expression. "Our sister is as wild as you are. Well, almost. But she isn't my problem...yet. You are."

Morgan pursed his lips and dropped his gaze to the floor. "No I'm not," he grumbled, wishing there wasn't so much revealing bitterness in his tone.

He had only come to know Roseford recently. They'd been kept apart as boys. Their father, the last duke, kept his by-blows far from his "real" son. Payments had come to keep everyone silent, rather than safe. Ten years ago, when his father died, Morgan had felt a genuine terror that those payments, which supported his education and his mother's small comforts, would dry up.

And yet they hadn't. Robert had continued to pay to support his father's bastards. He'd even managed to get doors opened for them in ways the previous Roseford hadn't tried. Morgan both appreciated his brother for making the effort...and resented him for wielding a power over him that Morgan couldn't make equal.

"We're only half-blood, Roseford," he muttered. "I'm not your problem."

"Yet here we are," Roseford said.

As he said it, a guard approached. At first Morgan thought he might be there to escort his brother from the premises, but instead the giant oaf of a man pulled a ring of keys from a chain around his waist. After a few seconds of fumbling, he opened the cell door and swung it wide, motioning Morgan from the unpleasant accommodations.

Morgan blinked at the offer of freedom and then glanced at his brother. "What?"

"Your debts are paid," the guard answered first, then flashed a rotten-toothed smile toward Roseford. "With our thanks for the extra, Your Grace."

Robert sniffed his response and turned, motioning to Morgan to follow. "Come along, Morgan."

Morgan looked around, but there seemed to be nothing he'd left behind in the nasty cell. He staggered after Robert, his stomach still roiling and his brain still a bit foggy from whatever had felled him last night. Normally he was capable of holding his liquor, so it must have been far more of a party than he recalled.

They weaved their way through the corridors, past men in cells in varying conditions. There were no words said until they exited the building at last and stood in the fresher air of the city. A cold rain drizzled down around them, and Morgan pulled his jacket closer and hoped he hadn't lost his fine great coat in his foggy night of sin.

Roseford's carriage came along at last. Roseford motioned him in, then said something to his driver before he joined Morgan. They were off in a flash and Roseford sat, silently staring at Morgan as they rode along.

If his brother had railed at him, Morgan would have preferred it. But when he sat silently, arms folded, gaze held firmly on Morgan's, it made him feel worse than he already did. Like he needed to defend himself.

"You were just as bad as me," he said at last.

Robert tilted his head back and let out a full, loud belly laugh. Morgan couldn't help but stare. It made his brother look younger, more wicked. He could see the man he would have liked to run the hells with, rather than the stern duke who held the purse strings and scolded.

"I was that," Roseford said at last. "I never ended up in Newgate, mind you...but close. I have changed, though."

Morgan shrugged. Everyone knew that story, even if he and Roseford weren't that close. "Oh yes. Your *great love*."

Roseford's eyes narrowed at his dismissive tone. "Yes. Katherine changed me. Or made me want to change myself, which is better. And you may scoff, but I would wish you the same luck that you could find someone like her."

"Hm," Morgan said, staring out the window into the distance. "Not interested."

Robert arched a brow. "You don't seem interested in much."

Morgan didn't respond as the carriage pulled through the gate of Robert's London estate and came to a stop on the circular drive. Robert cleared his throat as the carriage door opened. "Come in."

Morgan shifted. He was in no mood to be clucked over and lectured to by a man who had been known as a libertine just three years prior. He wanted to go home, take a bath and try to remember what exactly had put him in the state he'd woken in.

"No," he said. "I—"

Robert pivoted back and stuck his head into the carriage again. His dark eyes were lit up with emotion now. Frustration. Anger. Fear. Fear for him? Morgan couldn't believe that. They weren't that close. Why would Roseford care what happened to him, beyond how it affected his own reputation?

"It wasn't a fucking question, Morgan," Robert snapped. "Get your arse out of my carriage and come into my parlor. *Now*."

For a moment, Morgan thought to refuse. He'd had one fight in the last twenty-four hours, why not two? He had a feeling Robert could scrap, no matter how fine his waistcoat was. But in the end, he couldn't stomach it. He trudged from the carriage and followed his brother into the beautiful house for the dressing down he knew he deserved.

"Good morning, Jenner," Robert said, bright as could be.

Jenner inclined his head. "Welcome back, Your Grace. Mr. Banfield, I see you have no coat."

Morgan glared at his impassive face. "No coat, no gloves, no hat. I'm every bit the mess I seem to be."

"Very good, sir," Jenner said, without inflection or reaction. "Your Grace, Her Grace and Miss Oliver are in the blue parlor."

"Excellent. Will you have a bath prepared for my brother?" Robert asked.

Morgan huffed out a breath. "I don't need you to get a bath for me, Roseford. I can go home and do it myself."

Roseford ignored him and strode up the hall, leaving Morgan no choice but to follow. He heard feminine voices in the distance. Musical laughter. As they entered the room, he saw Roseford's wife, Katherine, sitting with their sister, Selina. Their heads were close together and they were giggling like schoolgirls.

"In the face?" Katherine was saying.

"Where else was I to do it?" Selina asked as she took a sip of her tea. "I wasn't trying to maim him, just put him in his place."

"I'm certain you put *any* man in his place without even trying," Roseford said as he swept into the room. The women got up and he crossed to press a brief kiss to Selina's cheek. Then he caught Katherine's hand and brought it to his lips. "I'm back."

"So I see," Katherine said, placing her fingers to her husband's cheek.

Morgan scowled. If his brother had brought him here in order to show him the joys of the bond he had with his wife, he was wasting everyone's time. Not that Morgan didn't like Katherine. He did like her, enormously. No one could deny her kindness and welcoming demeanor, nor question her utter beauty. She had come through a great deal, it was rumored, but she didn't seem embittered by it all. Morgan sometimes wondered how she did it.

"I found him," Robert said, motioning to Morgan, who still stood in the doorway.

Selina moved to him with a soft smile. She caught his hand and squeezed briefly. "Good morning. You look terrible and you smell worse."

"I hear I have you to thank for sending the nursemaid to collect me," Morgan said with a frown for her, even as he squeezed her hand in return.

I'm sorry, she mouthed, though she looked anything but as she flitted away to the sideboard, where she poured him coffee without asking how he took it. Unlike his relationship with Robert, his bond with Selina had been established years ago and had always been strong. They were so very alike.

Katherine approached him next. She flitted her gaze over him and her concern was written more gently on her face. "You weren't injured? You're well?"

Blood heated Morgan's cheeks at her question, asked with such sincerity. That connection she created with her kindness wasn't one he'd sought very often. So he flashed her a smile that pretended away any negative response to her query. "I'm right as rain, Your Grace."

Her lips pressed together and she looked unconvinced, but she nodded regardless. "So you say. I'm just glad you're here."

She seemed honest in that response even as she stepped away. She moved to Robert's side and touched his arm, lifting her gaze to him and creating a world of unspoken communication. Robert's expression relaxed and he smiled at her with pure adoration.

Then his gaze turned to Morgan and all the softness bled away. "I'm concerned about you," he said.

Morgan rolled his eyes and strode over to the sideboard. "I need a bloody drink."

"That's what started all this, isn't it?" Robert snapped, and Morgan felt him watching him as he dug under the sideboard for a bottle of whisky.

He came up with it in his hand and slammed it on the tabletop before he pivoted to face his brother. "I know I wasn't at my best," he barked. "I'm not a fool, no matter what you think of me. But I don't need a father, *Roseford*. And if I did, it wouldn't be you."

Roseford flinched, as did Selina at Katherine's side, and for a moment they all stood in the wake of Morgan's imprudent retort. One he wished he could take back as he saw its impact. Too much, too far.

The story of his life.

Robert drew in a long, shaky breath and Morgan waited to be kicked out of his parlor once and for all. Instead, his brother ran a hand over his face as if he were very tired. Then he said, "I would never try to be that to you," Robert said softly. "I'm too young, for one."

Morgan smiled slightly at the attempt at the joke. It cleared the room of some of its tension. "You're seven years older than me. Thirty-three is ancient."

Robert shook his head. Seemed he wasn't willing to play away the serious issues at hand as easily as it had originally seemed. He glanced at Selina and Katherine, almost with uncertainty.

"Morgan, when you started having trouble last year, when I got wind of...of the problems you'd caused. Of the consequences you were about to face, I never judged you, did I?" Roseford asked.

Morgan flinched. *That* was how the two of them had come to meet face to face. He'd gotten into some trouble with that same friend who had been at the club last night. Roseford had been the only place to turn in order to avoid...well, to avoid a dire outcome, indeed.

"You didn't," Morgan agreed through clenched teeth. "Though it appears you intend to do so now."

To his surprise, Roseford's expression softened. "No," he said quietly, holding Morgan's gaze. "I would never. Not only because I have no leg to stand on when it comes to behaving badly."

At the fireplace, Katherine let out a tiny snort and Robert shot her a playful glare.

"But also," he continued, "Because I have no idea of what would make you feel you have to behave in this manner. I know you've lost in your life—"

Morgan held up a hand. "I will not discuss that with you."

Robert inclined his head, though Morgan thought he saw a flash of hurt in his eyes before he hid it. "Very well. Perhaps one day you'll trust me with some part of yourself that isn't the act you present to the world. Or not. That's your choice. What *isn't* your choice is how your behavior affects those around you."

"Like you," Morgan sneered.

Roseford shrugged. "Yes. Me and our family name—"

"It's not my family name," Morgan interrupted.

"Morgan," Selina said softly from behind them. When he glared at her with the same ferocity he had gifted their brother, she shook her head. "Glare daggers at me all you like, but Robert is not the same as our father. He doesn't deserve such censure."

Morgan pursed his lips. "Perhaps not," he conceded with great effort.

Robert sighed. "I can take the censure, I assure you. My greater concern is that you are wrecking yourself and you have been for some time. Do you deny you are running through your money?"

Morgan folded his arms. "Checking up on me, I see."

"What choice do you give me?" Robert threw up his hands. "Yes, the account is one I can look in on and I choose to do so. It is obvious you need a settling influence, Morgan. To find your place in the world by one way or another."

Morgan stared at him, confused by the true worry of Roseford.

He didn't have many people left in his life that truly gave a damn about him. He didn't let most people close enough to care or to damage. He knew better than to be such a fool.

So he turned, as he always did, to frivolity to mask the darker emotions, to put up the wall he required. "Are you arranging a marriage for me?"

Selina snorted, and even Katherine laughed as she stepped up next to Robert and placed a hand on his forearm a second time. "I think your brother has something else in mind, Morgan."

"Have you ever met my friend Hugh Margolis, the Duke of Brighthollow?"

Morgan shifted at the question. His brother had a group of friends, everyone knew about them and their close bond. Everyone said they were like brothers...and Morgan hated that the description stung him. He didn't *want* to be brothers with Roseford. So why the hell did he care if Robert found other men to care about in that way?

"I think I've met him in passing," Morgan said with a shrug. "Stuffy fellow, yes?"

Robert laughed and glanced at Katherine like that was some great joke. "Once I might have said so myself. But no, just honorable. It's hard for people like us to recognize that sometimes, but there's great value in it."

"What does it have to do with me?" Morgan asked, stifling a yawn in the hopes his disinterest would move this conversation along. He wanted to get out of here and find a bath and a bed.

Robert held his gaze. "He's in the market for a new man of affairs."

There was something in his brother's tone that brought Morgan up short. "And?" Roseford didn't answer, just kept staring, and Morgan jolted in understanding. "Wait, me? You *can't* mean me."

But it was obvious that was exactly what Roseford meant. "It would settle you to have a vocation. Brighthollow intends to return to his country estate for a few weeks, so it would also take you away from London and its bad influences. You need that."

"What I need is a stiff drink and a fuck," Morgan muttered, and then jerked his gaze to Katherine. "Apologies, Your Grace."

Katherine fought a smile. "I have heard the word before."

Selina winked at him. "Wait, do you have no apologies for me?"

Morgan rolled his eyes. "*You* invented the word. And you can't tell me you support this nonsense. Me, going to work for some toff?"

Selina's playful demeanor faded and she shot Robert and Katherine a quick glance. The couple seemed to understand it, for Robert sighed and escorted Katherine across the room to the window, where they stood together, heads close. Katherine was talking to him, low and gentle. Soothing him, it seemed.

And Morgan was left with his sister. Selina slipped up to him and took his hand again. She smiled, but the expression didn't quite meet her eyes. She had softened, which was a rare thing, indeed. Selina, like himself, was expert at keeping herself separate from difficult emotions and tenuous connections.

Which meant she took this very seriously, indeed.

"Morgan," she said, her voice low. "Perhaps a few months ago, I would have stood here at your side and battled Roseford about this subject. I would have claimed everything was fine and the danger was manageable."

"You're not going to do that now?" Morgan pressed.

She shrugged. "A few months ago, Nicholas almost died. He's still in grave danger."

Morgan shifted. Nicholas Gillingham was one of the legion of their bastard siblings. He was Morgan's polar opposite: honorable, proud. He had served in the King's Army and been badly injured in the Battle of Toulouse, nearly died.

"How is he?" he whispered.

Selina blinked, as if she were fighting uncharacteristic tears.

"He's...better. There's still danger to his life, and pain. But every day his chance of survival increases."

Guilt ripped through Morgan. The last time he'd gone to see Nicholas was weeks ago. "W-Well," he stammered, fighting to retain some distance from the painful subject. "What does Nicholas have to do with the subject of my punishment for crimes against propriety?"

Selina hesitated and her voice trembled as she said, "I was at Donville Masquerade last night, Morgan. I saw you falling apart and it...it frightened me. I don't have many people in my life. I nearly lost one brother, I won't lose another."

Morgan swallowed. "Selina..."

"It can't hurt, can it? I mean, it isn't in either of our natures to—to *try*. But there may be something to it."

Robert rejoined them from across the room. "What do you say, Morgan?"

Morgan let out a sigh. In truth, his siblings weren't far off the mark. He was tired of London. Tired of gaming and whoring. Tired of looking over his shoulder for whoever he'd lied to or schemed against. Now he'd have to add the watchful, judging eyes of Roseford if he said no to this offer.

But if he said yes...well, then when he failed, at least he could say he tried, and perhaps that would appease Robert enough to keep Morgan's settlement coming each year.

"Fine," he ground out. "If this Brighthollow toff wishes to speak to me about the matter, I won't refuse."

To his surprise, Roseford's eyes lit up. As if he really cared what Morgan did. He clasped Morgan's arm and gave a gentle squeeze. "Very good. Now, Jenner should have your bath prepared. Why don't you take that, and I'll arrange for someone to go and fetch some clothing for you better suited for this sort of meeting. Then we'll go talk to my friend."

Morgan's eyes went wide. "Right now?"

"I know you, Morgan," Roseford said with a chuckle as he moved to call for his butler and get the ball rolling. "It's always now or never when it comes to you."

Morgan wished to argue that point, but how could he? Much as he hated to admit it, his brother was right. So now he had to find out if this situation was going to be now...or never. And if it was never, what would that mean for his future?

CHAPTER 2

"But *why* must our plans change?" Lizzie gasped as she rushed across the parlor toward her brother, Hugh, and his wife, Amelia.

They exchanged a worried glance, something they often did when they spoke with her. She loved them for it, but also struggled with it. She hated to cause trouble and sometimes it seemed that was all she did.

Still, Hugh took Lizzie's hands in his. "The plans aren't changing, not in truth," he said gently. "We are all still going to Brighthollow for the month. I will merely be delayed by a few days in joining you. Roseford has asked a favor of me, that is all. It will take a little time if it plays out as my friend hopes it will."

Lizzie worried her lip. She liked her brother's club of close friends. They were all wonderful men with even more wonderful wives. But though the Duke of Roseford was no exception and was never anything but kind to Lizzie, he'd once had a certain kind of reputation. She shivered.

"What kind of favor?" she asked softly, fearing the answer.

"Oh, nothing of concern, I assure you," Hugh said, waving his hand as if to dismiss the entire subject. "Trouble with his half-brother, Morgan Banfield. It seems the young man is a bit wild."

Amelia chuckled as she slipped an arm around Lizzie's waist to comfort her. "Serves Robert right to have a wild sibling to manage after what he put all of you through all those years."

Hugh joined in her laughter, but Lizzie couldn't. *Wild.* She didn't like that word or all the ugly things that often came along with it.

"Do you think you'll hire Banfield, then?" Amelia asked, drawing Lizzie back to their conversation.

Hugh shrugged. "I've looked into his background a bit since Robert first mentioned this weeks ago. He's clever, that's for certain, and I think he could do the job *if* he applied himself. I suppose I'll decide once I get a feel for him when they arrive shortly. If I do take him on, he'll come with me to Brighthollow to get his start, so perhaps you can have an arrangement ready for him there just in case."

"Of course," Amelia said. "I'll ask Masters to—"

Lizzie shook her head at how casually they were discussing this. "What do you mean you're considering hiring some...some *rake* to work for you in Brighthollow?" she asked, even though she knew she had no right to interfere in her brother's hiring of any employee.

Hugh's brow wrinkled at the passion of her response, and Amelia's arm tightened at her waist as if to hold her up. Lizzie almost felt as if she needed it.

"You needn't be so concerned," Hugh soothed her as he leaned in to kiss her brow, just as he'd done all her life when he wished to comfort her. "Banfield will work for me and he'll know his place. He won't trouble you if he does come. You'll be busy at any rate, won't you? With the garden?"

Lizzie tensed. The garden back in Brighthollow was the reason she'd given to Amelia and Hugh about why she wished to depart London in the middle of the Season and go to the countryside. Her late mother had designed but never finished it, and it was a project she did care deeply about.

But it also served as an excuse she could offer so that no one would badger her about how much she despised London and the expectation that she would be wooed and wed. The Season was only weeks old and she already wished to flee it.

"Yes," she said slowly. "I suppose all my time *will* be taken up with the garden."

Hugh nodded. "Now, the carriage is likely on the drive and loaded, so it is time for you and Amelia to depart." He leaned down to kiss her cheek and she returned the same to him.

"Be careful," she said softly, meaning the road *and* his meeting with this stranger she already did not like.

Hugh smiled with indulgence and motioned them to the door. Lizzie exited the parlor first, to give her brother and his wife a little more time for a private farewell. She adored them both, but sometimes seeing their close bond was...difficult. It was something Lizzie knew she would never have. Perhaps didn't deserve thanks to the mistakes of her past.

She smiled at her brother's London butler as she passed him in the foyer. "Thank you for everything, Murphy."

"We hope to see you very soon, Lady Elizabeth," Murphy said with a warm and genuine smile. "Safe travels."

Lizzie kept her own false smile on her face until she had been helped into her brother's fine carriage for the long ride back to Brighthollow. Murphy's words made her cringe even though they were meant kindly.

See her again soon?

She didn't want to be in London. She didn't want to return *soon*. She just wanted to stay in Brighthollow and play the pianoforte and take walks on the grounds she loved so much and read all the books from the library over and over again, even though she knew them all by heart.

But she wasn't old enough to declare herself a spinster and put her brother off on his attempts to bring her out of her shell. That meant she would have to endure and find these little pockets of respite where she could claim them.

Amelia climbed into the rig, her cheeks bright and her lips red. From being kissed, no doubt. Hugh definitely loved to kiss her. And Amelia seemed to enjoy it, too. Lizzie shivered. Kissing was fine, she supposed, but it led to trouble.

Hugh waved from the door as they rode off, and Amelia watched him intently from the window until they turned from the drive. Only then did she let out a shuddering breath before she smiled through tear-brightened eyes at Lizzie. "You needn't worry, love," she said as she dug for a handkerchief in her pelisse pocket.

Lizzie nodded as she found her own and handed it over. She adored her sister-in-law with all her heart and didn't want to worry her more than she knew she already did. Amelia was so kind. "I'm sure I don't. Hugh knows how to handle himself."

"But you still have concerns about this man coming to Brighthollow and disturbing your peace," Amelia said softly.

Lizzie worried her lip. There it was, the exact feeling that burned inside of her. Yes, Hugh could handle himself. So could Amelia. So could everyone else in her small circle of acquaintances and friends, it seemed. She was the only one who struggled. Or at least it felt that way.

"I suppose," she said slowly. "In the end, what does it have to do with me? Nothing at all. If Hugh does judge this Morgan Banfield as worthy for the job of his man of affairs, then I'll probably hardly see him, at any rate."

She would make sure of it, but that was hardly a necessary point to add.

Amelia smiled. "Indeed, that is likely true. He'll be very busy learning all the facets of his job that Hugh has handled on his own for so long."

Those words brought Lizzie up short. Her brother had taken on the duties of duke and as her guardian at such a young age. For

27

years he had handled it all, never complaining, never putting voice to any pain he might have suffered. When he met Amelia, Lizzie had loved watching him open up. Blossom was the word for it, though she doubted her brother would fully appreciate the flowery verbiage.

If Hugh wished to hand off some of his duties so he could enjoy time with his wife and the family she knew they were both hoping to start, who was she to behave like a petulant child?

"You'll only rarely cross paths," Amelia added, oblivious to Lizzie's thoughts.

Lizzie nodded and tried to clear her mind of her worries. They mattered little at the moment, and Hugh might not even hire the man. So there was no use preparing for the worst, even if it had become her nature to do so in the past few years.

"Did you bring the book?" Lizzie asked, pushing the difficult subjects out of the way as she vowed to enjoy the next few days with her friend. She and Amelia were rarely able to spend time alone, and she cherished it.

"I did!" Amelia said, and pulled from her reticule a novel they had each been interested in and decided to take turns reading aloud to each other on the trip to Brighthollow. "*The Children of the Abbey*! Are you ready for a tale of desperate romance and stolen inheritance?"

"Always," Lizzie said with a laugh that helped to dispel her fears.

Amelia opened the book to the first page and smiled across the carriage. "Then let's begin."

Lizzie settled back against the carriage seat and closed her eyes so she could better picture the story about to unfold. It would be a good way to forget her troubles. A good way to forget the world.

Morgan shifted in his place on the settee as he and Roseford waited for Brighthollow to join them. In the hours he'd taken to ready himself, his throbbing head had gotten a bit better and he no longer felt like he would cast up his accounts. He was almost human again. Or as close as he ever got.

The door to the parlor opened, and both Morgan and Robert rose as the tall, handsome Duke of Brighthollow entered the room. Morgan watched as his brother crossed to his old friend. The two men embraced, pounding each other's backs and exchanging warm and obviously genuine expressions of reunion.

Morgan had to fight not to turn away from it. Robert was all ease with his duke friends. Their club was his home, their friends his family. Morgan was...well, he knew he was a responsibility his brother didn't really want and not much more.

"Hugh, may I present my brother, Morgan Banfield," Roseford said, forcing Morgan to jerk himself to the present moment and out of maudlin thoughts.

Brighthollow stepped forward with a hand outstretched in greeting. There was no hesitance as he caught Morgan's hand and gave it a firm, certain shake. "A pleasure to officially make your acquaintance at last. I've seen you from time to time out in Town and I've heard so much about you."

Morgan stiffened as he sent his brother a look. "I'm sure Roseford's assessment of me highlights all my best qualities."

The warmth on Brighthollow's face faded a fraction, replaced by a slightly protective shadow. "Roseford has never expressed anything but consideration for you, Mr. Banfield. And I welcome you to my home. Please, do sit. Would you like tea or something stronger?"

Roseford shook his head as he retook his seat on the settee and Morgan settled across from him in a chair. "Banfield doesn't need anything stronger."

Morgan glared at him again. "So my nursemaid says. I'm fine, thank you for asking."

"Hmm," Brighthollow murmured, and took a place beside Robert. Now there were two sets of eyes focused on Morgan. Judging.

He didn't like the judgment. Never had. And he'd learned over the years that the best way to thwart it was through charm. He'd honed his skills in that arena well and good.

"I've heard you've a fine prospect," Morgan said.

Brighthollow puffed up a bit, just as Morgan had known he would. "We think it so," he admitted. "I would say it is the most beautiful in the world, but Roseford might argue."

Robert shrugged. "You know I can take or leave my father's holdings. Though I'd argue Ewan has the best of all our estates. He has the benefit of a sea view. That has to be worth something."

Morgan shifted again as the long friendship Robert and Brighthollow had shared with their club pushed him from the inner circle of the conversation. He wasn't certain who Ewan was, but believed he was one of the dukes his brother ran with.

"I'm sure Ewan would agree," Brighthollow chuckled. "But we are straying from the topic that has brought you here, even though Mr. Banfield opened a window to it a moment ago. I am in the market for a man of affairs. And Roseford says you might be the man for the job."

Morgan shifted. "He tells me the same thing. I-I suppose we must determine together if that is true. Can you tell me about your expectations?"

Brighthollow's eyebrows lifted, as if he were surprised Morgan had the wherewithal to question the offer. That didn't bode well to his potential employer's judgment of his sense.

"It's a large estate, with a great many holdings and tenants to manage." Brighthollow leaned back in the settee and folded his hands in his lap. "There are books to be kept, problems to be managed, people with questions that never seem to end."

"It sounds like a pleasure," Morgan muttered with a frown. God's teeth, he'd made a very nice life out of avoiding the very kind of responsibility being thrown out before him now.

"It is, much of the time," Brighthollow said. "I simply don't want to sugarcoat it. This isn't some estate that has been ignored or uncared for, so there's no expectation that you would bring it back from the brink. However, I don't want it to fall into disrepair or ruin. Too many lives depend upon its careful management."

"And who was doing that duty before?" Morgan asked. "And why did they leave their post?"

To his surprise, Roseford and Brighthollow exchanged a look, and then they both began to laugh.

He tilted his head at the strange reaction. "Did I say something funny?"

"The current manager is being fired because he wants to spend more of his time making babies with his lovely wife, I think," Robert teased.

Brighthollow inclined his head with a smile. "Though Roseford is a bit blunt about it, he does answer the question. I have been the sole manager of my properties since I took the title from my father twelve years ago. But Amelia and I have been married for three years and we are…" He smiled again. "Well, I have other priorities that don't allow me to take care of my estate as closely. Do you feel you would be interested in taking on the challenge?"

"Of course he'll take it," Robert said, giving Morgan a pointed stare.

Morgan jerked at the statement, said as if he were a recalcitrant child rather than a man well past his majority. "Roseford," he growled, unable to keep his annoyance from his tone.

Brighthollow cast a glance between the two brothers, and then he turned to Robert. "Roseford, why don't you give me a moment alone with Mr. Banfield? Please."

"Yes," Morgan said, glaring at his brother. "That's a very good idea."

Robert opened and shut his mouth. He clearly wished to argue against the request. But then he threw up his hands. "Very well," he muttered, pushing to his feet. "I suppose I will go observe your garden, Brighthollow."

He walked to the door, but there he turned and speared Morgan with a glance. It spoke volumes. It said *don't cock this up*. And Morgan bucked against the unspoken order. Robert might manage the estate that paid his bills, but he wasn't Morgan's father. No one had ever been that. Not really.

Once he was gone, Brighthollow got up and closed the door behind him. "So he won't eavesdrop," he explained with an easy smile as he retook his place on the settee.

"You know him so well," Morgan grunted.

"I do," Brighthollow said softly. He was silent a moment before he said, "You're very clever."

Morgan forced himself to hold the other man's stare. "I try."

That elicited a bit of a smile from his companion. "Roseford worries over you. A brother's prerogative, and one I understand better than most. But it makes me wonder if I should worry about you, too."

Morgan sat up straighter. There was something about the question, about the man who sat across from him, that made him want to prove something about himself. That was a new sensation and he wasn't certain he liked it much.

And yet…

"No," he said, and the mask he wore slipped a bit. "You wouldn't have to worry about me."

Brighthollow arched a brow. "Do you *want* this opportunity?"

Well, they had come to it and swiftly, at that, because the Duke of Brighthollow did not seem a man who minced around topics or played games. So the total opposite of Morgan, himself.

But this was a split in the road of Morgan's life. He recognized it with a clarity that rarely accompanied such moments. There were the two paths. One where he scoffed at the idea of a different life, where he continued on as he always had and probably irrevocably damaged his relationship with Roseford.

But life had not been...perfect...as of late. Roseford wasn't wrong when he said Morgan was troubled. He just hated that his brother could see it. That felt like vulnerability and Morgan had fought his entire life not to show any of that. Soft underbellies got knifed in his experience.

And that made him look at the other path that Brighthollow presented. One with a vocation that could provide instead of the dwindling inheritance Robert continued to bestow upon him. A future that went beyond gaming hells and brothels and a wastrel's existence.

"Mr. Banfield?" Brighthollow said, tilting his head to examine Morgan more closely.

Morgan blinked. "I-I haven't served anyone before," he admitted softly.

"I know." Brighthollow leaned forward. "But there is time to learn. I'll teach you."

Morgan swallowed. "You're doing this for Robert."

Brighthollow's smile softened. "Yes. Does that bother you?"

"If it's the only reason," Morgan said.

"I understand that. You must know that Robert isn't. I'd be a fool to hand over the keys to my kingdom just because of a friendship. In truth, I think you might be good at it. Everything Robert has told me about you says you would be if you applied yourself to it."

Morgan wrinkled his brow. So Roseford had spoken to Brighthollow about him before, it seemed. And with...with pride? Something in Morgan flickered that he did not want to feel.

He cleared his throat and words he didn't expect fell from his lips. "Then I'll do it."

"Excellent." Brighthollow pushed to his feet and extended a hand to Morgan. He stood and shook it, slightly dazed by how this meeting had gone. He'd had plans for it, but now everything had veered to the side. "I will stay here in London for a few days so you may make any arrangements you need. And I'll also invite Robert and Katherine to join us in Brighthollow."

Morgan shook his head. "For what purpose?"

"To ease the transition."

Morgan pursed his lips. He couldn't imagine having Robert around, parenting him over his shoulder, would be easy. But then again, having people there he knew *might* help. "Er, that is kind of you."

Brighthollow shrugged, as if the gesture meant nothing. Then he moved toward the door. "Well, let us see if Roseford is standing in the hallway with his ear pressed against my door? And then I'll let you go so you may put your own house in order. We can meet again, perhaps tonight for supper, and go over these new beginnings for us both."

Morgan followed him to the door in a daze. A new beginning. It had been a long time since he'd had one of those. He just hoped he'd know what to do with it.

CHAPTER 3

L izzie strolled along the pathway in the vast expanse of the garden behind the manor house, notebook in hand, although she hadn't been taking notes. There were many reasons for her inability to gather her thoughts.

Part of the distraction was that she loved being back home. The quiet of the estate, the beauty of the trees and fountains and flowers, it all made her feel so peaceful. She'd needed that after her recent time in London.

But it had been a week since she and Amelia had arrived home. They'd enjoyed many a casual stroll and happy supper and visit with shire friends. As time passed, though, she felt the expectations from her sister-in-law about the garden. When Hugh arrived with his new employee, probably shortly, he would likely have the same questions. After all, that was why she'd claimed she wanted to come here for a month during the height of the Season.

She sighed. Her parents had died when she was just eight. Her father, she admitted, she didn't miss often. He had been a distant and often unpleasant presence in her life, and Hugh had stepped into his role with grace and ease and kindness, even when she didn't feel she deserved it.

But her mother? Oh, how Lizzie missed her. And the garden, which had been the prior duchess's passion project, reflected her mother. Lizzie saw her in every flower, in every carefully trimmed shrubbery.

What if she managed it the wrong way? What if she planted something her mother hadn't intended? So she pored over the old, faded plans from decades ago and worried over it endlessly.

It made her restless here, and that was not something she enjoyed when it came to the sanctuary of home.

She let out a sigh as she trudged up the back stair onto the terrace that overlooked the garden. Through the glass doors that led to the parlor, she saw servants bustling and rushing. It could mean only one thing.

Hugh was home.

She smiled and pushed through the doors and into the house. In a few steps she was to the foyer and out the front door where servants were collecting in order to retrieve trunks and boxes.

She blushed because Hugh had already exited his carriage. He stood on the bottom step, arms around Amelia, and the two were kissing enthusiastically, regardless of the bustle around them. She was happy for them, of course. Amelia had been bereft without him for the past week. Lizzie had felt how her friend forced frivolity at times and watched the clock ceaselessly. Hugh had to have missed her, too. They were rarely parted and Lizzie knew how deeply he adored her.

But seeing the way they smiled at each other as they parted…it made Lizzie feel something darker. Something she hated in herself. She was *jealous*. Always jealous of her brother's happiness. Which made her a terrible person, she knew.

"And Amelia, this is Morgan Banfield," Hugh was saying as he motioned toward the carriage. A man was exiting it, and Lizzie's stomach leapt.

He was tall, broad shouldered and lean. When he unfolded himself from the carriage, it was a smooth, confident movement.

And when he looked up the stairs, first at her brother and Amelia, and then past them toward Lizzie...

Well, her heart all but stopped. He was exceedingly well favored. He had light brown hair that was thick and slightly mussed, like he'd been running his fingers through it, and dark chocolate eyes that swept over her in one motion. He also sported a beard, a shade lighter than his hair. The facial hair was most definitely not in fashion, so it surprised her to see it. But it certainly suited him and highlighted the angles of his jaw and cheekbones.

A tiny smile tilted one corner of his lips, and then he winked at her. The motion broke the spell and she jerked her gaze away, lifting her hands to cover her hot cheeks.

This libertine had just *winked* at her. And it threw her back to four years before, when her world had been torn to pieces by a man who was equally handsome and charming. Well, perhaps not *equally*.

What was wrong with her?

"Lizzie!" Amelia called out, glancing up the stairs at her. "Come and join us."

She stayed frozen on the top step for a moment, and then somehow forced herself to move. She made her way to the drive, where she kissed her brother's cheek in mute welcome and then girded herself for the inevitable introduction to the devil who had just placed himself on her family estate.

"Lizzie, this is Morgan Banfield," Hugh said. "My new man of affairs. Mr. Banfield: my sister, Lady Elizabeth."

"My lady," Mr. Banfield drawled as he extended a hand in greeting.

She didn't want to take it, but propriety and politeness did not allow her to refuse. She extended her hand. He took it, his ungloved fingers folding over her own bare skin, and she was enveloped in warmth for a moment. His hands weren't calloused, but they were a bit rough and she hated how the dichotomy of her soft skin against his sent a shiver of awareness up her spine. Feelings such as this brought nothing good.

She pulled her hand away and shoved it to her side. "Mr. Banfield. Welcome to our home."

Amelia smiled and everyone else seemed unaware of Lizzie's tangled feelings. Including Mr. Banfield, who looked away from her toward her sister-in-law.

"We have a chamber prepared for you, Mr. Banfield," Amelia said. "And I assume Hugh has been talking your ear off with details about the estate for three days. So I offer you a respite from his voice while you settle in."

"Well now," Hugh said with a teasing affront to his tone. "I thought you *liked* my voice."

Amelia linked her arm through his. "And *I* never asked for a respite from it."

They laughed and Banfield along with them. Lizzie somehow managed a smile even though the blood was rushing in her ears.

"There is much to learn, Your Grace," Mr. Banfield said with an incline of his head. "But I assure you, I'm up for the task."

"I think he might be," Hugh said with a quick glance at him. "And you'll have plenty of time to settle in and explore the grounds. Robert and Katherine will join us in a few days, as well."

Amelia smiled. "I received word just before you arrived that Ewan and Charlotte also intend on arriving at almost the same time."

"The Duke and Duchess of Donburrow," Hugh explained. "Old friends. A better man, I could not name."

"Then we will be a happy party, indeed," Mr. Banfield said, and shot Lizzie another brief look.

She refused to return it and instead stared at a loose thread on the cuff of her gown. If the house was filled with friends, she had to be pleased for that. Not only would she enjoy their company, but it would likely give her a barrier between her and this unwanted newcomer. He would be busy with learning the estate, she would be playing hostess at Amelia's side.

"Why don't we go into the house, then?" Amelia said. She

squeezed Hugh's arm and slid her hand through the crook of Lizzie's elbow. Lizzie felt herself guided away, into the house, away from the interloper that came to test her resolve.

But this time it was a test she intended to win.

M organ couldn't help but stare as the most beautiful woman he'd ever encountered was drawn inside by her sister-in-law. It was an odd thing to think of Lady Elizabeth as that, since she was so different from the woman who normally caught his eye.

He normally liked flashy women. Ones with confidence and experience like the ones he encountered in the hells. It was easier with them. They understood the boundaries of whatever arrangement he would enter with them. Most of them appreciated those boundaries as much as he did.

But Elizabeth? Well, this was not a woman you played about with. This was a *lady*, and not just because she was a duke's sister. No, she was fully of her station, that was clear from the way she held herself: a bit distant, standoffish. She had a delicacy to her, like a beautiful little bird who had been happily trapped in a cage all her life. She wouldn't understand a man like him. She would be shocked by him if she allowed him past the surface. Which she had been trained all her life not to do.

But she was utterly enchanting regardless of the imprudence of his attraction. She had pale blonde hair, done up in a simple fashion that framed her slender face perfectly and brought attention to blue eyes the color of a clear summer's sky. There was something sad to those eyes, something hollow and even a little pained that he marked and set aside in his mind.

She must have heard something about him before his arrival, because she didn't like him. He'd felt her disdain the moment he touched her hand, smoothing his thumb over the delicate bones and slender fingers that had fit into his own so perfectly.

But though she didn't know him, she'd darted her gaze away, lips pursed with displeasure. So it was evident she did not approve of her brother's choice of man of affairs. It made him wonder how he had been described to her by her brother or by Roseford. He might have to explore that more closely in order to know where he truly stood.

"And so what do you think of it?" Brighthollow asked as he stepped up next to Morgan and the two observed the big manor house together.

Morgan nodded. "It's a fine seat, Your Grace. Which I'm certain you already know."

Brighthollow chuckled. "I am biased, I suppose. As my wife said, you'll be given time to settle in. There will be a long period of transition, for your sake and for my own."

"Why for yours?" Morgan asked.

Brighthollow shrugged. "I've run my own estate for a long time. Letting go will not be easy, though it is necessary. My time is required elsewhere."

Morgan followed the duke up the stairs and into the foyer. There was a bustle of activity going on around them, but his focus was entirely on the retreating back of Lady Elizabeth as she and the Duchess of Brighthollow entered a parlor just off the foyer.

"Your sister is older than I assumed, based on your description of her during our travels."

Brighthollow's brow furrowed slightly. An interesting tell, given that it was clear he adored his sister. But something troubled him about the subject. Morgan wondered what, exactly.

"I suppose that is an old habit. Although Lizzie is twenty, I still sometimes see her as the little girl I raised." His smile was soft. "But don't let her know I said it. She wouldn't want to be seen as a child."

"Ah, if you raised her, I suppose that makes sense," Morgan said, filing the information away with all the rest, as was his habit. "And do I answer to Lady Elizabeth, as well as to you and the duchess?"

Brighthollow seemed taken aback by the question, and for a

moment he said nothing. Then he responded, "I...suppose. Yes. If Lizzie needed something you could provide, then yes, you would answer to her."

"Hmmm," Morgan murmured in what he hoped was a disinterested tone.

Certainly, his new employer wouldn't care for the thoughts Morgan was having about Lady Elizabeth. An innocent like her was lovely, for sure, but out of his reach for a variety of reasons.

"I doubt she would ask for your help, truth be told," Brighthollow continued with a deeper frown. "Although..." He seemed to consider something for a moment, then shook his head. "No. My sister is shy. You needn't trouble yourself with her. If she requires anything, Amelia and I are the ones who will provide it. You can focus on a great many other duties."

"Of course," Morgan said.

Brighthollow motioned for him to follow. "Now they have taken your trunks up to your chamber. I'll find someone to escort you there and allow you a few moments to gather yourself."

Morgan nodded his thanks, but as Brighthollow called for a servant, his mind kept going back to bright blue eyes. For a man drawn to trouble, he could recognize it when he saw it. And now he'd have to fight his impulses if he didn't want to create even more of it for himself.

Lizzie paced down the long hallway, hands clenched at her sides and body on high alert. She felt wound too tight and had been this way for hours, since the arrival of Morgan Banfield into her home. No, not arrival. *Invasion.* That was the right term. He had invaded like a Viking, fitting considering the beard, and then he'd...*winked* at her.

She shook her head. Oh, how she hated that one man, one stranger, one foolish little flit of an eyelid she couldn't get out of her mind, could affect her so. It was too much power for someone else to hold over her. And it was too much like the terrible past.

She huffed out a long breath as she neared the library and tried to find her focus. Here, at least, she would find peace. She always did.

Except as she entered the large room, with its high bookshelves and sweet little nooks and crannies for reading, she came to a sharp halt. The very man who had troubled her thoughts for hours was standing in her ultimate sanctuary, a book perched in his long, lean fingers. He had shed his jacket at some point, leaving him in a crisp white shirt, sleeves rolled to the elbows, and an intricately stitched waistcoat that fit his broad chest far too well.

His back was to her, so she had an opportunity to escape. Only she didn't. Instead she froze as he reached up to casually place the book back on the shelf an arm's length above him. His shoulders flexed against the white linen fabric of his shirt.

Once he had replaced the book, he turned and flashed a smile at her that revealed even, white teeth. It was not as if he was surprised to see her, he seemed to have known she was there gaping at him all along.

"Good afternoon, Lady Elizabeth," he drawled.

She shifted. He was being nothing but polite to her, and she still wished to run in the other direction. It was very rude to be that way when he'd done nothing directly wrong. She was just judging him by another man with another face. It was unfair and she knew it.

"G-good afternoon, Mr. Banfield," she managed to squeak out. She took a cautious step farther into the library. "Are you settling in well?"

He nodded as he looked around with a smile. "It is a fine estate, which your brother told me I could explore at my leisure. I was making the attempt when I was waylaid here. It is the best room of the house so far."

She blinked, for she agreed about the assessment. She didn't like being of a mind with him. It felt…a little like a trap. She cleared her throat. "The, er, music room is another of my favorite haunts."

Now why had she told him that? He certainly couldn't care about her tiny little interests. Nor should she offer them to him as if he were anything more than a stranger.

But to her surprise, his eyes lit up. "Ah, I have not yet found the music room. I assume you play pianoforte?"

She nodded. "I do."

"I have been known to play a tune or two, myself," he said with another smile. This one felt a bit more genuine.

She stared at him. He liked to read and to play piano? Those were not the activities she would have guessed were the favorites of such a man.

She pursed her lips at the connection she hadn't wished to find and changed the subject. "You are Robert's brother."

His brows lifted. "Yes. *Robert*. So informal with the great Duke of Roseford?"

Heat filled her cheeks at the observation and she dropped her gaze to the floor. "Well, I've known him almost all my life, so perhaps I am a little more familiar than I normally would be with a duke," she explained softly. "He and my brother are very close."

"Yes." There was a flicker of something…dark in his stare. Something a little sad. Then he masked it and smiled. As if this were all a game. For the first time, she noticed he had a dimple beneath those whiskers. "And *your* brother tells me I also work for you, my lady."

Lizzie drew back in surprise at that bit of news. "Work for me?" she repeated. "N-no, you must have misunderstood."

"Did I?" he asked, stepping a long stride closer. "You don't have things you need?"

Her lips parted in surprise. He was being playful, teasing. Flirting with her. And part of her was drawn to that fact. Drawn to this handsome man's charm. Just as she had been to another man. One who had lied so prettily and played her for the worst kind of fool.

She folded her arms and glared at Mr. Banfield, hoping he would see that she was not to be trifled with. "You forget yourself," she whispered, wishing her voice didn't tremble. "Good day."

She pivoted away from him before he could respond and stalked from the room. But the moment she was out of his line of sight, she ran. Away from the library, away from the man so invading her space.

And away from the unwanted flutter this conversation had put in her belly. She would do well not to feel such a thing. There was no good that could come of it.

M organ lay in the narrow bed in his small but serviceable chamber that night. It had been hours since his unexpected encounter with Lady Elizabeth. He should have been able to chalk that up entirely to being busy. After all, he'd had a household to meet and share a meal with. The servants had all been friendly—a little guarded, perhaps, but welcoming. Afterward, he'd busied unpacking and settling into his room. It was a huge estate—it was very likely one could go days without seeing the other inhabitants, and that wouldn't be because anyone was avoiding anyone else.

Except he had the distinct impression Elizabeth *was* avoiding him after their encounter in the library. He'd spent the remainder of his afternoon and evening watching Brighthollow every time they were in the same room, waiting for the moment when he would be sacked. It was clear the duke was protective of his sister, and if she said the word, Morgan would be gone.

But it never happened, and so he had to assume Elizabeth hadn't gone to her family and said the same words that she had left ringing in his ears in the library.

You forget yourself.

That was the story of his life, really. Forgetting himself.

Suffering the consequences. Wallowing in them. Sometimes reveling in them.

But this time he couldn't. If he wanted to keep this position— and for the moment he did—he was going to have to charm the duke's sister by being polite when he encountered her, not chase her off by going too far. By being himself. Now he just had to figure out how, exactly, to be someone else.

CHAPTER 4

Lizzie sat on the window seat in her study, feet tucked up beneath her as she stared out at the garden below. The garden that was accusing her because she had not done a single thing to improve it, not even in the two days since Hugh and Mr. Banfield had returned to the estate.

She could have lied and told herself that it was the excitement of the new arrival that had kept her from the work. Except that Mr. Banfield had not come around since that first day when she found him in the library. He'd been busy, settling in with the servants, learning about new duties with her brother. She'd only seen him once or twice in passing, and though she'd felt him watching her from time to time, he hadn't bothered her.

No, her own thoughts were guilty of that, but not the man, himself. But now the other guests had arrived. Lizzie had watched their carriages roll onto the drive that afternoon and the friends tumble out. She'd watched the usual warmth and brotherhood between Hugh and Robert and Ewan. Observed the laughter between the couples and the true friendship and bond. And then she'd sat up just a little higher and watched as Morgan shook his brother's hand with no more connection than he had with Ewan or Hugh. They weren't close, that was clear.

She jerked her head up at the memory and got to her feet. It was none of her business what the situation was between Banfield and Robert. Or Banfield and anyone else, for that matter. He was her brother's employee, nothing more.

She walked toward her escritoire in the corner of the room, ready to write down a list of things to do for the garden, when there was a light knock on her door.

Amelia ducked her head into the room. "There you are!" she said, face bright with pleasure.

Lizzie shrugged her thoughts away and forced a smile in return. "Were you looking for me?"

Amelia worried her lip a moment, and then stepped into the study and shut the door behind herself. She leaned against the barrier a moment and Lizzie felt her sizing her up. Fretting over her. The focused attention was uncomfortable and she shifted beneath it.

"Are you well?" Amelia asked at last and with great care to her voice, as if she thought just the question would shatter Lizzie.

Lizzie fought the urge to sigh. She wasn't glass, no matter what her family thought. "Of course," she said, and broadened her false smile a fraction.

Amelia's brow wrinkled. "It is just that you have been so quiet since our arrival in Brighthollow."

"I'm always quiet," Lizzie said, clenching a fist at her side gently and trying to maintain eye contact when what she wanted to do was run away.

"So you aren't...troubled?" Amelia pressed.

"No!" Lizzie burst out, a little too loudly, a little too quickly. She ducked her head and repeated it, this time with more control. "No. Not at all. There has been so much excitement with all the newcomers, I'm sure it's just that."

Amelia nodded slowly, but from her expression, Lizzie wasn't certain her sister-in-law believed her explanation. But she didn't pursue it and instead smiled brightly. "Speaking of newcomers, I'm sure you heard that Robert and Katherine and Ewan and Charlotte have arrived."

"Yes," Lizzie said, and now she could breathe again, for this topic was far less fraught. "I saw from my window a short while ago."

"Well, we were about to have tea once the ladies settled in. Won't you come join us?"

Lizzie nodded and linked her arm through Amelia's without hesitation. "Of course."

Amelia led her out of her study and down the hall toward the parlor. As they entered, Lizzie smiled. It was all laid out perfectly, but of course it would be. Amelia had taken to her duties as duchess with enthusiasm in the three years she and Hugh had been married. It was as if she were born for the role...and for the man. Despite a difficult beginning, now it felt like everything was in place for the pair.

"Later I want to talk to you about something," Amelia said. "Hugh and I wish to discuss it with you together."

Lizzie's goodwill fled as she pivoted to face her friend. "What is it about?"

Before Amelia could answer, the door to the parlor opened and Katherine, the Duchess of Roseford, and Charlotte, the Duchess of Donburrow, entered together, laughing at once. Whatever Amelia was going to say was lost as the two women rushed forward, greeting Lizzie and talking about what they wanted in their tea.

Although Lizzie felt anxious as she glanced at Amelia and wondered what in the world she could want to discuss with her, it was impossible not to feel comfortable in the room with the three women. All of Hugh's friends had married exceedingly well, to women who were perfectly matched to them. Katherine and Charlotte were no exceptions. Katherine kept the once-wild Duke of Roseford in line, and the man seemed to adore her for it. And Charlotte had developed an intricate hand language with the Duke of Donburrow, who had been unable to speak since birth.

Both women were kind and welcoming, funny and sharp. And though their friendship was more firmly with Amelia, Lizzie never felt anything but welcomed by any of the duchesses in their friend circle.

Welcomed, yes. Though not exactly comfortable. After all, the common factor for them all wasn't their position, but the fact that they were all in love. Every duchess was head over heels for her duke. They all had faith that the future was a beautiful thing where that love would not, *could not* die.

And that was what kept Lizzie on the fringes of their circle more than anything. She wasn't like them. She never would be.

"And how is Morgan settling in?" Katherine asked as she took her cup from Amelia with a smile. Lizzie stiffened at the mention of their unwanted new addition. "Robert has worried about him greatly, though he likes to pretend he isn't fully invested in his half-brother's success."

"He has settled in well enough," Amelia said. "He's only been here a few days, but has been studying Hugh's books."

"Tell me more about him," Charlotte said. "I'm endlessly fascinated by Robert's pursuit of his half-siblings."

Katherine nodded. "Well, Robert's father is where they all got their wild streak. He was an unkind man, but he must have had charm like his sons and daughters, for he never had a deficit of lovers at his door." She glanced at Lizzie. "I'm sorry, my dear."

Lizzie shrugged one shoulder even though her throat felt like it would close at the uncouth subject. "I'm fine."

"The old duke supported his by-blows, obviously," Charlotte pressed.

Katherine frowned. "Financially. And I think there were some he tried to influence personally. But there was little relationship there. Robert decided a few years ago that he wanted to change that. He has always continued the financial support of the estate, but also begun to forge relationships with his siblings where he can. Some are…easier than others."

Lizzie frowned at this new bit of information about Morgan Banfield. "I assume this means Mr. Banfield is one of the difficult ones," she said softly. "Does that bode well for Hugh and his goals?"

Katherine glanced at her from the corner of her eye and then toward Amelia. "Don't mistake me. Morgan is…yes, he is a challenge at times. He's wild, but that's not his entire personality. He's very intelligent and a good judge of other people. It's amazing sometimes to watch him call out the truth of a person with just one look."

Lizzie's lips parted. This man could read people so easily? She didn't like that idea. She didn't want to be read by a stranger. She didn't want the truth that she protected so jealously to be revealed by a cavalier person like Morgan Banfield.

"That's a good skill for a man of affairs," Charlotte mused. "The ability to read people could mean he will sense their intentions all the easier. Ewan can do the same, I think. See into a person's heart."

"Yes," Katherine said. "Morgan is also of an artistic bent. He plays the pianoforte beautifully, though it's almost impossible to get him to do it for company. And he is…good. I just see it in him, behind all the other foolishness he chooses to share with the world. In the end, I think he is much like Robert before…"

"Before you," Charlotte said with a laugh the other two women joined in. Lizzie couldn't bring herself to do the same, especially when Charlotte added, "That would solve the problem, wouldn't it? We just need to find this Mr. Banfield his Katherine and he'll come right in line, the best reformed rake in the country."

"Second best," Katherine said with a giggle. "I refuse to think that anyone else could reform better than my Robert has. But perhaps you're right. We need to match the young man, that is all."

Lizzie had been shifting as this conversation unfolded, but now she couldn't stay still any longer. With a gasp, she got up and paced away to the sideboard, where she fiddled with the teapot as she tried to regain her equilibrium.

"Lizzie, are you quite well?" Amelia called out, and concern was thick in her tone.

Lizzie glanced back to find all three women staring at her with open, warm expressions. They were so loving and nonjudgmental. She knew she could talk to them about anything, and yet what would she say? That Morgan Banfield made her nervous due to his mere existence? That sounded so foolish and churlish when the man had done nothing more than harmlessly flirt with her a little in the library.

So she pushed her thoughts aside and shook her head. "I'm very well, pardon my woolgathering. I'm only thinking about a project I'm working on."

"What project is that?" Charlotte asked, her eyes lighting up with interest. Everyone in their circle knew that the Duchess of Donburrow was always finding something new to pursue. She seemed to be an expert at every pastime she tried.

"The garden," Lizzie admitted, and her anxiety eased as she said the words. Yes, that's what she needed to do. Refocus. Nothing else mattered but this, did it?

"Hugh and Lizzie's mother left a redesign behind at her death," Amelia explained more fully. "We found the plans last Christmas, and Lizzie has been determined to see them through this summer, which is why we came here."

"Rather than finish your Season, my dear?" Katherine asked, her brow wrinkling with confusion. "I would think you'd want to dance away at balls and return to this in the autumn."

Before Lizzie could answer the question, she saw Amelia give her head the very tiniest shake, and the look that came over Katherine and Charlotte's faces was humiliating. She knew their entire circle was aware of her fall from grace years before. Their club didn't keep secrets from each other. No one had ever spoken of it to her beyond Amelia and Hugh.

But seeing the dawn of understanding felt like it yanked her past from under her feet and caused her to fall flat on her back. Her breath came shorter and she dug her fingernails into her palms as she fought to remain light and carefree.

"I do not care much for London," she managed to choke out.

Amelia got to her feet and hustled over. She took the pot of tea Lizzie didn't even realize she was still holding and freshened first her cup, then Amelia's own. She smiled at her kindly. "You know, perhaps this would be a place where Mr. Banfield could assist you. Katherine says he is of an artistic bent. I'm certainly not."

The room laughed, for if Charlotte was a master at any craft she tried, Amelia was the opposite. Everyone had received her crooked needlepoint for one holiday or another. Lizzie tried to join in on the inside joke, but her throat was closing all the faster.

"Mr. Banfield said something about assisting me, as well," she said with a shake of her head as she tried to forget the way he'd held her stare, the cheeky wink that had haunted her ever since. "But I don't *need* help."

Katherine's smile fell. "That's too bad. I think Morgan does."

Lizzie gaped at those words. Morgan Banfield needed help? She wanted to doubt it, but she'd never known Katherine to be anything but honest, and her expression was filled with genuine worry. Everyone had talked about Mr. Banfield being wild and also…lost.

She frowned. It was in her nature to help others. It always had been. Now she was torn between a desire to offer a hand to another in need…and to avoid the touch of a person who terrified her because he was just too…too much. But perhaps that would be the buffer she needed. All those years ago with Aaron, she had been tricked by the game he played. She'd believed in him simply because he told her she should.

But now things were different. She knew exactly what Morgan Banfield was. She wouldn't be fooled by any costume he put on or game he played. Unlike all those years ago, she would be stronger. More distant. It would be a good test, at any rate, wouldn't it? After all, she was expected to marry at some point. She wanted to be a mother, and that was how it happened. This would be practice for exposing herself to a man who would try to flirt with her. Practice for keeping herself distant from whatever he pretended to want.

"Well," she said with a small shrug that didn't reflect how difficult all this was to her. "Perhaps. His input couldn't hurt, at any rate, and it will help him learn about the property."

Amelia stared at her, and there was no mistaking her surprise that Lizzie had capitulated to the request. She tried not to let her feelings be hurt by that expression and smiled at her sister-in-law.

"That would be very kind of you," Katherine said. "Thank you, Lizzie."

"I'll speak to Hugh," Amelia said. "Before supper. And since Mr. Banfield will be joining us for our meal tonight, perhaps you'll find a chance to speak to him about it yourself."

Lizzie nodded, but was pleased when Amelia retook her place on the settee and she and Charlotte started talking about a book they'd both recently read. Now that the attention of the room was no longer focused on her, she almost sagged with the effort this conversation had required.

Had she truly agreed to spend extra time with Morgan Banfield? In the guise of helping him, of all things? Perhaps it would all work out and nothing bad would come of it. But she couldn't help but believe she was making a terrible mistake.

And she could only hope it wouldn't be the kind that left a permanent scar.

CHAPTER 5

Morgan sat at the end of the long dining table, smoothing his fingers along the heavy fabric of the napkin in his lap. This was his third night in the service of the Duke of Brighthollow, but the first time he had been asked to join the family for supper. He had no doubt it was thanks to his brother, for Roseford sat across from him with Katherine at his side. On his opposite side was the Duke of Donburrow. The infamous Silent Duke signed his words and his wife, Charlotte, translated the hand language he'd been told they'd shared since childhood.

It was a fascinating thing to watch them move as such a unit. Morgan had already begun to pick up on a few of the words here and there, and he practiced signing them in his lap below the table. He had little else to do, in truth. After all, he was invited to sup with them, but he didn't belong in their circle. He was an outsider.

He stood at the glass in the cold, watching as his brother and his friends laughed and joked and exchanged stories. They were a family, more so than he and Robert had ever been.

His gaze slid down the table. On the far opposite side sat Elizabeth. She was part of the family, certainly. Seated beside the Duke of Brighthollow, she often laughed at her brother's jokes or smiled

THE LOVE OF A LIBERTINE

warmly at his friends. But there were times when he could see her join him on the fringes of their circle. Times when he watched her shrink into herself a little, as if she were trying to disappear.

She glanced down at him as if she noted his attention to her. When she saw he was staring, her cheeks filled with pink color and she dropped her eyes to her nearly empty plate and fidgeted with her silverware.

He made her nervous. Interesting.

Of course he had to remind himself, yet again, that Lady Elizabeth was not his type. She was too quiet, too shy, too innocent. He didn't run around destroying the futures of those who were untouched, it wasn't his nature. So he couldn't let his boredom and lack of comfort in his new place in the world alter his goals and the rules by which he lived.

Elizabeth was out of reach. That was the end of the story.

"I hear the topic of the garden came up today," Brighthollow said as the final course was placed in front of each guest.

Nuts and dried fruit, sprinkled across a vanilla-flavored ice cream. The dessert was all the rage at present, and difficult to come by, so to have it was a casual example of how beautifully managed and well-funded this estate was.

And now Brighthollow wished to hand over that managing to Morgan. And not for the first time, Morgan wondered if he was the kind of man who wanted to take care of checking the icehouse to be certain it could provide ice cream for a party of eight.

"—and since Mr. Banfield already offered to help her, we thought that might be the best opportunity," the Duchess of Brighthollow was saying.

Morgan jolted as he realized he'd been dragged into the very circle where he'd claimed to himself that he didn't belong. He looked around the table to see if he could glean the particulars of the conversation. They'd brought up the garden, of all things. And that he should help someone. The only *her* he'd offered to assist was Elizabeth, in their truncated encounter in the library days before.

He glanced over to find her eyeing him from the corner of her eye with an almost guilty expression. "I would certainly be happy to help Lady Elizabeth with her garden project if she'd like the assistance," he drawled, holding his gaze on her until she was forced to acknowledge him with a slight nod.

"Th-thank you," she said, her voice only barely carrying down the long table.

"I will find you when the gentlemen rejoin the ladies and we can discuss what it is you need," he added.

She nodded and her eyes moved away, while her cheeks were suddenly pink. He would have smiled at creating that pretty blush, but for the fact that when he stopped looking at her, he realized her brother was watching him closely. Brighthollow was not an easy man to read. It took effort generally, but in that moment there was no work required to see his concern.

Blast, Morgan would have to be more careful. Playing around was one thing, but getting sacked less than a week into this odd venture was another entirely.

For a short time, conversation was drawn away and then the dessert plates were cleared. As Elizabeth got up, Morgan noticed her briefly glance his way again before she took Amelia's arm and the two strolled out of the dining room together, down toward the parlor where the ladies would have their sherry.

The men separated off in another direction, toward the billiard room and port. Robert found his way to walk side by side with Donburrow, which left Morgan with his employer. Brighthollow moved with a quick, purposeful gait toward the billiard room, his gaze straight ahead.

"Lizzie's garden is very important to her," he said as they neared the room.

Morgan pressed his lips together. The tone made it clear that Brighthollow was warning him. "Yes, I get that sense," he said, keeping his tone carefully neutral as he tried not to picture bright blue eyes and blushing cheeks.

"I will advise you to be careful with my sister," Brighthollow added as they entered the room together. "She is not to be trifled with."

Morgan wrinkled his brow at the choice of words, at the deep concern on Brighthollow's face. But before he could pursue the topic further, Robert crossed to them with his own concerned expression. "Is there a problem?" he asked.

Morgan fought not to roll his eyes at the protective instinct in his brother. "No. His Grace and I were just talking."

"I was only reiterating how seriously I expect Mr. Banfield to take his duties," Hugh said, his gaze holding Morgan's.

"Of course he will," Robert said, and now his eyes shifted to Morgan, too. Two dukes, staring him down, their messages dueling across their faces. He would have laughed if he didn't want to shrug off the shackles created by both and simply run into the night.

"Don't let me keep either of you from your port," he said, motioning toward the sideboard where the bottle had been left out by some helpful servant.

Robert looked like he would argue, but Brighthollow caught his arm and the two ended up chuckling as they crossed to pour drinks and set up the billiard table. Morgan let out a long breath as he was finally left alone to his own devices.

But not for long. The Duke of Donburrow edged up to him, a small silver notebook in his hand. *They are an intense pair,* he wrote in a neat, even hand.

Morgan read the message and smiled as he used one of the signs he'd picked up from watching Donburrow and his wife interact. "Yes."

Donburrow's eyes went wide and his smile broadened. *Not many pick up our language. Only our children thus far.*

"Well, I'm observant," Morgan said with a chuckle.

I can see you are that, Donburrow conceded, and he leaned back to examine Morgan a bit closer. Unlike when his brother or Brighthollow did it, Morgan felt no discomfort at Donburrow's observation. Though he did wonder what the other man saw, for he had fewer tells than even Brighthollow.

Don't let them scare you off, he wrote.

Morgan looked at his employer and his brother, standing by the billiard table, heads together as they seemed to be involved in serious conversation. Robert cast his gaze toward Morgan and his lips thinned slightly.

Morgan gritted his teeth and, mixing in sign, he said, "I'm not afraid of anyone."

Donburrow nodded slowly and wrote, *Come, let's play a game, shall we?*

Robert had racked the balls, and Donburrow and Morgan joined them. They paired off, he and Donburrow against Robert and Brighthollow. For a while, Morgan forgot his worries and simply focused on a game he was very good at. When their team bested his scowling brother's, he couldn't help the grin of triumph that tilted his lips.

"You owe me a rematch," Robert muttered. "But for now, I say we rejoin the ladies."

All three dukes seemed vastly pleased to rejoin their wives. Another interesting tidbit, since Morgan knew so many men who would do anything to avoid their spouse. But the dukes were all in love, just as it was rumored all over London. Somehow that knowledge made Morgan uncomfortable.

They entered the parlor where the ladies were gathered together. The three duchesses were giggling over something by the fire and Elizabeth stood alone by the window, staring out into the very garden she wanted help from Morgan with. As the other men moved to their wives, Morgan edged toward her. She wasn't paying attention and didn't note his approach.

Which gave him a moment to observe her. She was truly lovely. Her face was the kind ships had been launched for in long ago pasts. The kind painted as a great beauty, no matter the era, in which she was found. And yet her full lips were pressed together in an expression of displeasure. There was tension to her shoulders, to her back, like she was always waiting for something bad to happen.

He knew that kind of tightly sprung apprehension—he'd seen it before, he'd felt it before. It almost always accompanied a past where the bad thing had already occurred. Where one was waiting for it all to come crashing down again.

So what had happened to Lady Elizabeth? What could have happened to a lady so sheltered and obviously loved by her close-knit family?

She pivoted to face him, and her gaze flitted over him from the top of his head to the toes of his boots. She swallowed hard and her pupils dilated ever so slightly. His body reacted to the look, though he didn't want it to do so. He knew that look too. It was another expression he hadn't expected on the face of such a lovely innocent.

Desire.

But then it was gone, and her mouth went tight again and her shoulders pushed back. "Is it your habit to sneak up on people, Mr. Banfield?"

He shrugged as he joined her to look out the window, being careful not to push too much into her space. For both their sakes. "I didn't think I was sneaking. The three dukes came into the room with such a clatter in their hurry to find their wives that I assumed you must have been alerted to our presence. And where else would I go but to you?"

She let out a tiny gasp and pivoted to face him again. "Why would you come to me?"

Her hands were shaking. It was such a strong reaction that Morgan actually took a step away from her. "The garden, my lady," he said, gentling his tone. "At supper I said I would come to discuss it with you after the party reformed."

That same pretty blush entered her cheeks again, but this time he thought it was for a different cause. Embarrassment. And he found he didn't like it quite so much when it was linked to pain and not to being merely flustered.

"Of course," Elizabeth breathed. "How silly of me."

"Not silly," he reassured her quietly, and found himself wanting to touch her arm in comfort. His fingers flexed at his sides the desire was so strong, but he didn't do it. He had no right, after all. He had no place.

Elizabeth glanced over her shoulder. The dukes and duchesses had paired off as couples. Every single one of them looked to be in intimate conversation, as if they had been separated for days rather than less than an hour for drinks and billiards. Her lips pursed again and she refocused on Morgan. "I suppose now is as good a time to discuss it, given the distraction of the other guests."

He smiled. "They are very attached, aren't they? All these couples so powerfully connected is uncommon, I think, in your class."

Elizabeth worried her lip a fraction, which of course drew Morgan's attention to it. A very full lower lip, indeed, when she wasn't pursing it flat. A kissable set of lips, to be sure.

"I suppose it is uncommon," she said slowly. "And yet all my brother's friends have found such a harmony in their marriages. It's lovely for them. No one should be anything but happy, for they all worked hard to earn their happiness."

"No one should be," he said, focusing on that careful turn of phrase. "But I suppose being surrounded by people so desperately in love can be...challenging."

"When you are alone?" she said softly. "When you will always be alone? Yes."

The moment she said the words, her gaze snapped up to his. Filled with terror, filled with regret. She lifted a hand to her lips as she stared at him. Then she cleared her throat and whispered, "I ought not to have said that. Not to anyone, especially not to you."

His brow wrinkled at that last bit. Why especially not to him? He wanted to ask her, but then he saw the tears glittering in her eyes. He saw her true, powerful discomfort. And he couldn't bring her more of that. He couldn't prove himself as untrustworthy as she apparently believed him to be upon first glance.

"Would you like to talk about the garden instead of this topic?" he asked.

Her hand lowered and she stared at him a beat. Then she nodded. "That would be best."

"It was your mother's project, yes?"

She seemed to be struggling to gather herself. "Yes. She was not the kind to be satisfied with just hosting parties and managing the household. She liked a project and the garden was hers." A shadow of a smile tilted her lips, and Morgan caught his breath. She was even lovelier when she wasn't bracing for some unknown attack.

"She is not still with you?" he asked.

She bent her head. "No. She died long ago and the garden fell to the wayside. But I found her plans not that long ago, Mr. Banfield. I wish to execute her vision."

He nodded slowly. Here he'd thought they were just talking about planting a few shrubs or clearing a space for a fountain. What Elizabeth actually wanted was far more personal.

"Why don't we meet in the morning and walk through your garden?" Morgan asked. "I'll better understand your wishes if we are standing in the middle of the space. Bring those plans if you can, so we can review them. Afterward we can talk more about it."

She stared up at him, holding his gaze like she was trying to determine something about him. Finally she said, "Very well. I rise earlier than the household. Shall we say eight?"

Morgan flinched. His life in London often had him lounging abed until luncheon. But he supposed those days were over if he were going to take on the duties of a man of affairs. He might as well start getting used to it.

"Eight o'clock in the garden," he repeated.

She worried her lip and then began to edge away from him, tiny side steps. "I should—I should rejoin the party. Until tomorrow, Mr. Banfield."

"Until tomorrow, Lady Elizabeth."

He watched her go, her hands shaking as she walked away. She slid up beside the Duchess of Brighthollow, almost hiding behind her and Katherine, but not really participating in their conversation. But Morgan felt her eyes move to him from time to time.

He felt her watching. And he wondered what would happen when they were well and truly alone together.

CHAPTER 6

Lizzie stepped down from the terrace steps into the garden and drew in a deep breath of the clean air around her. She loved the smell of her mother's garden, she always had. It was roses and honeysuckle, wet green leaves and earthy soil. The scents she always associated with a woman long gone, but never forgotten. Now when she took them in, tears pricked her eyes.

But she was not going to let Morgan Banfield see that moment of vulnerability, so she blinked the tears away, pushed her shoulders back and took a few steps down the path into the garden. She looked around for him, peering around bushes and into nooks and crannies, but he was nowhere to be found.

She huffed out a breath. "Probably lazing around like the true rake he is," she muttered as she moved toward a flat stone bench beside her favorite statue in the garden. She smoothed the wrinkles from the folded plans and then stepped back to look over them.

"You are very serious."

She jumped at the deep voice right at her elbow and pivoted to find Morgan standing there, looking down at her. He was informal in another white shirt rolled to the elbows and a black waistcoat.

His beard was neatly trimmed and it looked soft this close, like it would feel good against bare skin.

She blinked and took a step away from him. "You startled me," she gasped, trying to find breath when there seemed to be none left.

He smiled and her heart stuttered even though she knew it shouldn't. He had a truly lovely smile because it felt so genuine and warm. Like it pulled her in. She didn't want to be pulled in. Being pulled in was dangerous, as dangerous as noting that woodsy smell of him or the fact that his warmth curled around her when he stood so near to her.

"We did say eight o'clock, my lady, did we not? Unless you wagered I would not make it." He arched a brow in challenge.

She opened her mouth to deny the charge, but then she shrugged. "I did guess you might have forgotten our meeting. I suppose that was an unkind assumption, I apologize."

"You needn't," he said with a low chuckle that seemed to make its way into her bloodstream. "I am a bad bet, my lady. You might have been right more than half the time."

She worried her hands together before her, uncertain how to respond to his playful magnetism. Part of her wanted to laugh. He brought that out so easily. But…it felt dangerous to do so.

He seemed to sense her discomfort and stepped away, granting her space as he turned around in a circle to look about him. "It's already a beautiful space," he said.

She nodded. "My favorite on the estate, truth be told. This spot in particular."

He focused his attention on the little nook where they stood. "Let me guess, you curled up on the bench where you've laid your designs and read before the statue."

She couldn't help her smile then, for he had guessed entirely right and it brought her back to long, lazy days where she'd done just that. "Persephone and I shared a great many stories, yes."

His eyes widened a little and he looked a bit closer at the statue.

Lizzie found herself watching him instead of following his gaze. He took in the lines of the marble young woman's face, beautiful and soft as she glanced downward with an almost coquettish smile.

"Persephone, eh?" he said, his voice a little rougher now. "I would not have pegged you for a devotee."

"She made the god of the underworld love her," she said softly as she shifted her attention from him to the statue she had long loved. "She found the good in Hades. And according to legend, she is the reason for all these flowers and trees. Life and death, light and dark. What is not to like?"

She felt him watching her, and she shifted beneath the sudden regard. Heat suffused her cheeks and she caught her breath as she lunged toward the plans. "At any rate, I have my mother's designs. Now that you are in the space, perhaps we can discuss them at greater length."

He did not follow her for a moment. She still felt his gaze on her back and she waited for him to say something more about the statue or the myth or anything else that would peel away a layer she'd wrapped around herself for protection.

But he didn't. Instead, he stepped up to join her. He leaned in, examining the plans carefully. "Hmm, yes, I see. She wanted to change the plantings. Moving the bushes and trimming them should be easy enough. Now what about this?"

He pointed to a gazebo that was to be built in the far corner of the garden, right beside the exit of the hedge maze and near the place where the garden met the long, rolling hills of the remainder of the estate grounds.

"What about it?" Lizzie asked.

"Why not move it?" he pressed, skimming his index finger across the plans gently. He seemed to be trying to divine a location and then he settled on the opposite side of the garden. "Here. It makes more sense with the path line."

She scowled and reached out to push his hand away. "No."

He straightened up and stared at her. "No? Just no?"

She folded her arms and glared at him. "We—we are not altering the plans, Morgan." She caught her breath at the inappropriate slip of the tongue. Had she truly called him by his Christian name? What was wrong with her? "*Mr. Banfield.*"

He was silent for a breath and then he cocked his head. "Morgan. And why not?"

She hesitated. It was a good question. In truth, when she thought of where he wished to place the gazebo, it probably did make more sense and would be more useable for garden parties and small gatherings with friends. And yet she didn't want to do what he suggested.

And she didn't trust him enough to tell him why.

"It's none of your business," she whispered, snatching up the plans and folding them gently.

She waited for him to argue. Or to become angry at her reticence, certainly her unexplained peevishness deserved a set down. But he did neither of those things. He just watched her, dark brown eyes tracking over her face, down to the plans, as if he were assembling the puzzle of her without any effort at all.

She fought to stand her ground in the face of that.

"I believe I have misread the situation," he said at last. "Elizabeth, I thought you wanted my creative input on your project."

She ignored the fact he had just called her by only her Christian name and worried her lip. "I...do. I-I did."

He tilted his head. "But you don't want me to change anything."

"Er...no?" She said it as a question because when stated out loud it did seem ridiculous. And patently unfair to him.

He twisted his face and then scratched his head in confusion. "I don't understand."

Lizzie's breath was coming short. She couldn't seem to find it as the garden closed in around them. If she explained herself, she would reveal too much to this stranger...this rake. Revealing too much would give him ammunition if he wished to hurt her in the future. She'd seen that before, she'd felt the brutal sting of it.

She didn't wish to repeat the action. Not now, not ever.

And yet he was asking for an answer, it wasn't an outlandish request. So how could she tell him the truth without giving him anything?

"Elizabeth?" he whispered, and he stepped a little closer. His gaze held her captive, his concern seemed real. And she felt a strange desire to step into him, to let him curl himself around her.

Was she so weak as to know the consequences of such a thing and still desire it? Was that her nature, to be a fool for men such as this one? Such as Aaron Walters? *Were* they the same?

She didn't know what would have happened next, in the quiet of the garden, with his eyes drawing her in and her shaking body trying to convince her to surrender the truth. But she didn't have to find out. Because before she could make an utter fool of herself, she heard Amelia's voice in the distance, and it broke the spell.

"Lizzie?" Amelia called out.

Lizzie took a long step away from Morgan, covering her hot cheeks with her cold hands. "We're here!" she cried out in return. "Near Persephone."

"Of course you are," Amelia said with a smile as she rounded the corner and entered the nook in the garden.

As she did so, Morgan stepped away, Hades moving closer to the statue, farther from Lizzie, and she felt the coldness of the morning air once more. It was like a jolt of awareness and it settled her racing heart and flipping stomach at last.

Distance seemed the only way to do that. And so she would have to make sure she maintained it when it came to this man. She knew how, after all. She just had to remember.

A s the Duchess of Brighthollow reached them, Morgan forced a welcoming smile to his face. In truth, he wished the woman hadn't come. Elizabeth had seemed on the edge of saying something important to him. Explaining why she was so determined to stick to the plans she'd dug up from some dusty box in the attic rather than making something new. He might have guessed it was mere sentimentality, but it felt like something more.

Now she had distanced herself once more. He supposed that was for the best. Although it was in his nature to read those around him —a skill he didn't even try at, it just happened—perhaps in this case it wasn't the right thing to do. Elizabeth didn't wish to be read. That was clear in the way she turned away from his seeking eyes. The way she put up barriers.

Whatever had hurt her in the past was not his affair. The best he could do for both of them was to honor the boundaries she put up. To behave as the servant he now was. Nothing more.

"Good morning to you both," the duchess said as she reached out to squeeze Elizabeth's hand. "I wanted to see how the garden plans were coming."

"We've only just begun," Elizabeth said, casting a glance toward Morgan. Her blue eyes flitted over his face and then darted away just as swiftly.

"I think we're figuring it out," Morgan added with a quick smile for Her Grace that he hoped would keep her from pressing. It was obvious Elizabeth didn't need to be pushed at present, whether that was well intended or not. "Does His Grace require my assistance?"

That brought a flash of pink to the Duchess of Brighthollow's cheeks and a smile to her lips. "His Grace is, er, still abed. So you are free to continue your work. I just wanted to see if you needed anything. Once you've firmed up your plans, Lancaster and the rest of the gardening staff are ready to put them into motion."

Elizabeth nodded. "Very good. Thank you, Amelia."

The duchess wrinkled her brow. "Are you well, Lizzie? You look a little pale."

"I'm fine," Elizabeth said, and she paced away toward Morgan. Her gaze caught his and she held it there. "Just ready to move forward."

Her Grace looked concerned and more than a little confused, but she inclined her head. "Very well. I'll leave you to it then. Oh, but don't let me forget to discuss the assembly ball in three nights' time! I want to compare what we will wear."

Morgan watched the light dim in Elizabeth's gaze a fraction and her shoulders roll forward just a bit. "Yes," she said with what felt like forced humor. "I will speak to you about it at the luncheon later."

"Good day, then," the duchess said, and sent one more quick glance first at Elizabeth and then at Morgan before she turned and walked back up the path that led to the house.

Once she was gone, Elizabeth let her gaze move to his face again. She held it there, even, though not entirely certain. She cleared her throat. "My mother designed every inch of the plans I showed you earlier, Mr. Banfield. I don't want to do anything she wouldn't have desired. I'm executing her vision, nothing more, nothing less."

Morgan had a world of things to say to that statement. About the past, about the future, about living someone else's life. But he wasn't close enough to the young woman who stood before him to say those things. And if he did, it would be reaching out to her in a way he had already vowed he wouldn't.

He was a servant. She was the lady. It was his job to do her bidding, not question it or soothe her or help her beyond the boundaries put up between them.

So he nodded. "Very well, Lady Elizabeth. I understand. May I take that copy of the plans?"

She clutched the folded papers against her chest a bit tighter. "Why?"

He flinched at how defensive her voice became. How her gaze

narrowed as if she knew without doubt that he would hurt her. Take something from her. Destroy something she cared for.

He gentled his tone. "I want to examine the work a bit more closely. Then I'll put together a schedule for what will be done and when and at what potential cost. Afterward I can present it back to you and to the duke, if the expenses require his approval."

Her lips parted. "Oh." She shook her head as she held out the plans with hesitance. "I-I suppose that makes sense. I wouldn't have thought of such a thing."

He took the papers with a smile. "There's no need for you to do so. That's why your brother asked me to help. I suppose this project is also a way for me to prove my mettle. To him and, I hope, to you."

She stared at him, eyes widening a fraction. "To me? Why would you wish to prove yourself to me?"

"Because," he said, inching forward a fraction, even though he didn't make a move to touch her. She still sucked in a breath regardless. "I don't like to see you look at me as if I'm a potential enemy, Elizabeth. If all goes well, I may serve under your brother for a long time. I don't want you to…fear me."

She hesitated, then her lashes lowered and she stared at her clenched hands. "I-I'm not afraid of you."

She said it. She lied. He knew that as well as she did. But he didn't push. "Well, then whatever negative emotion you associate with me, how does that suit? I want you to see me as a…a friend. Someone you can count on if you need something done. If I can prove that to you by doing your bidding in the garden, then it will be worth it." He held out a hand. "Will you allow me to try?"

She stared at his outstretched fingers, then slowly extended her own hand to shake. When they touched, there was almost an electric sizzle in the air that Morgan had not expected. A heat that flushed up his hand, his arm, filed into his blood, pumped into every nerve ending. He lived with that touch.

And that was a terrifying notion. He swiftly released her hand, clenching his hands together as he forced a smile for her. "Very good. Now I'll leave you and get to work on this. Good day, my lady."

"G-Good day," she whispered, her voice almost not carrying as he turned and walked away from her. This woman, this slip of a woman who wasn't even his type, was turning his world on its head.

And he wasn't sure if he should like her for that fact. Or avoid her like a plague that would ultimately destroy him. But he'd have to decide soon enough. And he feared once he did, there would be no turning back.

CHAPTER 7

Lizzie sat at her desk in her study, a half-written letter to an old friend there, waiting for her. In truth, she was having a hard time composing what to say. She wanted to tell her friend about what was going on in her life and yet...

The truth of that wasn't something she felt she could fully put in words. She wasn't sure how to explain it to herself, let alone another person. Not unless she wished to fully expose herself, that was.

It had been three days since her meeting with Morgan in the garden. Three days and she hadn't been able to stop thinking about him. About that dimple hidden behind those soft whiskers. About the way he looked at her, focused on her, always reading her with what seemed like no effort whatsoever. She couldn't stop thinking of the way he'd asked her about Persephone and picturing him as a handsome Hades reaching up to her from the underworld. Beckoning her to darkness she feared...and craved.

Not to mention it had also been two nights and she had dreamed of the dratted man on each one. Benign dreams where they were walking through the endless garden. And less benign ones where his arms came around her, his lips lowered to hers, his hands clenched against her skin.

She jerked her head up to break the thoughts and sighed. It was very annoying to feel this way when she knew full well the consequences of such wicked desires. She could tell herself it was just because he was a new person in her life, handsome and compelling and born to draw women to him like bees to honey.

She could tell herself her thoughts were so desperate because she was surrounded by loving couples who often didn't realize doors were cracked or that sounds carried in the hallways. Knowing how much they each loved and desired each other was enough to put strange thoughts into anyone's heads and dreams.

Yes, Lizzie could tell herself all those very rational things. And none of them rang true. None of them explained her emotions quite as well as that she simply had a weakness for wicked men. That Morgan Banfield had come into her life to prove to her that she could not be trusted, no matter how much time had passed since her last fall from grace.

She sighed as she pushed her unfinished letter aside. Only that didn't help clear her mind, for under the sheet was another reminder of Morgan. A note she'd received from him that morning.

Because, despite how wicked she knew him to be, despite the fact that rakes and libertines were known to be lazy layabouts, the man *had* been working, just as he'd vowed, on the garden. He was doing things for Hugh, but each morning he sent her a missive with a list of things to do, an order in which they would be done, and a price sheet for materials. He had neat, even handwriting. Occasionally he drew a sketch and asked if it pleased her.

All of them pleased her. So she signed off on those things or made notes on changes and sent them back.

Work hadn't begun in the physical sense, but she could see that his strategic organizing would make everything flow smoothly and quickly once it did.

Once there was no garden to use as an excuse to hide here in Brighthollow, Lizzie had to assume she would be ferried back to London to continue the Season. Morgan would stay here to manage the estate, just as he had been hired to do. And that would be the end of all of it.

There was a light knock at her door and Lizzie jumped at the sound. She twisted in her chair. "Come in."

Amelia did so, with a bright smile for Lizzie. "Good afternoon. I wanted to come speak to you about the particulars regarding the assembly ball tonight. Have you thought about what you'll wear? I'll pick something to complement your gown if you know."

Lizzie pushed to her feet and shifted with discomfort. Amelia had been making little noises about the assembly gathering for days. Charlotte and Katherine had joined in, all of them loudly declaring what fun would be had, as if somehow Lizzie didn't know about these things. As if they could change her heart by saying the same words enough times.

Only her heart had not been changed.

Amelia frowned when she didn't answer right away. "You—you don't want to go. You've been avoiding the subject since I first brought it up, and I hoped you would come around to it. But you don't want to go."

"I don't," Lizzie admitted. "You know how those things are. Everyone in the county will be there since you and Hugh are in residence and you'll be bringing two additional ducal couples to the fray. They'll push in and talk too much and ask for too many dances and it all seems..." She dipped her head. "It's too much."

"I know you don't love these gatherings," Amelia said carefully. "I know they are silly sometimes, and overheated and the punch is bad. But they are also a way to meet and thank Hugh's people for their hard work and support."

Lizzie folded her arms. "It isn't as if I don't make myself available. I visit the village regularly and call on a great many friends and tenants."

"Of course you do," Amelia rushed to agree. "I only mean... Lizzie, I worry about you. Your desire to avoid all gatherings like this, I fear, will limit your choices in the future."

Lizzie shifted. "I assume you mean my marital choices."

"Yes, to be blunt about it. It isn't that anyone expects you to marry tomorrow. You are young and have many years to find the right person. But if you refuse to look or make any attempt, then how will you ever do so?"

"Hugh will arrange a marriage for me eventually," Lizzie said with a little shrug that dismissed her darker feelings on the subject. "We will discuss what match will make the most sense from a financial perspective and a title advantage. I will meet the person and if I feel I could get along with them on a basic level, then we'll marry."

Amelia stared at her, lips parted with surprise and, it seemed, horror. "*Lizzie!*"

Lizzie shook her head. "What? That is how it is done in our world."

"Perhaps in some corners of our world, but never ours. You cannot want such a bloodless, loveless union. Not when you are surrounded by friends who are made so happy by love! By passion. You cannot tell me that you want something less than a true union of the heart."

"I *don't* want that," Lizzie insisted, though there was a twinge of regret in her heart that she shoved away so the words rang strong and true.

"A great many people have said the same," Amelia insisted, worrying her hands before her. "But you know love is true. That it's real."

"I also know it isn't for me," Lizzie said as firmly as she could muster.

Amelia stared at her, eyes wide and shiny with tears that didn't fall. Tears of pain and pity and loss. Lizzie hated that she had put them there, but this had been a conversation a long time in the making and perhaps it was best to have it and be done with it.

Amelia cleared her throat. "Perhaps you could—"

Lizzie held up a hand to interrupt her. "I know you mean well. I

Now Amelia's jaw set and the expression on her face went from

love you more than anything for it. But I cannot risk what you are describing, Amelia. I won't."

Now Amelia's jaw set and the expression on her face went from grief to anger. "I hate that Aaron Walters did this to you. I hate that he took something you feel you cannot get back."

"Virginity is not retrievable," Lizzie said, and felt her cheeks heat with a blush.

"It's not your virginity I'm referring to," Amelia said, arching a brow.

"Well, I'm not sorry," Lizzie declared, brightening her tone as best she could. "I mean, I am. Of course I am. But what I went through...it brought you to Hugh, didn't it? So there's...something good from the bad, and that is enough for me."

Amelia was silent for a beat, and then she whispered, "We want you to be happy, my love."

Lizzie stepped forward and took her sister-in-law's hand. She lifted it to her heart, and for a moment the two women simply held stares, connected as they had been since the first moment Lizzie met Amelia. They'd been true sisters ever since, and she knew Amelia would feel her heart if she allowed it.

"Then let me stay home," Lizzie said softly. "I am not up for the assembly tonight. I *will* do it some other time."

Amelia's breath left her lips in a shuddering sigh, but Lizzie knew it was a sound of surrender. She'd won this battle, though it didn't feel like a triumph of any kind. When she saw Amelia's pity, it felt more like a defeat. "If that is what you want, I will speak to Hugh."

"Very good," Lizzie said with a sigh of her own. "Come, I was thinking about going to the music room to practice my pianoforte. I'll walk with you to my brother's study."

Amelia nodded and the two linked arms as they exited her private parlor and walked down the hall together. "You won't make a fuss with Katherine and Charlotte, will you?" Lizzie asked as they neared Hugh's study.

Amelia shook her head. "I'll tell them you felt under the weather. A slight headache."

Lizzie was going to answer her, to thank her for her discretion, but she was distracted as Morgan rounded a corner from the opposite side of the hall and came toward them with a long, certain stride. He was wearing a jacket today, and the buttons strained slightly against that broad chest.

He smiled as he saw them standing a few feet from Hugh's office. A bright, wide smile that made Lizzie want to return the expression, no matter how fraught her morning had been. But she fought the urge and merely inclined her head in his direction as a greeting, then squeezed Amelia's hand and slipped away from the both toward the music room. She hoped there she could find a little peace.

It seemed the last place it existed for her in this house. And she needed to lock everything out, especially Morgan Banfield, and find that peace again.

~

M organ and the duchess stood together, watching as Lizzie walked away down the hall without anything more than an acknowledging nod in their direction. The duchess let out a tiny, almost imperceptible sigh of worry and then gave him a strained smile.

"Good morning, Mr. Banfield. I assume my husband is working away in his study?"

"Good morning, Your Grace," he returned as he opened the door and motioned her to enter first. "Please join us. I know he will enjoy the interruption if it is you who creates it."

"Banfield, did you find that ledger?" Brighthollow said without looking up from his desk.

"I did, Your Grace. And I found something else I thought you might wish to see," Morgan said, and the duchess laughed.

JESS MICHAELS

That brought Brighthollow's head up from his work, and his expression softened with pure pleasure as his gaze fell on his wife. "I will take this interruption every day," he said, pushing to his feet and motioning Morgan to the desk.

Morgan stepped away to take the seat that Brighthollow had abandoned and dipped his gaze into the ledger to give the pair a moment of privacy.

"You do not know what a light you bring into this room," Brighthollow said as he kissed his wife's hand and drew her a little closer. "That gown is beautiful. I always convince myself you cannot be so beautiful, that I must have conjured you as a dream, but then you come into the room and prove me very happily wrong."

The duchess rested a hand on his chest with a smile. "You are a charmer today. How goes the work?"

Brighthollow sent a quick glance back at Morgan. "Very well. It seems I drag ledgers all over this house, so Mr. Banfield is being so kind as to retrieve them for a long-needed review."

"It is no trouble," Morgan said, keeping his gaze in the books. "I believe we have them all here now."

"And what about you?" Brighthollow asked, his attention returning, always and forever, to his wife. "Did you talk to Lizzie?"

Morgan froze, quill balanced above the ledger, at the mention of Elizabeth. He glanced up briefly and saw the duchess's concern plain across her pretty face.

"I...did. She cried off the assembly ball tonight, just as I feared she would." The duchess let out a shuddering sigh.

Brighthollow's shoulders rolled forward. "I see. I had hoped you could convince her."

"I tried," Her Grace said, and there was a hint of tears thickening her voice. "Oh, Hugh, she still blames herself for—"

Morgan tensed and lifted his gaze again, but she cut herself off before she could reveal anything of value to him. But now he had a hint of something he hadn't known before. Elizabeth blamed herself for something. What, he couldn't imagine. What could a gentle and genteel lady such as she have done that required self-blame?

He couldn't imagine she'd ever had a wild streak or done anyone harm. It wasn't in her nature. He knew that after spending five minutes in her company.

Brighthollow cupped his wife's cheek, and Morgan realized he was wiping a tear from her skin. Then he sighed. "I'll talk to her about it."

"I don't know," Her Grace said. "We've talked it to death, haven't we? I see her panic every time the subject is broached. We need to reevaluate our plan, I think. Perhaps just leave her be for a while."

"Wait too long and her moment might pass," Brighthollow mused.

"Push too hard and she'll shut us out forever," his wife whispered. "Things are going to change soon, Hugh. For all of us."

Brighthollow seemed to consider that a moment. He cast a quick glance at Morgan, who continued working away as if he hadn't heard a bit of this conversation. That was what servants did, wasn't it? They faded into the woodwork, pretended not to see or hear or imagine.

That was his place now. Even if it wasn't his nature.

"You're right," Brighthollow said, and leaned in to gently kiss his wife. "We'll discuss it later. Perhaps tonight with Charlotte and Ewan. They might have advice."

The duchess squeezed his hand. "Perhaps. I'll see you later. Good afternoon, Mr. Banfield."

She slipped away, and Brighthollow came to the opposite side of the desk and sank into a chair. For a moment, he stared straight ahead, his gaze blank as if he were in some faraway place. Thinking of Elizabeth, it seemed. Worrying over her, for that was clear as anything.

Morgan couldn't help but think of his own brother. Robert was making attempts to connect recently. This assistance in obtaining the position here was one example. But he couldn't imagine Roseford crashing himself on the rocks with such power as Brighthollow did for Elizabeth.

He found himself a little jealous of their powerful bond.

"Is there anything I can do?" Morgan said, not looking at Brighthollow but keeping his focus on the line of numbers before him.

"No," Brighthollow said, and his sharp tone made Morgan glance at him. The duke had speared him with a focused glare. "Let us discuss the ledgers, shall we?"

Morgan inclined his head, giving over to whatever his employer desired because there was little other choice. But his mind was left to ponder what he'd overheard regarding Elizabeth. That she was in trouble of some kind intrigued him. And even if he shouldn't, he wanted to find out exactly what kind of trouble it was.

CHAPTER 8

Silence was Lizzie's only companion as she took a long stroll down the hallways of the house. The entire party had left for the assembly ball an hour before, and at first she had enjoyed the quiet and peace of only the occasional servant bobbing by and the tick of the clock as she worked on her needlepoint.

The joy of silence had lasted a while. Except in the past quarter of the hour, she had begun to feel...restless. A little *lonely*.

But that was ridiculous, of course. She wasn't lonely. Being alone was a perfectly wonderful state to be in. There was nothing wrong with it.

Which was how she'd found herself walking down the halls toward the library. She'd find a friend in a book, just as she always did. That would quiet the regrets in her mind.

"Not regrets," she growled at herself through clenched teeth. "I have no regrets. I didn't want to go to the ball, I didn't want to exhibit for a passel of people. I wanted to be by myself, and by myself I..."

She trailed off as she entered the library and found Morgan Banfield among the books for the second time since his arrival. He was sitting before the fire, a book in hand, but he looked up as she entered the room. His dark brown gaze swept over her from head to toe before he shut the book with a soft thud. "Good evening, Elizabeth."

She swallowed hard. "You—you shouldn't call me that."

He blinked, almost as if he hadn't realized he was doing so. Then he pushed to his feet and tossed the book onto the side table. With a shrug, he said, "That's probably true. But I've spent my life not following rules. This transition to doing so isn't always easy."

Those words were a stark reminder and Lizzie folded her arms as a shield before her. "Yes. I can see that about you."

"Directives, though," he drawled as he came closer by a long step. "Those I'm exceedingly good at. Do you want me to be proper, *Elizabeth*? Because if you do, I will. But I think perhaps we might be… friends at some point."

She bent her head. He was testing her. The universe was testing her, it seemed, by sending him here and making him exactly as he was. What she should do, of course, was to set him down and demand he address her properly, whether in private or public. What she should do was walk away from him and find something else to do with her time.

But she didn't. Because he asked her what she wanted and right now what she wanted flew to the top of her mind, taunting her. She wanted to talk to him. She wanted to hear her name from his lips. She wanted to be…imprudent.

Even though she knew the consequences of such a thing.

"My friends…" She caught her breath. "My friends call me Lizzie…*Morgan*."

He arched a brow and a smile tilted his lips. "And is that what you want me to call you? That childhood name?"

She hesitated. She'd been Lizzie so long, she hadn't really ever thought about it in those terms. "I suppose it is my childhood name. Hugh always called me Lizzie and then everyone else did the same for as long as I can recall."

"But I don't think you're that person anymore," he said softly.

She tensed because there was a hint of knowledge in his stare. He didn't guess that—he knew that. How, she wasn't certain. Was it just because he was so observant or had he heard something? Had he been told something? Her cheeks heated at the thought.

"No," she said, straightening her shoulders. "I suppose I'm not. Time and experience changes us all."

"That it does," he said. "So shall I call you Lizzie like the rest? Or Elizabeth?"

She worried her lip for a moment. How did he do that? How did he just spew a few words and turn her on her head? Demand she look at herself in some new way? It was exceedingly frustrating.

But he was still waiting for an answer to his question, so she squeezed her eyes shut and whispered, "Elizabeth."

He gave just the hint of a smile, then turned and picked up the book he'd discarded upon her entry. He crossed to the shelf and placed it back where it belonged, and without looking at her said, "Were you looking for something?"

She swallowed. Here was her opportunity to walk away. To lie and say she just saw the light beneath the door or that she didn't come in for anything.

Only she didn't. She stepped closer, hating herself for not being able to resist. "A book to pass the time," she admitted.

He pivoted and speared her with another of those close glances. "Because the others are at the assembly ball," he said. "And you didn't go."

She pursed her lips. He was challenging her, or it felt that way. And she went on the defensive immediately. "I didn't want to," she snapped, perhaps more sharply than she had intended to.

"Why?"

She glared at him. "Why do you have so many questions?" she burst out. "Why are you always watching everyone?"

His eyebrows lifted at the unexpected outburst. "Am I?"

She huffed out a breath. "Please don't play me for a fool. Of course you are, I see it every time you're in a room. You look through me, you look through everyone. Like you're trying to see everything."

He shifted slightly, and for a moment she saw a slip of the mask he always wore. His eyes darted away from hers. So he didn't like to be seen, even if he could see. Well, it served him right.

He cleared his throat. "Perhaps we all have different ways of…coping."

She was shocked at the response, given so softly and so directly. "Coping?" she repeated.

He shrugged, and she saw his struggle in maintaining a nonchalant distance at this topic. "Of course. You hide. I…see. They're both ways to keep the darkness away, aren't they?"

Her breath was short. She could hardly find it as she stood staring up at this man. This utterly confusing, fascinating man who shouldn't be in her library. Who shouldn't call her by her first name. Who shouldn't speak of darkness because it wasn't a polite dinner topic.

But he did and was all of those things.

"For a while," she admitted.

There was a flutter of a smile on his face, but it was not accompanied by pleasure. No, it was a pained expression. "I suppose we are both finding that out. Demons are a difficult thing."

She edged a little closer. They were still three long paces apart, but it felt like the room shrank every time either one of them took any quarter.

"What are your demons, Morgan Banfield?" she asked, even though she shouldn't want to know. Shouldn't pry.

He arched a brow and leaned a little closer. "I'm not sure you want to know the answer to that question, *Lizzie*."

That nickname was a slur from his lips. An accusation that she was too innocent to understand.

So she stepped up once more, closing the gap further, and put her hands on her hips.

"I asked the question. Perhaps *you* are too afraid to answer it."

~

There was a fire in Elizabeth's eyes that Morgan hadn't seen before. A challenge to answer his own when he had expected a retreat. People so rarely surprised him that he wasn't prepared for this slip of a woman who rocked him on his heels.

No one ever asked him about his life. No one ever saw past the façade he had so carefully crafted during years and years of necessity. But here Elizabeth was. And he felt the strangest urge to...tell her. To strip himself open and let her see everything ugly. Maybe it would be better for both of them in the end, at that.

She would surely run if she knew the truth. Stop stalking him across the library with those blue eyes like sapphires.

"You must be able to guess, my lady," he drawled, reverting to casual flirtation because it was his safest place. "With a brother like mine. With a father like mine. I'm an infamous bastard, Elizabeth. Isn't that demon enough?"

She lifted her chin, and now it was she who peered closer, deeper. His trick, turned against him by a woman he had underestimated. She was quiet, but it was evident she was watching all the time, just as he did. Noticing while she remained unnoticed. Except by him.

"For some men, I would say it was demon enough. But *you* seem to revel in the reputation of your family."

"Do I?" he asked. "Have I done so here?"

"Well...no. You've been nothing but proper here. And yet I've heard talk. Rumor. You were brought here because of your wild side, weren't you?"

He shook his head slowly. Seemed his brother would talk, even if he pretended to want to help Morgan. He would poison this woman to him, perhaps her family, too.

"I suppose I was," he admitted.

"And that *never* seems to trouble you. So I think your demon is something deeper."

He flinched. "You know so little, here in your ivory tower where your brother lets nothing touch you."

Now she turned her face and he saw a flash of desperate pain. She covered it, but there it had been, plain as the brightest sunny day.

"And you know even less," she muttered, and turned as if she would leave. "You owe me no explanation, Morgan—Mr. Banfield. I will leave you to whatever troubles you."

She took a step toward the door and he found himself lunging after her, reluctant to allow her to walk away. If she did, she would never come back. She'd convince herself to never, ever come back.

"My mother was a courtesan," he said, the words feeling heavy as they exited his lips.

She pivoted to face him, her eyes wide. "I see."

"Everyone saw," he spat. "She was one of the most celebrated women of her generation. A shining jewel in the crown of any man who paid for the benefit of her company. She was the best, and that is why the last Duke of Roseford wanted her so badly. To stake a claim on what everyone else desired." He glanced at Elizabeth and those wide eyes. "You must think very little of a woman like her."

She drew back with a shake of her head. "No. I am not of that world, so it's difficult for me to picture her life. But it's not hard to imagine the choices she likely had to make. How a woman would end up in circumstances such as the one you describe and would make the best with what she had. You may think you see, but you don't know me, Mr. Banfield. I would never judge her or any other person for what they did to survive."

He stared at her, shocked by the acceptance she offered. There were few of her rank who would do so. Even the men who had drooled all over his mother would have spat on her if she dared enter their hallowed halls. His father included.

"I apologize for judging you," he said softly. "I simply wouldn't have assumed a lady of your background would take such a view."

She swiftly cast her glance away. "Demons, sir. You already

spoke of them." She didn't allow him an opportunity to press her on that. "Is she still with us?"

"My mother?" he asked, and his throat got suddenly dry. "No. She died six years ago."

Her expression softened. "I'm sorry."

"So am I."

"How?"

"Consumption, they say," he said with a shake of his head. "But it wasn't that. She died of a broken heart, courtesy of my father. That man claimed things of beauty and then crushed them so no one else would get a chance to enjoy them. She was part of that. When he left her, she never recovered. I watched her wither for decades. His name was the last on her lips when she left this earth."

"Oh, Morgan," she whispered, and now she moved closer again. The soft scent of her skin wafted up to tickle his nose as she closed her fingers around his forearm. Orange blossom.

He stared down into that beautiful upturned face. "I learned a great deal from her," he whispered. "To watch people. To read them. Those skills have kept me one step ahead a great many times. They've kept me safe."

Her lips parted slightly, and then she tightened her hand on his arm. "You are safe here."

"Am I?" he whispered, and he could no longer resist the desire to do something very foolish. Very dangerous. He reached out a hand and traced his fingers along the gentle line of her jaw. The need to touch her was just too powerful to deny. The need to take a tiny piece of this pure, lovely thing that he didn't deserve.

"Morgan," she whispered, his name a warning and a prayer and a question all at once.

He leaned in, the room blurring around them as all there was became her. He waited for her to step away, to tell him no. But she didn't. She didn't even as his breath stirred her lips.

She didn't when he claimed her mouth at last.

~

Morgan was kissing her and it was…so, so lovely. She was mesmerized by the soft brush of his whiskers against her chin, the pressure of his firm lips, the faint taste of whiskey and mint that flowed into her as he parted his lips and traced the crease of her mouth with the tip of his tongue.

She opened. She knew how this dance was danced. But this was very different than it had been all those years ago. Or at least, she had remembered it differently.

Aaron's kisses had been insistent, wet, sometimes a little painful with their force. But Morgan…he was something different. He didn't claim. He could have, of course. He was far bigger than she, far more experienced, despite her past. He could have had her on her back on the carpet without even losing breath if he wanted to.

But he seemed in no hurry to do anything but just…taste her. That's what he was doing, after all. Leisurely exploring her mouth with his tongue, swirling and sucking and washing her away on a very gentle current.

She clung tighter to his forearms, trying to find purchase in the tide. The world was turning, burning, and there was an ache deep inside of her for something more. More and more of his mouth and his arms as they gently wrapped around her and molded her firmly against his chest. She felt the accelerating thud of his heartbeat echoing her own, felt the clench of his fingers against her spine as he let out a very soft sound of pleasure and deepened the kiss yet again.

She was about to be lost. She felt it in every fiber of her being. If she didn't pull away, she would end up making the same mistakes she had all those years ago. Worse mistakes because surely her brother wouldn't forgive her again. Amelia would look at her with judgment, not love. Lizzie would destroy everything important if she let this happen.

So she pressed her hands flat against his chest and pushed. To her surprise, he released her immediately, opening his arms as he stepped away to give her space and purchase.

He said nothing, simply stared at her from that one long pace away, his expression utterly unreadable. She fought to regain her footing, gripping her hands at her sides as she struggled to slow her breath.

"I-I can't do this," she panted at last.

He nodded slowly. "Even if you want to."

She jerked her gaze to his and her cheeks heated. He knew she wanted to. A fact, not a question. He wasn't wrong. "Especially if I want to," she whispered. Then she straightened up and let out a long sigh. "I-I want you to know I'm not sorry it happened. It's just that I…can't."

"Very well," he said. "Than I have just one important question for you."

"Wh-what is that?" she stammered. Her entire body tensed, waiting for whatever awful thing he would say now. What accusation he would lodge or threat he would make now that he had the upper hand over her.

Except he didn't go hard and cruel. He smiled at her.

"How do you feel about piquet?" he asked.

She blinked. "The…the card game?"

"Yes. It's a two-hand game, so we can play just us. And it will help pass the time we were both looking to fill since you no longer wish to do…" He waved a hand between them. "That."

Her lips parted. "You aren't going to argue with me about *that?*"

"Why should I?" he asked. "I vastly enjoyed kissing you. You aren't sorry we did it. You asked me to stop, so we did. There's nothing more to say. Neither of us did something wrong, did we?"

She hesitated. Kissing him should have felt wrong. But it didn't. Pulling away had always felt wrong in the past, like she was wrong to refuse. But now it didn't either. She was confused, but not guilty. "I-I suppose not."

"Then what stops us from playing a round of cards as friends?" he asked. "Unless you don't wish to be friends with me."

She hadn't considered that as a possibility, even though he'd mentioned it before. Morgan Banfield had been a confusion, a distraction, a frustration...but she'd never considered truly making him a friend. She rather liked the idea, really. Everyone else around her was part of a couple, in love and unable to imagine that anyone else had a different path. Why not be friends with this man? If his employment with her brother worked out, they would see each other a great deal. Why should it be awkward or uncomfortable?

"Very well. I would like to be...friends."

"Excellent." His grin was bright and genuine. "I will fetch a deck of cards. You see if you can find some buttons."

"Buttons?" she repeated in confusion.

"To wager with," he called out as he exited the room. "I do not trust you, my lady, and I do not wish to lose what little blunt I have left."

She stared at the door he'd just departed from, stunned into silence for a moment. But then she couldn't help but laugh. And laugh she continued to do as she went to seek out the buttons for their game.

Morgan leaned back in his chair with a chuckle as Elizabeth threw up her hands in defeat. "I'm terrible at this game," she giggled.

He grinned as he took in the cards and began to shuffle. "It's because your face is too honest."

"My face is too honest?" she repeated. "What does that mean?"

"It's a game of trickery and deception," he said. "And you always look so guilty when you lie. Meanwhile I am very charming and you believe everything I say."

Elizabeth tilted her head back and she laughed harder. Morgan stared while she was distracted. It had been a few hours since their kiss in this very room. He would be lying if he said he hadn't been thinking of it.

But he'd also enjoyed their time together. Elizabeth was kind and intelligent, she was witty and quick to laugh once she relaxed. She was, in short, everything lovely. And he liked her.

She pointed at the pile of buttons before him. "I'm glad we didn't play for real stakes, or I would have been stripped of my pin money."

He kept the smile on his face even though her words struck a bit closer to the bone than perhaps she knew. After all, he'd been stripped of more than pin money by gambling and carousing. And ended up here. Which suddenly didn't seem so very bad.

"Another round to try to win it back?" he teased.

"My God, you are like a barker in the park." She affected a deeper voice. "*Step up and you'll surely win this time, my lady!*"

"But surely you will, Elizabeth," he said. "Don't I look trustworthy?"

"And what is going on here?"

They both jumped at the voice at the library door. They got to their feet at the same time and Elizabeth pivoted to face the intruder. It was the Duke of Brighthollow, along with Donburrow and Robert. All three were staring at the scene before them. Brighthollow looked...concerned.

"Hugh, gracious how late is it?" Elizabeth said as she stepped toward her brother. The guilt she hadn't displayed after their kiss was written all over her face now.

Morgan didn't care for the expression.

"Very late," Brighthollow said with another glance at Morgan. "I'm surprised to find you up. The ladies retired when we returned. The gentlemen were going to have a quick drink before we joined them."

"Oh, I lost track of time," Elizabeth said. "I should probably go up, as well."

She turned back to Morgan and met his eyes. She smiled, and for a moment all he could think about was the intoxicating peaches-and-cream taste of her mouth. The little sigh she'd made when he parted her lips with his tongue. The clench of her fingers against his arms as she reached out for more. Allowed him to take more.

He blinked to clear his mind and returned the smile, though his own felt strained.

"Good evening, Mr. Banfield," she said. "Thank you for…for the company."

He inclined his head. "My lady."

She exited the room, and for a moment everything was silent. The Duke of Brighthollow stood in the door, staring at him, eyes narrowed. Then he cleared his throat. "I think I'll forgo that drink, lads. I need to speak to Amelia about something before she falls asleep. Good night."

He pivoted on his heel and marched from the room without another word. Donburrow's eyes went wide and he motioned his head toward the door. Robert nodded. Morgan sucked in a breath as he and his brother were left alone.

He thought of what Elizabeth had said about his wild streak. He needed to speak to Robert about that. But he wasn't up for it tonight, not when his entire body felt on edge thanks to Elizabeth. Thanks to his own poor judgment that he refused to regret.

Robert pulled the door shut behind him and leaned back against it. He folded his arms. "Do you want to tell me what's going on?"

Morgan bent and began gathering up the cards and buttons that proved his evening with Elizabeth. "I won at piquet," he muttered.

Robert slapped a hand back against the door, and Morgan jerked his gaze up to find his brother shaking his head at him. "What's happening between you and Lizzie?" Robert clarified.

Morgan sighed. "Nothing. We spent a little time together. Nothing more."

He expected his brother to rail at him, but Robert merely smiled. "Hmmm. I wonder how many times I said the same thing over the years. I was just spending time with her. It didn't mean anything. None of it means anything. And then it does."

Morgan pursed his lips. "It's vastly annoying to be the brother of a reformed rake, you know."

Robert snorted out a laugh and the tension in the room bled away a fraction. "Because I can read your intentions? Yes, that's always troublesome, I agree. I despised it when my friends did it to me over the years. But now I'm going to offer you some advice and you'll be equally annoyed by that. I only hope you'll take it."

Morgan shrugged. "There's no stopping you. Go ahead."

Robert pushed off the door and stepped closer. The teasing was gone from his expression. "Tread lightly, Morgan. There are things in this world you cannot trifle with."

Morgan set his jaw. He hated that his brother was closer to the mark that he should have been. He hated that the advice rang true.

He stepped away and went back to picking up the cards. "Fuck off, Your Grace."

Robert snorted out a laugh and said nothing else as he left the room. When he was gone, Morgan set the items in his hand down and stared into the fire. As much as he hated to admit it, Robert wasn't wrong. He was in dangerous waters now.

He'd have to tread extremely lightly from now on.

CHAPTER 9

Morgan stood at the edge of the area in the garden that had been cleared for the gazebo and watched as the workers staked out the edges of the new building. He ought to have been focused on that work. Focused on the goal at hand and his job as overseer of it.

Instead, his mind kept flitting, insistently and at the most inopportune times, to Lizzie in the library the night before. Lizzie's lips. Lizzie's gaze as she stared up at him.

"Mr. Banfield?"

Morgan jolted for he realized that the head gardener was at his elbow and had said his name more than once. He turned to face the older man with a contrite nod. "I was woolgathering, Mr. Lancaster, I apologize. What do you need?"

Lancaster stretched his back and watched the men work for a moment. "It will be a fine building when it's finished."

"Indeed," Morgan said.

He had been uncertain about Lancaster's feelings toward him since he had swept in and taken charge of a project in the garden the man had tended for decades, but the gardener had not been anything but polite and helpful. The entire staff was, in truth. He felt welcomed by them, though he wasn't entirely in their society. Just as he wasn't entirely in the society of the duke and his family.

He was stuck in between. And that was…isolating.

Lancaster said, "Now that the lads have begun their work, I wondered if you might join me a moment? I have a question about an area in the garden that hasn't been discussed yet."

"Of course," Morgan said. He followed Lancaster down the twisting paths, and finally they reached a little area in a corner of the garden. It was brown and dead, old vines twisting against the ground and brittle bushes shedding leaves and sticks across the grass.

"Oh," Morgan said. "I'm shocked a change to this part of the garden wasn't in Lady Elizabeth's plans."

"Since she's following the last duchess's sketches, I suppose it wouldn't be," Lancaster said with a sad frown. "There was a deep frost that lasted too long a few years back. We covered most of the plants, but these got forgotten somehow and died. Still, since we're doing so much work, I wondered if you had a thought about this place?"

"You want my opinion?" Morgan asked. "You certainly know more about every leaf in this place than I could ever hope to."

Lancaster smiled at him. "Perhaps that's true. Perhaps that's why I want your opinion. Sometimes fresh eyes are the brightest. You have good instincts, Mr. Banfield."

Morgan tried to ignore the way his chest puffed up with unexpected pride. He rubbed his chin. It was a pretty little corner of the estate grounds, to be certain. A great many guestrooms looked out over it, if his judgment of the layout of the chambers above him was correct. So it needed to be special. And since this area didn't fall into Elizabeth's strict adherence to her mother's plans, he also felt he might have a bit more leeway in design.

Just months ago, he might have scoffed at that idea. But since his arrival here, he'd come to—and he couldn't believe he was admitting this, even to himself—*like* his work in the garden. He liked working with the living things, liked the smells of the grass and the flowers and the trees. He liked creating something that would last for more than just a few hours. Something that would change and grow of its own accord.

"If she's not considered this area, perhaps this is a chance for us to do something special for Lady Elizabeth," he mused. "Make this a surprise for her."

Lancaster nodded, and Morgan could see he liked the idea. If the servants accepted Morgan, they adored Elizabeth. Her name was said in hushed reverence and he was certain at least three footmen were half in love with her. How could they not be?

"What do you have in mind?" Lancaster asked.

Morgan shut his eyes, drawing out what this corner could be in a few broad strokes. And connecting it to Elizabeth, as well. When he thought of her, the scent of her skin was one thing that sparked his memories, and he smiled as he looked at the older man again.

"Do we have access to orange trees?" he asked.

The corner of Lancaster's mouth quirked up. "I think it can be arranged."

"Good," Morgan said, stepping forward and sweeping his arm in a semicircle along the wall. "I think we could plant them here. And then let's talk about a fountain…"

Lancaster pulled out a small notebook and began scribbling as Morgan lost himself in something he never would have guessed could draw his attention. Not just the garden, but the woman who had inspired such a change, and such a desire to create something as a gift for her. He only hoped she'd like it when it was finished.

And that he wouldn't reveal too much of himself while he was making something that was just for her.

L izzie stared into her teacup, her mind leagues away from the parlor. It had been three days since that searing kiss with Morgan in the library. She'd tried to minimize it, but she couldn't lie and say something like that didn't matter. She'd tried to forget it, but that was impossible too. She still sometimes tasted Morgan's lips on hers. Being in the same house as he was made it impossible to just lock that memory away.

And so she was left with the thoughts and the distraction and the questions that hatched in her mind. How had they come to this? Would he ever do that again? Did she want him to?

"Do you want to, Lizzie?"

She blinked as Charlotte repeated the very question in her own mind. When she looked up, she found Amelia, Katherine and Charlotte all staring at her with equal expressions of concern and expectation. Her distraction had yet again caused her trouble.

She forced a smile. "I'm sorry. I have such a flighty mind as of late. What are you asking me?"

"We were speaking about London," Katherine said, tilting her head as if to examine Lizzie more closely.

"Yes," Charlotte said. "Amelia was talking about getting all the duchesses together and having a private showing of Madame Lorraine's newest fashions for winter. Do you want to be part of that?"

Lizzie shifted. "Madame Lorraine does make the most beautiful clothing, but..."

"But?" Amelia pressed.

"It's hard to make plans for London when we are here in Brighthollow, isn't it?"

"Well, we aren't staying here forever," Amelia said with a light laugh. "The remainder of the Season is to be had, with friends to be met and balls to attend."

Her sister-in-law sounded so hopeful that Lizzie wanted to slither to the ground and roll beneath the settee to hide from her expectations. After all, she didn't want to go back to London. She didn't want to leave her home. To leave Morgan.

No, not Morgan. She shook her head at the wayward thought. Her reasons for wishing to stay in Brighthollow had nothing at all to do with her brother's man of affairs.

"Your pale cheeks worry me," Charlotte said, pursing her lips. "My dear, surely the idea of the Season doesn't cause you this much distress."

"It...does," she squeaked. "I so appreciate the thought to include me and the desire to see me participate in what comes naturally to all of you."

"Not all of us," Charlotte assured her gently. "Ewan has always been uncomfortable with the city. With practice he has become more at ease, but I know he doesn't care for these things any more than you do."

Lizzie drew in a long breath. Ewan had been mute since birth. He had been treated badly by his family and sometimes by those in Society. She felt the accusation in Charlotte's comparison, as if she shouldn't feel apart when she'd always had a place in the world she shunned.

"I just don't know," she began, but before she could try to explain herself better, there was a light knock on the open door behind them.

The group as a whole turned, and Lizzie caught her breath as she saw Morgan standing in the entryway, his gaze trained on her and a broad smile on his handsome face.

"My apologies for the interruption, Your Graces. I am about to go see the progress in the garden and I wondered if Lady Elizabeth might wish to join me and see the headway the workers have been making on the gazebo."

Lizzie pushed to her feet, smoothing her suddenly damp palms on her skirt. "Yes, of course. I'd love...I'd like to do that, if my friends don't mind me so rudely abandoning them."

Amelia's brow wrinkled and her gaze slowly shifted from Lizzie to Morgan and back again. "We don't mind at all," she said, her voice soft. "I'm certainly looking forward to seeing what you two are cooking up back there."

Lizzie was already moving across the room to join Morgan at the door. She cast a quick smile of farewell to the duchesses before he swept his arm forward as if to tell her to take the lead.

She did so, feeling the weight of his presence beside her as they strolled up the long hallway together. This was their first time alone since their game of piquet and she felt...shy. The world had shifted between them, after all. How was she to behave normally when she knew what his mouth felt like when it pressed to hers?

"Mr. Banfield?" Masters called out before they could reach the exit to the terrace and the stairs there that led to the garden.

Morgan gave her an apologetic nod and turned back. "Yes, Masters?"

"A missive just arrived for you from London, sir," he said as he held out a note.

Morgan's brow wrinkled and Lizzie immediately saw the flash of concern on his face. He took the note with a quick nod and glanced at her. She could feel he was torn between being polite to her and seeing what the letter was about.

"Of course you should look at it if you believe it might be important," she said.

He looked down at the missive a second time and then said, "Come, we'll step onto the terrace, at least. Might as well not waste a perfectly beautiful day."

They exited into the sunshine and Lizzie stepped away a fraction to allow him some privacy in his letter. Or at least, that's what she should have done. Only she couldn't help but glance at him from the corner of her eye as he broke the seal on the folded sheet of paper and let his gaze drift across whatever had been written to him.

His mouth tightened and his shoulders stiffened. He stared at the letter a moment, then folded it and stuffed it in his pocket.

"Do you need to—to handle that?" she asked.

"No." His tone was gruff, dismissive, and she found herself moving even further away from him. He'd been all friendly regard, and then this wall had been erected with just one single word.

And it reminded her, in a flash of awful memory, of Aaron Walters that horrible night her brother had found them on the road to Gretna Green. Her lover had been sweet, kind, and then cold as steel as he dismissed her and all they had shared. That moment where she realized she'd been played for a fool was one she often thought about.

She shook off the memory and thrust her shoulders back. She and Morgan had kissed, yes, but there was certainly nothing that connected them beyond that slip in judgment. She couldn't fool herself that there was.

"Well, then I think you should lead on, Mr. Banfield," she said, retreating back to formality because it felt safer. "Show me what you wanted me to see."

He nodded and they went down the stairs together. A few turns through the garden, and as they came around the last corner, she saw it. The frame of the new gazebo, just as her mother had designed it in her plans all those years ago.

Lizzie couldn't help her excitement. She clapped her hands together with a gasp of glee. "Oh, Morgan!" she burst out as she pivoted to face him. He was standing just behind her, and she rested her hand on his chest to steady herself.

He stared down at her and then the corner of his lips tipped up in a half-smile. "I'm glad you like it."

"I do," she whispered, but she was no longer looking at the gazebo.

His smile faded and his pupils dilated. Slowly he lifted a hand and brushed a lock of hair from her forehead. The brush of his bare knuckles against her skin made her shiver with sensation. What did this man do to her? How could he so easily wrap her up in these desires she'd feared for so long?

He bent his head and all her pretense of putting up a wall between them fell away. Even though she knew it was folly, she found herself lifting to him. Their lips met and her hand gripped into a fist against his chest as she parted her mouth and let him in. He cupped the back of her head, tilting it so he could deepen the kiss. She sank into the feeling, letting her guard drop as she finally got the thing she had been dreaming of for days.

But just as quickly as he'd drawn her in, he stepped back, steadying her before he dropped his hands away from her. "You told me no before," he said, his voice thick and raspy. "My apologies, Elizabeth."

She stared at him, shocked that he even remembered she'd told him this was something they could not do, let alone honored the request. One she regretted in this heated moment.

"Don't apologize," she said, shoving her shaking hands behind her back. "I know this isn't a good idea…probably. But…but…"

His smile returned. "Oh, Elizabeth, better not say *but* or I'll kiss you again."

She laughed at his gentle teasing. The tension between them faded a fraction, though she still wanted that damned kiss more than ever.

He offered her his elbow. "And now, I want to show you something else."

She blinked. "More than the gazebo?"

His eyes danced with excitement. "A surprise. Come along."

He drew her away from the framed outbuilding and down a winding path through the garden. They twisted and turned in companionable silence until they reached a corner of the garden that had once been a mass of rosebushes her mother had planted before Lizzie was even born. They had been touched by a frost a few years before and never fully recovered, no matter how Lizzie or the expert gardeners under her brother's employ tended them.

But now all those half-dead plants were gone. They'd been

replaced by a little half-circle of orange trees that surrounded a bench. There was also the base for a small fountain opposite the bench that hadn't been there before. It wasn't complete, but she could see how charming it would be in a short amount of time.

Had this little circle of protection existed in any other garden in the world, Lizzie would have been enchanted. She loved orange blossom—she even had her soap infused with the scent—and the sound of the trickling water was soothing and happy, indeed, and she could picture it here.

But this *wasn't* her garden. It was her mother's garden. And now the late duchess's dead roses had been removed and their intended place had been filled by something...different.

Tears stung her eyes and she pulled away from Morgan's arm with a shake of her head. "I-I told you we were to remain firm to the plans I discovered, Morgan! Why did you do this?"

She didn't wait for his response, but turned away and rushed from the little corner, fighting tears and a looming sense that she had done something wrong, both by allowing this to happen...and by loving what Morgan had created for her.

Morgan stared at Lizzie's retreating back as she hustled away from the corner of the garden he had specially designed for her. He was utterly confused. She was always so gentle, so bound to please others, even to her detriment. But the moment he changed anything in her mother's garden, something deep within her snapped.

He saw where she had gone and for a moment he longed to follow. Then he pushed his hand into his pocket and felt the folded missive he'd shoved there earlier. He didn't need to look at it to know what it said.

You can run, but you can't hide. I know where you are.

Morgan shook his head. The note was a stark reminder that his life did not, could not, mesh with a woman such as Lady Elizabeth. He should just let her be angry and leave it at that, for both their sakes.

Only he couldn't. He smashed the letter down deeper in his pocket, as if that could push the past further away, and then he marched toward where he'd seen Elizabeth go. The place where he'd originally found her here days ago, the Persephone corner, as he'd begun to call it.

He entered the space and found she had sunk onto her bench and was staring at the statue of Persephone, her expression blank. At least she was no longer crying.

He took a step closer.

"I'm sorry," she said before he could speak. She glanced toward him, her expression filled with an expectation that she would be chastised. Only he didn't want to do that. He just wanted to understand, even though it wasn't his place to do so.

"You needn't be." He slowly sat down beside her on the bench. It was narrow, so it forced them to be close together, closer than he'd imagined when he thought to join her. But it was done now, and he would just have to ignore the fact that her knees brushed his and it made him so aware of her presence.

"You must think me a fool," she whispered, and her head bent.

He shook his head as he tucked a finger beneath her chin and lifted to force her gaze back to his. "No, not a fool. I admit I don't understand the strength of your reaction when it comes to this garden, though."

Her breath came short as she stared up at him, and he could see her running equations in her head. Ciphers to determine if he was honorable enough to share something obviously private and painful. He found himself leaning forward, wondering if he'd be found worthy. Wondering how a woman like her could *ever* find him worthy.

At last she worried her lip and whispered, "I suppose you shared something of your past with me, didn't you? About your mother, in fact. It is only fair to do the same."

"You don't owe me something just because I told you about my mother," he responded. "Tell me if you wish to do so, not because you think I expect a quid pro quo."

Her eyes widened in surprise and then she clenched her hands together on her lap. "No, I-I want to tell you. So you'll understand. So someone will understand *something*."

His brow wrinkled. She was so close to her brother, he hadn't expected that Elizabeth would say something that indicated she felt...isolated. Misunderstood. He certainly related to that, no matter how far apart their worlds might be otherwise.

"Take your time," he encouraged, and didn't stop her when she got up and paced away to the statue of Persephone. She reached out and traced the lines of the stone woman's face and then shook her head.

"I was eight when they died," she began. "It was an accident. One moment I had parents, the next I was orphaned. A blink that changed everything about my life."

"That must have been frightening," he whispered, trying to picture her as a little girl, grieving and afraid.

"It was, at first," she admitted. "But Hugh stepped in. I knew he'd be a good duke—he was always so clever and even-handed. But he turned out to be so much more. Despite how young he was, only twenty-one at the time, he embraced the role of *father* with great aplomb. I was lucky to have him, I still am."

"Still, you must have missed them."

"My real father was..." She sighed. "He was not a very nice man. He refused to allow any weakness from us. He had little use for me, as I was not his heir, nor qualified to be a spare. He spent all his time and energy and cruelty on Hugh. So when he was gone, I felt little except for a regret that he could not have been...better. But my mother?"

She turned away and her hands clenched at her sides. "I did miss her, terribly. I still miss her. I long to tell her about my small triumphs. And when terrible things happen. Things like—"

She cut herself off, and Morgan straightened. There was that hint again, that little whisper about something that had happened to this woman that no one wished to reveal. Every time it came up, he found himself wondering more and more about it.

"Well, I just wish she were here to advise me sometimes." She forced a smile as she looked at him again and he saw the false brightness on her face. "Not that I don't appreciate the relationship I've developed with Amelia or the kindness of the other duchesses."

"But they aren't your mother," he said. "No one could ever ask you to take any other relationship and pretend it could replace that one."

"I suppose not. I've always longed for ways to connect with her." She gave a soft chuckle. "For the first year after she died, I used to stop by her portrait in the gallery every night. I'd drag a chair across the room and climb up to kiss her cheek. Once I fell and nearly broke my head. The servants went into a panic and Hugh found out what I was doing. Then he gave me a miniature of her for my own bedside. I talked to it for years and years. But I never felt quite so connected to her as I did after I found the garden plans last winter."

Morgan drew back. There it was. The puzzle piece he'd been missing, and it snapped into place and completed the picture perfectly. "It was a real connection."

"Yes." She nodded. "I could talk all I wanted to a portrait, but there was never any message back. But the garden plans, that is like seeing her heart. Hearing her voice again. It is a guide to exactly what she wanted. And I'm the conduit to give that to her." She shook her head. "What if I do it wrong, though? What if I don't complete her vision as she wanted it? What if we make changes like you did when you removed her roses and she wouldn't have approved?"

He caught his breath. Now he truly understood her reaction to what he'd done. And though he'd meant the surprise as a happy one, he still regretted not discussing it with her first, considering the consequence now.

He hated to see her trapped in the past. Trapped in the approval of a woman who had been dead for over a decade. A woman he had to believe would wish only good and happy things for her only daughter.

He stepped up to her slowly and caught her hand between his. He lifted it and pressed it against his heart as he held her gaze evenly. "If the vision isn't entirely hers, then it will be partly yours."

Her brow wrinkled. "I'm not sure that helps, Morgan."

He smiled at her confusion. "I didn't know your mother, but I would wager you must be rather like her."

A blush filled her cheeks with warm color. "If I am, that would be a compliment of the highest order. She was lovely and so kind."

His smile broadened. "Then you are her true heir, Elizabeth, for you're both those things and more. I can't imagine she would want you to punish yourself over those plans. Yes, I'm sure she would love the idea that you found her incomplete vision and are working to make it a reality. But I must believe she'd also love the idea that the garden would ultimately be a shared vision, something that contained you both."

Her eyes widened. "Wh-what do you mean?"

"If she had lived—" He paused when Elizabeth's eyes filled with tears. She gripped his hand tighter and he pulled her a fraction closer in support. "If she had lived, you two would have redesigned this garden many times, don't you think? You would have planted and replanted. You would have changed things to suit you both. If you loved the garden as much as she did, she would have brought you into that world and shared it."

She blinked. "Yes. I suppose she would have."

"Then she would want you to have a place here as much as she did. Don't you think?"

She worried her lip a moment, and he could see her pondering that, rolling it around in that amazing mind of hers. And then she smiled. For the first time since they had begun this conversation, the expression wasn't sad or filled with tension or regret. She truly smiled, and it was like someone had lit the world up with the brightest sunshine.

His chest filled with pride that a few little words from him could do that. It felt like the greatest accomplishment of his life.

"You're right, of course," she whispered. "When you say it, I can picture it perfectly. That past that should have been, that future that would have been. And I suppose it wouldn't hurt to bring a tiny bit of myself into whatever we do here."

"I think it would be wonderful," he corrected her.

She turned into him, and suddenly they were chest to chest. Her upturned face was such a temptation, and he fought to keep himself from taking her lips yet again. He had almost won the battle when she lifted on her tiptoes and wrapped her hand around the back of his neck. She drew him down and this time she was the one who pressed her lips to his.

Morgan was a strong man. He'd fought to be so out of necessity. But in this moment, he had no way to battle this woman. He let his breath out in a harsh sigh and surrendered to the gentle insistence of her tongue as she darted it against his lips. The kiss deepened and his entire body pulsed with growing need for her.

This was only getting more desperate now, this desire to be near her, to touch her. It couldn't end well. And he didn't give a damn. Not when she was kissing him.

She stepped away with a blush, and the spell over him faded. It was reckless to let this happen, of course. To keep kissing her in the bright light of day in the garden where anyone watching from the house could see. It was going to get him sacked at best. Called out to duel at worst, and he had to assume Brighthollow was a good shot. Men like him always were.

"Thank you," she whispered. "You helped."

His resistance faded at that simple phrase. He didn't think he'd helped very many people in his life. Hurt some, certainly. The note in his pocket proved that. But helped?

He swallowed back the strong reaction he hadn't expected and offered her his elbow. "Of course. Now, what do you think of going over those plans again? Perhaps we can see where we might put a bit of you."

She hesitated a moment but then slid her hand into the crook of his elbow. "Do you know those tall bushes on the east lawn?" she suggested.

"Yes."

"What do you think about trimming them into the shape of animals?"

He glanced down at her with a laugh as they headed toward the house and her study where she kept the plans for the garden. "Animals."

"You know, little bunnies. Cats."

"Foxes," he suggested.

"Oh, to stalk the others!" she said with a giggle that warmed his heart in a way he shouldn't have allowed.

"I like the way you think," he said.

They were about to head up the stairs toward the terrace above when Brighthollow started down toward them. Elizabeth slid her hand from Morgan's arm as she stared up at her utterly unreadable brother.

"Oh, Hugh," she said, and Morgan heard the tension in her voice. She was obviously worrying over the same thing he was. Had they been seen?

"Lizzie," Brighthollow said, and arched a brow down at Morgan as he stopped in the middle of the staircase. "Might I have a word with you?"

She swallowed. "Of course. I'll join you."

She hurried up to her brother and took his arm. At the top of the stairs, she glanced back at Morgan. Her blue eyes were wide, not fearful, but concerned. And lovely. And he couldn't help but watch as long as she was still in view.

But once she was gone, he shook his head with a curse. He was in a lot of trouble. Not because Brighthollow might sack him, but because the connection he felt toward Elizabeth Margolis was not going to lead to anything good, that was for certain. And he hated the idea of it leading to something bad.

CHAPTER 10

Lizzie stepped into her brother's study. They parted and he crossed to the sideboard to pour himself a drink, while her throat closed with anxiety. And so she filled the uncomfortable space between them by talking.

"Did you see the gazebo starting to go up?" she asked. "It's almost entirely framed out—I wasn't expecting that to happen so soon. I think we should paint it, what do you think?"

"Lizzie," Hugh said softly.

She pretended not to hear him. "Or perhaps let the natural color of that pretty wood remain? And a table inside, do you think? Or benches around the perimeter? It's so hard to say. Mother only sketched in the gazebo's placement, so I suppose this is a way to put me into the garden."

"Lizzie," he said a second time, and this time he stepped toward her so she couldn't pretend not to see his concern or hear it in his voice.

"What is it?" she asked.

He shut his eyes and let out his breath on a shaky sigh before he asked, "Did I make a mistake in bringing Morgan Banfield here?

She clamped her mouth shut and clenched her fingers so they would no longer shake. It didn't work, of course—now it was her entire hand shaking. Her entire body.

But she fought to remain calm. She didn't want Hugh to see how moved she was by that question. By the fear that question invoked. "I don't know what you mean," she said at last.

He lifted his eyebrows. "I've seen you two together several times since his arrival."

"We're…we're working on the garden. Of course we must be together. You asked him to help me. That's…all there is to it." She tried not to think of Morgan kissing her. Hugh would read something on her face if she did that. He knew her so well.

"Is it?" Hugh leaned in closer. His voice was so gentle. "Lizzie?"

She froze, for that was the tone of voice he'd used when she was a little girl and he knew she'd done something naughty. She had learned not to lie to him because he always seemed to know the truth. Because she respected him enough not to do so.

But Hugh was protective. Even more so since that terrible incident with Aaron. If he knew that she and Morgan had connected far more deeply than mere conversation about a garden, Hugh would surely sack him. And she didn't want that. More to the point, Morgan didn't deserve it. He'd been respectful of her boundaries. He'd never forced anything on her.

Today, she'd been the one to start the kissing, hadn't she? At least the last time. So she couldn't, in good conscience, do something that would cause Morgan grief.

"Hugh," she said with a swallow. "You are seeing things that aren't there." She took her brother's hand. "I-I wouldn't do anything untoward that would cause you anguish again. And Morgan Banfield has a certain reputation that should…scare me."

Should. And did. But also drew her. She had to question if that made her weak, but she ignored it. This was not the time to analyze her secretly wicked soul.

Hugh nodded. "I suppose that is true. You've avoided any man of questionable reputation since...well, since before." She sensed his relief and it cut her to the bone to know she'd worried him. She had done that once before and seen his pain as a consequence. He'd tortured himself for months after her fall. He'd almost ruined everything with Amelia as a result.

"I'm sorry," she whispered.

He shook his head. "I'm protective, as you know. Amelia has tried to break me of the habit, but I only...I do love you, Lizzie. And I only want your happiness and security. That is always on the top of my mind."

She smiled at her brother. This man who had raised her with such a loving heart. Seeing his worry drew her up short when it came to Morgan and those kisses. Perhaps she had gone too far, not just for herself, but when it came to those who cared for her.

"I know you always have my best interest at heart," she said. "And I adore you for it."

He seemed to shake off the worry, probably for her sake as much as his own. "You say they have the gazebo framed out. I'm very curious what all you're doing in the garden. Will you tell me about it?"

She pushed thoughts of Morgan away. "Why don't you walk with me and I'll show you?"

Hugh nodded. "I'd love that. Lead the way."

She did, taking him back to the garden she'd recently abandoned. To both her relief and her disappointment, Morgan was already gone. That meant she could focus on her brother. And try to forget the longings Morgan had awoken in her.

In the end, they were dangerous for them both. And it was probably time to have a conversation with him once and for all about ending whatever bond they were forming.

Morgan stood in the parlor, staring at the note he'd received earlier in the day. Since parting with Elizabeth in the garden hours before, he had been more focused on the threat that note contained.

He had enemies, of course. His wild ways had resulted in bad gambling losses...and wins...and a plethora of grumbling husbands from all corners of the country. It had also resulted in broken relationships. People he'd once been close to whom he had betrayed and harmed. He flinched at the idea, self-loathing filling him along with the memories.

In the end, though, his bad behavior meant he had no idea who might be threatening him. Or over what.

He only knew it was a reminder that he might try to find respectability, but there would always be a past to catch up with him.

"Chickens will come home to roost," he muttered as he tossed the note into the flames and watched the words be devoured. "And the past can never be fully overcome."

"That sounds ominous."

Morgan turned and sighed as Robert entered the parlor. He was alone, so there was no buffer to be had between Morgan and his brother. At present, he thought they needed one.

"You would know," Morgan muttered, and stepped away from the fire so his brother wouldn't see the last remnants of the threat. It would be fully ash in a matter of seconds.

"I suppose I do have a past," Robert said with a shrug. "And sometimes I'm reminded of it with an unpleasant confrontation in a ballroom or club. But for the most part, I'm able to leave it behind. Or the parts of it that no longer serve me. I'll never be fully tamed, but Katherine seems to like the wildness that remains. You could have the same experience if you want it."

Morgan stepped closer and glared at Robert. "Can I? Can I really, if someone who is my supposed ally is going around talking to people about my past? Never allowing me to let it go?"

Robert's brow wrinkled. "Are you talking about me?"

"Of course I'm talking about you," Morgan snapped. "Why the bloody hell did you arrange this, Roseford, if your intent was to sabotage me?"

Robert took a long step back, and his expression was a combination of pain and anger. He reached behind him and slammed the parlor door to give them privacy, and then he folded his arms. "What the hell are you talking about? How have I sabotaged you?"

"A few days ago, Elizabeth talked to me about what she called my wild past," Morgan admitted. "How in the world would she know about that unless someone had told her? Told *everyone* about where you found me in London before you went to Brighthollow?"

Robert stared at him a beat, two. "Yes, I did speak to Brighthollow about your...behavior. And when you say it, I suppose I should have discussed that with you first."

"You goddamned well should have," Morgan growled. "But you didn't, and I can only imagine why you'd go behind my back."

Robert clenched his hands at his sides. "I don't know what you think I intended, but there are two reasons I spoke about your past. First, I thought I owed Brighthollow the truth before I asked him to consider you for his man of affairs. The man is my friend and has been most of my life."

"Ah, yes. Your *true* family. All those dukes," Morgan spat.

Robert flinched. "They *are* my family. I would have nothing, I would *be* nothing, without them. But you are my family, too. Or at least I'd like you to be if you could pull your head out of your arse long enough to see I'm not our father. I'm not your enemy."

"So you say," Morgan barked. "But you have our father's title and you hold the purse strings just as he did, so pardon me if I get confused about the similarities."

He didn't expect Robert to charge him, so he wasn't prepared when his brother pushed him back. "You don't know a fucking thing about our father or about me!" he shouted, right in Morgan's face. "You don't know anything about what I've done to prevent that devil from having any quarter in my life."

Morgan shoved him in return and Robert staggered. "I know enough."

Robert's face twisted and Morgan prepared to get punched, and knew he probably deserved it. But before the argument could escalate even more, Lizzie rushed into the room.

The two men backed away from each other as she said, "I could hear shouting from the hallway. What is going on?"

Robert stared at Morgan and Morgan stared back. The moment felt like it stretched out forever. But then Robert turned away. "Nothing, Lizzie. My apologies for upsetting you. Excuse me."

He left without another word, without a backward glance, and Morgan pivoted away to the fire. He hated that he and Robert had gotten so heated so fast. Hated that there was so much beneath the surface between them that could bubble up instantly.

"Morgan," Lizzie said softly.

He turned to find she had come toward him a few steps. She was halfway into the room now, and she was watching him. Waiting for an explanation, he thought. One he could hardly give.

"It's not your concern, my lady," he gasped out.

"Probably not," she conceded. "But I'm making it my concern. Why were you fighting with Roseford?"

Morgan bent his head. "I just…realized the other night that Robert has…said things about me. And I don't like that he's bringing my past up with others. It feels like he's trying to destroy me."

His brow wrinkled. "Then why would he help you get this position?" she asked. "If he wanted you to fail, he could have abandoned you wherever he found you."

"Gaol, my lady," he admitted, because at least he wanted her to hear it from his lips. "He helped to extricate me from Newgate before he brought me to your brother."

"Oh," she gasped and the color faded from her cheeks. "I-I didn't know."

"At least that's something," he muttered, and ran a hand through his hair.

"Morgan," she said softly. "It's obvious you and Robert have a connection that is...fraught. I'm sure you have reasons for that, for it seems you both had a difficult relationship with your father. And not being raised together must complicate things."

He shrugged. "I suppose."

"But...but I can tell you from the outside it is obvious that Robert cares for you. He wouldn't have brought you all the way here and vouched for you with Hugh if he didn't *care*."

Morgan shook his head. "Well, that's a very rational thing to say."

She laughed softly. "I suppose that thwarts your desire to see him as an utter villain."

"It does." He found himself smiling slightly. "Somewhat irritating of you, my lady. I was very happy stewing in loathing for my brother."

"My apologies then," she said with a soft laugh. "I should not have disturbed a good stew."

He leaned in, catching a whiff of orange blossom that took him to fantasies that were unfulfillable. "I forgive you," he whispered.

Before she could respond, the rest of their party joined them and Morgan stepped away from her. It was so odd how he could feel so upset, so angry in one moment, then a few words from Elizabeth could change his mood and his thoughts.

"Have any of you seen my brother?" he asked, casting Elizabeth a quick glance. She gave him a small smile in return. Encouraging. Comforting.

"I saw him go out on to the terrace from the east parlor," the Duchess of Donburrow said. "Katherine followed him."

"Ah. If you don't mind, I think I'll seek him out," Morgan said. "I was not finished talking to him and I think I owe him something."

"We'll be here for a while," Brighthollow said. "You'll join us when you're finished with your conversation and we'll all go in to supper."

"Very good," Morgan said as he exited the room and walked down the hallway. As he entered the east parlor, he saw the shadow of his brother and Katherine past the glass doors that led outside. They were standing close together. Katherine had her arm around him.

Morgan sucked in a breath and stepped onto the terrace. The couple turned and Robert scowled as he returned his attention to the garden below.

"Good evening," Morgan choked out. "You look lovely, Katherine. May I speak to Robert alone?"

She shook her head. For the first time since Morgan had met her, she didn't look welcoming toward him. She looked protective.

Robert had that. Robert deserved it. Morgan knew it when he got past the complications of their brotherly bond.

Katherine smoothed her hand across Robert's back once more. "I'm not sure I should leave you two alone. Will you come to blows or will one of you throw the other off the terrace?"

"No," Robert said, and glanced at her with a look of chagrin. "For my part, at least, the answer is no."

Morgan inclined his head. "I don't have any intention of carrying on."

Katherine considered that for a moment, looking back and forth between the men. Then she nodded. "Very good. I'll see you two in a moment." She leaned up to kiss Robert's cheek. When she whispered something to him, Roseford's expression softened.

Then Katherine slipped into the house and the brothers were alone once more.

"I-I overreacted," Morgan admitted, though the words choked him. "I'm...sorry."

"No. Well, yes," Robert said, facing him without moving toward him. "But I deserved it, I think. I shouldn't have talked about your past without discussing it with you first. I'm sorry, as well."

Morgan blinked. He hadn't expected that. He almost didn't know how to respond. But at last, he nodded. "Apology accepted."

Robert let out his breath in a long stream. "And I overreacted, as well. My feelings about our father are...complicated. And being compared to him is like my greatest fear come to life."

Morgan's eyes went wide. Because Robert had been raised by the man, he supposed he'd never fully considered his brother's past. His brother's pain. That was a failing, he could see that now.

"You aren't like him," Morgan said softly. "I met him once, you know."

Robert drew back. "You did? Usually he made note of such things in the files he kept on each...each..."

"Bastard?" Morgan said softly.

"Each child," Robert finished.

Morgan let out his breath in a low whistle. "Great God, what he must have said about me."

"They aren't that detailed," Robert offered. "But if you'd like to see yours, I'm happy to turn it over to you when you are next in London. What did he do when you met?"

"I was at school. He paid for my education, so there I was, the bastard son of a courtesan surrounded by fops with true connections."

"That must have been difficult," Robert conceded and there was nothing but kindness in his tone.

"At first," Morgan said. "But I learned to...entertain them."

Robert gave a small chuckle. "Yes, I can see that your charm would serve you well. As it does now."

"The previous duke materialized one afternoon. I was drawn out of my studies, taken to this room and left alone with a man I'd only ever seen in passing and in the miniature my poor mother kept beside her bed." He sighed. "He just...*stared* at me. He stood in that room and stared at me, and when I tried to speak, he stopped me."

He flashed back to that day. He'd felt so small next to this man. He'd known Roseford was his father, but there had been no affection when the duke looked at him. Up and down, circling him like Morgan was a pony to be evaluated at market.

"He started drilling me with questions about my studies, about my marks in school. After I answered he said perhaps I wasn't entirely worthless, and then he left and I never met with him again."

Robert flinched. "How old were you?"

"Nine," Morgan said.

Morgan stepped up next to his brother, and for a moment they stared out over the garden together. He could see the shadow of Elizabeth's gazebo in the distance. He thought of her and he felt a little...better.

"It is difficult knowing what he was," Morgan continued. "And that I meant so little to him."

"None of us meant anything to him," Robert said. "That's not meant as comfort, mind you. Nor to dismiss what you experienced when he took the whim to meet you. I only say it out of understanding. He was a cruel man, unable and unwilling to control himself. He took what he wanted, he never thought of the consequences. He caused nothing but destruction."

Morgan flinched. "I have inherited that from him."

"So did I," Robert said. "Until I chose to be better."

Morgan glanced toward the house where Katherine had departed a few moments before. "Because of her."

"Aye. Anything good I've managed to become is because of her," Robert said softly.

They were silent for a moment, but there was no animosity to it. At last Morgan cleared his throat. "Earlier...before we started pushing and swearing, you said there were two reasons you spoke about my past. What was the second reason?"

Robert's expression softened a bit further. He pivoted to face Morgan and closed any distance between them physically. But it felt even deeper than that.

"Because I was *worried* about you," Robert admitted softly.

"You...you were?" Morgan asked.

"Yes. Of course." Robert shrugged. "I don't know how to be a good older brother. I never had an example in my life. There is no one more qualified to offer sound advice about the subject of siblings than Brighthollow. He all but raised Lizzie, and their relationship is very close. So yes, I spoke to him about you long before I asked him to consider you as an employee, in the hopes he could help me be...better."

"I see," Morgan breathed. It was harder to be angry at Robert for turning to a friend for support. For trying to find a way to be there for Morgan.

"I'm sorry Lizzie heard anything about it. Perhaps she gleaned some information from him or from Amelia about your past. Perhaps Katherine mentioned it in passing, I don't know. But it was not cruelly meant. I am not our father."

Morgan shook his head. "I...I know that in my heart. I have just hated that bastard for what he did to my mother, for what he did to me, for so long."

"I understand that," Robert said, and clapped a hand on Morgan's shoulder. "Someday you'll get me very drunk and I'll tell you what he did to *my* mother. What he did to *me*. And we'll sob into our tankards and come out closer than ever. But not tonight."

"No," Morgan agreed. "Not tonight."

"Let's join the others before they send a search party in the fear that we've killed each other." Robert motioned to the door, and they exited and walked up the hallway together. "I must mention that you seem to have had some good influence on you since we talked in the parlor. I cannot imagine who that could have been."

"That's enough, Roseford," Morgan muttered, but he found himself smiling regardless.

His brother stopped. They were a few feet from the parlor where the others were gathered. Morgan could hear their voices drifting out into the hallway.

"Honestly, Morgan, I only want for you to be happy. Stable. And while I like Lizzie, I do wonder at the ramifications if you happen to…to like her too."

Morgan bent his head, for his brother was only saying out loud what he already knew himself. "Yes."

"You must know this already, for you are so very clever, but you can't play here," Robert continued. "You can't shit where you eat and expect Hugh to smile and say nothing. After everything Lizzie went through—" He stopped himself.

Morgan wrinkled his brow. Everyone kept alluding to that, even Elizabeth herself. Something in her past. Something that made all those around her so very protective.

"What did she go through?" he asked.

Robert shook his head. "It's not mine to say. I like to think I learned my lesson about speaking out of turn about someone else's past."

Morgan felt a swell of disappointment but also understanding. He couldn't fault Robert for not repeating the mistake he and Morgan had nearly come to blows over.

With a sigh, he stepped a bit closer to the parlor door and saw Elizabeth. She was at her brother's side, talking quietly to him and to the Duchess of Donburrow. She was so lovely. But Robert was correct that she wasn't the kind of woman a person could trifle with.

"I…understand what you're saying," he choked out. "And perhaps I do need to distance myself from Lady Elizabeth in order to stop things from becoming…confused."

Robert clapped him on the shoulder. "You must do what you think is best. Let's rejoin them."

His brother entered the room, but for a moment Morgan hung back, just continuing to watch her until her gaze darted to him like she sensed his presence. Her brow wrinkled and then she smiled in question, in support. She smiled so sweetly that his rotten remnants of a heart thudded.

He didn't want to step away from the strange connection he'd made with this remarkable woman. But if he didn't, he feared the father he and Robert had discussed on the terrace would find a new life in Morgan, himself.

And he didn't want that even more.

CHAPTER 11

Lizzie sat at her desk in her study, her mother's plans for the garden laid out before her. Now they were marked up, containing her notes with a few changes. Morgan's responses in that firm, even hand. She stared over the conversations she'd shared with him through this method and smiled.

Still, she felt restless. The communication on the plans was the bulk of how she'd interacted with Morgan. At least since the gathering a few nights before when she'd found him fighting with the Duke of Roseford. He'd maintained his distance since. She'd done the same.

And though she knew that was for the best, it still felt like a loss, somehow. A regret that she could add to all the others until the pile felt overwhelming.

There was a light rap on her partially open door and Amelia poked her head into the room. "Lizzie?"

She forced a smile and got up to wave Amelia in. "Yes?"

Amelia shifted as she rested her hand on the doorjamb. Her gaze darted about and wouldn't focus on Lizzie. "I wanted to talk to you about something."

Lizzie lifted her brows. She didn't like this. "Er, what is it?"

"Well, Charlotte and Katherine and I got to talking two nights ago, while you were playing pianoforte after tea that day it rained? It was lovely, by the way. Your playing is always so lovely."

"Amelia," Lizzie said. "Why are you trying to soften me? What is going on?"

"There's going to be a ball tonight," Amelia burst out. "Here."

Lizzie caught her breath. "A ball, *tonight*?" she repeated. "What are you talking about?"

Amelia at least had the wherewithal to look chagrined. "It was such a last-minute thought. It isn't going to be big, just a small gathering. Some of the local gentry and our party. One of Hugh's friends from an adjoining county is coming. It will be delightful, I assure you."

Lizzie stared at her. Amelia looked as though she'd done something wrong and even though that wasn't entirely true, there was still a twinge of pain that accompanied the news. Amelia had not only decided this without talking to her, but planned it with her friends, rather than with Lizzie.

"Why wasn't I included in the discussion?" Lizzie asked softly.

"I know you have little interest in such things," Amelia said with a blush. "And you've been so involved in your garden preparations."

Lizzie nodded, as if accepting that answer, even though she doubted it to her core. She knew Amelia didn't think she could handle the preparations for a ball. It was one more example of how her family tiptoed around her, like she was glass. And not solid glass either. More like an important family heirloom that had already been chipped or shattered, then repaired and placed back on the shelf. It was for looking, not using or enjoying.

She hated it. She hated the idea of a ball, too, but the other was worse.

She cleared her throat. "Well, of course I am very excited about the gathering," she lied. "Is there any way I can help with the preparations?"

"No, just bring your lovely self and try to have fun," Amelia said. "Now I must go speak to Masters. I'll see you at tea later today, yes?"

"Of course," Lizzie called out because Amelia was already ducking away, leaving the door open behind her.

Lizzie walked to the fireplace. She stared into the flames and clenched and unclenched her hands at her sides. Pressure felt like it was building inside her. Pressure over her family's view of her, pressure over what she'd done to cause it, pressure over the attachment she didn't want to feel toward Morgan Banfield, and pressure because she didn't want to lose that attachment either.

It seemed she lived in a world of in-between. Never quite belonging, never quite finding her place. "Bloody hell," she muttered.

"Well, that's unexpected."

She pivoted to find Morgan standing at her doorway, lounging lazily against the doorjamb with a grin on his handsome face. She blushed as she realized he'd heard her curse and bent her head. "Excuse me, I didn't realize I wasn't alone."

"Apparently so," he said with a laugh. "But don't stop on my account. If you're upset—" He stopped talking and his brow furrowed as he looked at her. He straightened and stepped into the room. "You *are* upset. What's wrong?"

Lizzie spun away from him. Of course, he would materialize to tempt her and then see right through her. Of course he would, because that was just her luck. Just her weakness.

"It doesn't matter," she muttered.

"I'm afraid it does." His voice was closer now and she peeked over her shoulder to find he was just a long step away. He could almost reach out and brush his fingertips along her bare arm. She wanted him to do just that. She wanted him to kiss her even though she recognized the folly in that.

She sighed. "It's nothing important," she assured him. "It's just Amelia's ball tonight. She...sprang it on me just now and I wasn't expecting it."

"She sprang it on you?" he repeated.

Lizzie laughed at the look of surprise on his face, even though she felt no humor in the situation. "Yes, they...they do that sometimes?"

"Why?"

She lifted her chin and tried to maintain a little dignity. "To force me to attend."

His lips parted and for a moment there was a flash of anger that crossed his face. Defensive...of her? "That seems...uncharacteristically cruel of the duchess," he said.

"No," she said swiftly, to defend her beloved sister-in-law. "Amelia would never, *ever* be cruel to me or to anyone else. It isn't that I *can't* go. It's just—" She cut herself off. How did she say this to this man who saw everything? How did she tell him without him seeing the past play out on her face? "It's complicated."

He did exactly what she feared. He leaned in and those dark brown eyes flitted over her, easily taking what she fought so hard to conceal. His frown deepened, concern lining his face. "Why is it complicated, Elizabeth?"

Her lips parted. His question was said in such a warm, hypnotic tone, and he looked so accepting. As if she could whisper the truth to him and find a safe place to fall after the inevitable collapse. Worse yet, she *wanted* to whisper what she'd done, what she was, all her secrets.

And that was, of course, exactly why she couldn't. She had already determined it was time to distance herself from this man who saw too much. If she wanted to maintain her sanity, she had to do it now.

"Morgan," she whispered. "I think we should...talk."

He arched a brow with a half-smile. "Nothing good comes of that sentence, does it?"

"And yet we must regardless," she said, and motioned to the chairs before her fire.

As he moved to them, she went to the door. She stared at it.

Propriety said to leave it open. That a lady such as herself shouldn't be alone with a gentleman. Especially one she had so inappropriately kissed over and over again. Especially one who always looked like he would devour her if he had a chance.

But propriety and privacy were two different things. She didn't want the world to hear what she was about to say. And that need to protect the sweet moments they'd shared won over everything else. She pushed the door shut and his pupils dilated when she did so.

"Please sit," she asked as she did the same. He joined her and was silent as he waited for her to take the lead. It wasn't a natural state, but she struggled to do so regardless. "Morgan, I…we…" She shook her head. Gracious, she was an educated, literate person. Why was it so hard to find words?

"Take your time," he soothed, and she watched his hands twitch in his lap like he wanted to reach out to her.

She drew in a few breaths and found some tiny center in the storm of her emotions. "It is obvious there is something between us."

He nodded. "Of course. All those stolen kisses don't lie."

She almost sagged in relief. When she'd pictured addressing this with him over the past few days, she had feared he would behave as though what had happened between them meant nothing. That she was imagining things.

"Yes, and those stolen kisses have been…wonderful." Her breath caught and she fought again for calm. "And unexpected. I don't—I don't regret them, Morgan. But I do fear their consequences. At the very least, what we've done could cause you to lose your employment."

His mouth tightened a fraction, but that was his only reaction to the statement. "Yes, you are correct. If your brother found out about all the kissing, I'm sure he would sack me within moments. And call me out if I wasn't lucky."

She nodded. "There would be consequences for me, as well." She dipped her head as she tried not to picture Hugh's disappointment in her. How he would feel when he realized she hadn't learned her lesson the first time she made such a dreadful mistake. It would change their relationship irrevocably. How could it not?

"I see," he said, noncommittal.

She shifted in her seat. It was best just to say this. Just to have it out and be done with it. But heavens, it was difficult. Especially when he was so close and so handsome.

"Morgan, I think it would be best if we distance ourselves," she burst out in one smashed-together sentence.

His stare remained even for a breath and then he nodded slowly. "I'm glad you said so, my lady. While what we shared was very pleasant, it was dangerously imprudent. And I think you are correct that ending it now is better than allowing our attraction to confuse matters, or endanger either of our futures."

She blinked. That was it? He was just going to accept what she said? Even look...relieved that she'd said it? It was ridiculous, because she should have been happy they were on the same page in this matter. That he didn't get upset or angry or argue against her words.

But she wasn't. Looking at him and seeing how little any of this had meant, it...it hurt her feelings. She pushed to her feet and paced away, smoothing her hands along her skirt as she tried to regain some purchase on these hateful emotions that flooded up in her.

"Very good," she forced herself to say as she turned back to him with a small smile. He had risen to his feet when she did, and he stood, hands clasped behind his back, feet spread wide. He looked completely unaffected.

"Yes," he agreed. Then he stepped forward and held out a hand to her. "Lady Elizabeth."

She hesitated a moment. She wasn't wearing gloves. This would likely be the last time she ever touched her bare skin to his. Should she allow it? Refuse it? Savor it?

Trembling more than she'd like, she extended her hand. He clasped it in his and shook it gently. Electric heat flowed between them as he stared down into her face, those dark brown eyes holding her captive. His thumb moved, stroking over the knuckle of her index finger. She shivered, but then he released her and she wasn't certain he had even done that on purpose.

"M-Mr. Banfield," she choked out.

He cleared his throat. "Well, I should rejoin your brother. I will see you tonight at the ball, I'm certain."

She nodded. "Yes. Tonight."

He gave her a rather formal half-bow, then he pivoted and exited the room without so much as a backward glance for her. She gasped out a breath she hadn't realized she'd been holding and crossed back to the chairs before her fire where she collapsed with a sigh.

That had gone as well as she could have ever hoped for, and yet she felt a desperate, aching sense of disappointment. For whatever pleasure Morgan—no, *Mr. Banfield*—had gleaned from their attraction, it had taken him no effort to walk away from it.

"Perhaps I can take a lesson from that," she muttered to herself as she smoothed her skirts once more. "Perhaps I should learn to be more detached, as he is."

She straightened her shoulders and drew in a few breaths. It didn't help. She still felt wretched about the entire ordeal. She pushed to her feet and paced the room a few times, shaking out her hands and trying to think of anything else in the world. But there was nothing else, only this.

"That is that, then," she muttered to herself. "It is better this way. Now you must focus on matters at hand."

"Lizzie?"

She turned to find Hugh in her doorway, staring at her as if she had sprouted a second head. And why not? He had caught her wandering her study, talking to herself.

"Oh, Hugh," she said, forcing a smile. "You caught me wool-gathering."

"It seems so. Did Amelia mention the ball to you?"

She frowned. His concern was right there, written across his face. She really was the family difficulty, it seemed. And she didn't want to be, not anymore.

"She did," she said, brightening her tone. "And, in fact, I was just about to go up to my chamber and speak to Nora about what I shall wear and how I will have my hair done."

Hugh nodded, but his brow was still furrowed. "Very good."

She moved toward the door and patted his arm as she exited the room. They walked up the hallway together in what she felt was an uncomfortable silence. But as they reached the stairway, she glanced at him. "Mr. Banfield was looking for you, Hugh."

He jerked his gaze to her. "Was he?"

"Yes. He stopped to briefly discuss the garden and then said he would join you. I assume he's in your study."

Hugh examined her closely and then nodded. "Well, I will join him then." He leaned in and kissed her cheek. "I hope you will save a dance for me tonight."

"You know I only ever dance with you," Lizzie said with a laugh. "But I will save as many as you'd like."

"Very good," he said. "I'll see you later today."

Then he was gone, heading up the long hallway to find Morgan. And leaving Lizzie to grip the banister until her knuckles went white. She had spent the past few years in such a fog and now she was seeing the consequences of that.

But it was time to change it all. Time to reenter the world with a bit more confidence, if only to keep her family from worrying. If only to keep the unwanted feelings toward men like Morgan Banfield from forcing her to make another mistake.

CHAPTER 12

"You look lovely, Lady Elizabeth," Nora said as she slid the last jewel-encrusted pin into Lizzie's hair and stepped back.

Lizzie looked at herself in the mirror and stifled a sigh. She *looked* ready for a ball, that was certain. *Felt* was another story, but the appearance mattered.

She wore her favorite gown, a gray-blue silk elaborately threaded through with silver. Her hair was done elaborately, curled and lifted and pinned through with sapphire and diamond hairpins she had inherited from her late mother. She never wore them, but tonight she wanted to. They completed the costume, after all.

The costume of a woman who had not a care in the world. Perhaps if she pretended hard enough, that would be true.

"You did a lovely job," Lizzie said with a smile for Nora.

Nora blushed and curtseyed. "Thank you, my lady. Do you need anything else?"

Lizzie almost laughed. There was a question she couldn't answer appropriately. Not tonight. "No, I'm fine, thank you."

"I hope you have a good time."

Lizzie took a deep breath as her servant departed, then followed her into the hallway. She had made it a few steps when she saw

Katherine, the Duchess of Roseford, coming down the hallway from the opposite direction. Her heart leapt a little. Of course she adored her friend, but Katherine was Robert's wife. Morgan's sister-in-law. Seeing her was like a slap-in-the-face reminder of what had happened this afternoon.

"It's good practice," she muttered to herself, and forced another smile for Katherine. "You look beautiful, as always," she said as they met at the top of the stairs. It was a true statement. Katherine was one of the most beautiful women Lizzie had ever known. Tall, with dark hair and eyes, she always exuded a natural confidence that made people turn toward her whenever she entered a room. Lizzie rather envied her that.

"As do you," Katherine said, and leaned back to look her up and down. "That color brings out your eyes, my dear."

Lizzie's cheeks heated and she ducked her head. "Thank you."

Katherine linked arms with her and they started down the wide staircase together. "Robert went down early to have a drink with the other men."

"Ah," Lizzie murmured, but couldn't help but wonder if that included Morgan. The two had fought a few nights before, but since then she'd noticed a shift in them. Some kind of truce, it felt like. And she was happy for Morgan. She knew the benefits of a close relationship to a sibling and she wished him nothing but the same. "Well, I'm sure he'll enjoy seeing you sweep into the ball in all your lovely glory."

Katherine tilted her head back and laughed. "You do know Robert's flare for the dramatic. Shall we enter in our glory together?"

Lizzie hesitated and looked up the hall toward the ball. The doors were open and she could see the room was already busy. Music filtered out into the house along with the buzz of lively conversation. "Oh, I don't know. I'm not sure I have much glory, especially next to all of you duchesses."

Katherine turned to face her and her expression softened. "My dear, you are lovely, both inside and out. I recognize confidence is difficult. Especially when one has been through something… painful. It was very difficult for me to return to Society after my first husband's death and all the talk about it."

Lizzie's lips parted. The duchesses on the whole were such a powerful, elegant and confident group that she sometimes forgot many of them had difficult pasts. It was easy to when they didn't seem to be troubled by them as she was by her own.

"I had all but forgotten," she whispered.

Katherine smiled. "Well, you are the only one, I assure you. My point being that I understand your hesitation. But as a fellow survivor, may I give you some advice?"

Lizzie's cheeks felt hot, but she nodded regardless. "I would be very happy to hear it."

Katherine took her hands and glanced down at her. "Don't let the bastards win."

Lizzie couldn't contain her shocked laughter at that statement. "I thought you were going to tell me to make the best of it and smile."

Katherine waved a hand of dismissal. "Bugger that. I suppose, yes, smiling and making the best of it is part of not letting them win. But what I mean is that you have this beautiful, powerful light inside of you, Lizzie. Anyone who gets to know you can see it, is warmed by it. And it was muted by what happened to you. But it wasn't extinguished. I'd hate to see you put it out yourself from some fear or worry or anything else that keeps you up at night. You deserve so much better."

Lizzie glanced toward the ballroom again. She'd hidden from such places for a long time, even when she was in them. But in that moment she felt a stir of stubborn rebellion. One she hadn't allowed herself more than a handful of times in her life.

"I will try," she said.

Katherine smiled and then caught her arm again, and they moved toward the ballroom together. "Very good. Now let's dazzle them, shall we?"

~

Morgan couldn't help but watch Elizabeth as she glided across the ballroom floor in the arms of her brother. She looked glorious, in the blue gown that made her eyes pop like sapphires. A gown fit for a queen, and she wore it well as it skimmed across her curves, accentuating everything graceful in the way she moved and talked and existed in the world. She smiled at something Brighthollow said and the candles that lit the dozens of chandeliers in the big room were dim in comparison.

She was impossible *not* to stare at, and he knew he wasn't the only man in that room doing so. A fact that both pleased him and tweaked him even though he hadn't earned his jealousy. She wasn't his. They'd made that fact perfectly clear hours before in her study when she'd stepped away from him.

Her words had been ringing in his ears ever since and distracting him from his duties. How many times had he read the same line in those ledgers today? It felt like a hundred, and he still couldn't have told someone the total amount Brighthollow took in from his tenants' wheat crops versus years when barley was planted.

But could he say how many sparkling diamonds and sapphires were scattered throughout Elizabeth's golden hair? Probably down to a one. It was not a good thing, but there it was.

The music ended, and Elizabeth smiled as she took her brother's hand and they left the dance floor. Brighthollow spoke to her, then moved off. The moment he did, her eyes darted across the crowd and settled on Morgan.

This was the problem about tonight. She kept watching him, despite her words that they should end their flirtation. She watched him, and he saw on her face that she still wanted all the same things he did. Circumstance and position separated them from that, but it remained, no matter what she said or did to the contrary.

It made him long for so much more. To kiss her again. Or at least to touch her. And that siren's song in her gaze was too much to

THE LOVE OF A LIBERTINE

resist. He found himself moving toward her around the perimeter of the ballroom floor. The next dance had begun, a waltz, and it would be too late to join it. But after they could certainly take a turn in a quadrille. Not too intimate. A dance that could be taken up as friends, couldn't it?

At least that was what he said to himself as he got closer and closer to her. Her eyes widened at his approach, dilated with a welcome he longed for, despite the complications of it. But before he could reach her, before he could speak to her for the first time that night, his approach was interrupted by a young lady who stepped in front of him and into Elizabeth's space.

"Lizzie!" the young lady gasped as she caught Lizzie's hands in hers.

Morgan turned away slightly, as if he were not approaching, and waited for their interaction to be finished. Perhaps this was a good thing. If Elizabeth was not interested in speaking to him, if she was stronger than he was, she could use this interloper as a means of escape. Then he would know where he truly stood, at any rate.

"Lady Jocelyn," Elizabeth said, and there was a tension to her tone that he didn't know whether to attribute to him or to the young lady she was addressing. "I have not seen you in so long."

"An age!" Lady Jocelyn said. "*Everyone* talks about how you have not been out much in Society. And how you left London in the middle of the Season. I *do* hope there's not anything amiss."

Elizabeth swallowed and her gaze swiftly turned toward him, then darted away. He saw the depth of her pain in it, though. "I have a project here that takes my time," she said, her voice faltering. "I am surprised to see *you* out of Town. I know you adore the pleasures of the Season."

Lady Jocelyn waved a hand. "My grandmother has taken ill, so my father demanded we come to the shire to call on her. I don't know why I couldn't have stayed behind with my aunt as chaperone. After all, what can I do for my grandmother?"

Elizabeth's eyes were wide now and she cleared her throat. "Offer the comfort of your company?"

The other woman looked confused by the suggestion. "What good will that do? At any rate, I have insisted we not stay long. The other Diamonds of the First Water will not be stopped in their search for a husband. I cannot fall behind or I shall end up like—"

She stopped, and Morgan straightened. He saw the cruel little smirk on her face and how Elizabeth's gaze dropped even further. And it was enough.

"I do beg your pardon, ladies," Morgan said as he stepped up the rest of the way.

The two women turned toward him, and Lady Jocelyn glanced up and down his body. He saw her interest but also her dismissal. He wasn't important enough for her, it seemed. Elizabeth, on the other hand, looked both joyful at his interruption...and utterly humiliated.

"Mr. Banfield," she said softly. "Lady Jocelyn, may I present my brother's man of affairs, Mr. Morgan Banfield."

"How do you do?" the other woman said with a sniff. "I am surprised to see the duke's man at a ball. What an odd thing country manners are."

Elizabeth's brow arched and some of her humiliation faded. "Mr. Banfield is the brother of the Duke of Roseford, Jocelyn," she said, her tone tart and pointed. "We are lucky to have such an esteemed gentleman as he to take a position in my brother's household."

Morgan smiled at her quick defense of him, earned or no. It made him all the more desirous of saving her from this nasty creature. "Well, I have come on the duke's behest. Your assistance is required. Will you come with me? I do apologize, Lady Jocelyn."

The other woman glared at him. "It is no trouble. I do hope I'll get a chance to see you again before my return to London, Lizzie. I'll be sure to call and catch you up on all the gossip you miss by hiding out here in the country."

She said the last word as if it were a curse. Elizabeth ignored that and inclined her head before she turned to Morgan. "Please lead the way, Mr. Banfield."

He wanted to touch her. God help him, he wanted so desperately to take her arm and allow her to lean on him as they walked away. But he couldn't offer her that comfort. Their positions were far too disparate and it would surely cause talk. Something he could see now already followed her, though he couldn't guess why. Elizabeth was so quiet and genteel. Who could possibly whisper about her?

Except everyone kept dancing around the subject of what had happened to her. Something he still didn't understand. Something he *wanted* to understand as he guided her into the hallway and down into one of the empty parlors far from the music and dancing and unwanted friends.

The moment they entered the room, she stepped away from him, dragging in deep breaths as he leaned back and quietly shut the door behind them. He watched her as she paced, her hands gripping in and out of fists at her sides.

"Well, Lady Jocelyn is a pleasure," he said, his tone dry as dust.

It elicited the desired response, for she stopped pacing and pivoted to look at him. She smiled and her shoulders relaxed. "Isn't she? I've known her since we were little girls. As you heard, her grandmother has a home just a short distance from this estate."

"Ah yes, the beloved grandmother," Morgan mused. "Her concern for the woman was touching."

"The worst part is that her grandmother is wonderful. So kind." She shook her head and for a moment she seemed distracted. "I will have to call on her. Have a basket put together for her comfort."

Morgan smiled at her easy kindness. "You are a wonder, Elizabeth."

She blinked and her attention returned to him. "A-a wonder? What do you mean by that?"

"Do you really not know? Can you truly not see what a revelation you are?" Morgan asked. When her expression remained blank, he laughed. "Then allow me to explain. That wretched woman obviously upset you, and I know you don't want to be at this ball the duchess arranged. And yet you are instantly distracted by checking on the well-being of an acquaintance."

Elizabeth waved her hand dismissively. "That isn't remarkable by any means. It's just caring about another person."

He stepped closer. "You have been sheltered in your time on this earth if you think that caring about another person isn't always remarkable."

He expected her to smile, but instead she backed away. "I'm not sheltered," she muttered.

His brow wrinkled. The trouble had reentered her face. The same expression he'd seen when that horrible Lady Jocelyn was needling her about not being in London. Like a cornered animal who feared the bite of a predator.

He stared at her, knowing he should make some excuse to walk away. Leave her to her peace. Perhaps send in one of the duchesses or her brother to comfort her because it wasn't his place.

But he didn't. He couldn't. Not when she was standing there with those amazing blue eyes locked on his, her hands worrying and trembling in front of her.

"Why do you hate London?" he whispered.

Those same eyes widened and the fear entered them yet again. "M-Morgan," she whispered.

He shook his head. "I am not the kind of man who would or could judge you for whatever it is that plagues you. And I…I want to help you, if I can. Perhaps talking about it would help."

She swallowed. "I don't know."

He stepped closer, and at last he let himself reach out to take her hand. She was wearing gloves. So was he. It didn't matter. Electric awareness still shot through him, making him want things he shouldn't have.

"Morgan," she repeated, but her voice trembled with the same desires he felt coursing through his body.

"Why do you look afraid whenever someone talks about gossip?" he pressed. "Why does everyone dance around your past?"

He saw her struggle with the answer he demanded. He saw all that fear and heartbreak and regret she held inside of her flash across her face in an instant.

And then she bent her head. Bent to his will, and he knew what she would say even before she whispered, "Very well. You want to know the truth? Then you'll have it. And you might regret hearing it as much as I'm certain I'll regret telling you."

CHAPTER 13

Although a great many people knew her secret, mostly kind friends she trusted to her core, Lizzie had only ever spoken of what she had done to two. Hugh, because she'd had to give him some of the information after he'd been forced to chase after her through the night. And Amelia, because she adored her sister-in-law and because it turned out they shared a chapter in the book of Aaron Walters.

Now she stared up into the dark, welcoming gaze of Morgan Banfield and prepared herself to confess again. Perhaps it would be better. Part of Morgan's interest in her had to do with the fact that he saw her as sheltered and innocent, as opposed to what he'd encountered in his once wild life. But when he knew what she'd done, what she was, perhaps that would end this connection once and for all.

She drew a shaky breath and sank into a chair before the fire. "I met him at one of those assembly soirees here in Brighthollow," she began.

His eyes widened. "*Him?*" he repeated.

"*Him*," she repeated. She held his gaze and saw he understood. "Aaron Walters was his name, not that it matters. I didn't want to be there. Even before…*it* happened, I was shy around people I didn't know well. I still am. He was handsome and he approached me, which shocked me. He asked me to dance."

"And did you?" he asked.

She shook her head. "I told him the same thing I told everyone: I don't like to dance. Mostly that makes the young men back away."

His brow wrinkled. "Idiots."

She smiled despite herself and was shocked that she could. Normally this story made her feel like she couldn't breathe. Like she was trapped in the past all over again.

"Well, this particular idiot suggested we take a walk in the garden if I preferred it. I thought I shouldn't. I knew I was too young for such a thing. But he was so…kind. So I said yes."

Morgan swallowed. "I assume that began a courtship."

"Unofficially, yes." She sighed at the memory. "Hugh wasn't at Brighthollow at the time, he was in London, and no one expected me to do anything wicked. I was probably allowed more leeway than another girl might have been and I betrayed the trust everyone had in me. I met with him in secret. We took rides around the lake and talked and picnicked. It was…it was romantic on the surface."

"On the surface," he said, and there was a wariness to his tone. "He wasn't what he seemed?"

She tried not to allow bitterness into her tone, but it was in her heart and it was impossible not to show. "He was not. But I didn't know it. I was so foolish and blind and…and so desperate for love that I ignored any warning signs. He led me by the nose all the way until the day he asked me to marry him."

Morgan stepped back, his eyes wide. "You married him?"

"Well, I was only sixteen. I told Aaron that we should speak to Hugh. That there was no rush. But he was insistent. He said that my brother would never accept him because he wasn't moneyed or titled. He said the only way to convince him was if we eloped. It would force Hugh's hand and we would be happy in the end."

When Morgan's lips parted, she nodded. "Oh yes, I know. Not a very gentlemanly suggestion. I *knew* it was wrong. But he told me I had to decide right then. If I said no, he would take it that I didn't care as much as I had declared. That I had been playing him for a fool, and he would leave and never come back."

"Blackmail. That bastard," Morgan muttered.

She bent her head. "I was too foolish to see the manipulation, I suppose. And so I agreed. It was such a long ride to Gretna Green. And…"

She trailed off and pushed from the chair. Her cheeks flamed as she walked to the window, looked down at the garden in the darkness. Her mother's garden. Her mother who certainly would have been so ashamed of what she'd done.

She heard Morgan move closer, and then she felt him. He stepped up behind her and, without speaking, wrapped his hands around her forearms. In the wavy reflection from the window before her, she saw him looking down at her. She felt his strength and his warmth and all the things that drew her to him. Was that a repeated mistake or something real this time? Did she even know the difference?

Did the difference even matter?

"You don't have to tell me what he did," he whispered.

"You are a man of the world," she replied, and hated that her voice cracked. "I'm sure you can guess. What do you think he did?"

He was silent for a moment, hesitant. Then he said, "Made you believe that you would be wed, so you might as well do the thing you'd been warned against your whole life. I think he took your virginity."

She bent her head, staring at the ground as she relived that experience. Quick and perfunctory and unpleasant. Tears filled her eyes and she nodded. He turned her then, slowly and gently, and she was forced to look up at him.

But there was no judgment to be found on his face. No pity. Nothing but understanding and concern and acceptance. She blinked to see it there, unexpected in this man who had been brought here from gaol in order to end his wicked ways.

Right now he didn't look wicked. But he was very close and his hands were very warm on her bare arms and he made *her* feel wicked.

She let out a breath in a long sigh. "Yes. I gave myself to him and the deal was sealed. There would be no going back. I felt the shift in him right away. He got harder, more cocksure. Less the man who was gentle with me. I suppose I realize now that was who he really was. The rest was just an act to get what he truly desired. My dowry. My brother's connections."

"Did you make it to Gretna Green?" Morgan whispered.

"No." Memories returned again, sharp and terrible. "The night before we were to arrive, Hugh appeared. He'd been making chase, it seemed. Come to rescue me, though it was too late. Aaron showed his true colors then. He...laughed at me."

Morgan flinched, as if that statement pained him as much as it had torn her to shreds that awful night. Even now she sometimes woke to Aaron's words ringing in her ears, his smirk dancing across her field of vision.

"There was nothing to be done. To protect me, Hugh paid for his silence. I was ruined and I returned home."

"Where is he?" Morgan asked, and his voice was now low and dangerous. "Tell me where he is and I will do what your brother could perhaps not out of a desire to protect your good name. I will rip him to shreds."

She shut her eyes and shook her head. "He is dead. About a year later, he did the same thing to Amelia. Made her think he was a man worthy of her. Hugh found out about their engagement and he was overwhelmed by guilt. So he stepped in, taking her from Aaron. They fell in love and they are very happy, but ultimately there was a fight. Aaron lashed out and tried to hurt Amelia and Hugh, and he was killed in the melee."

Morgan's jaw tightened and he brushed his hand across her

cheek. She found herself leaning into his palm. Taking some of his strength. Wishing she had more of her own.

"His death must have been complicated for you."

Her lips parted in surprise that he would guess that. No one else had. Her brother and Amelia had been supportive, of course. Tender, gentle. But they didn't fully understand her emotions. And she had chosen not to share them. So the thing she was about to say was a secret she had always held close to her heart.

"It was," she admitted. "I had once told myself I loved this man, enough to run away with him. Enough to give myself to him. Whatever he'd done, however I felt later, that had once been true. Then he was dead. So I felt grief and pain, anger and betrayal, and also relief all at once. I hated myself for all those feelings and for what I allowed him to do to me."

"That isn't your fault," he said, so swiftly that there was no doubt he believed it down to his core.

She shook her head, for she had certainly heard that before. It wasn't her fault, it wasn't her doing, it wasn't because of her.

"Of course it was my fault," she said, straightening her shoulders and stepping away from the comfort she hadn't earned and shouldn't take. "I snuck out to meet with him. If I'd thought that was the right thing to do, I wouldn't have done it like a thief in the night."

"You were a young woman feeling the flush of attraction, emotion," he said. "Thinking he was...decent."

She shook her head. "Don't absolve me. I *left* with him when I knew it was wrong. I gave him what he wanted instead of protecting my future. *I* ruined everything."

"Wait, you said Amelia had a similar interaction with the bastard," Morgan said. "Do you blame her for her interest?"

"Of course not," Lizzie said. "He made himself into what she wanted and she couldn't see what he was."

"So you will give her that grace, but not yourself," Morgan said, lifting his brows. "Not well played, Elizabeth."

THE LOVE OF A LIBERTINE

She frowned. "The difference is that Amelia didn't go as far as I did."

"Because she didn't, er..." He seemed to struggle. "I can only think of vulgar ways to describe it."

Lizzie's face felt like it was on fire. "*Yes*, because she didn't allow him to bed her. She wasn't weak like me."

"Desire is not a weakness," he said. "And she seems to share it in spades with Brighthollow, if the fact that they can barely keep their hands off of each other is any indication."

Lizzie dropped her gaze. She didn't really want to discuss that with this man. Her brother's relationship was something private. Though Morgan was right—Amelia and Hugh did little to hide their powerful physical connection from the world at large. Three years into their marriage and it hadn't lessened or waned.

"Need, desire, passion," she whispered. "For me they will lead to nothing good. I don't enjoy them and I refuse to surrender to the danger they pose ever again. *That* is why I can't go around kissing you, as much as any other reason. What you make me want is wrong."

His frown was dark and deep, and he shoved a hand through his hair out of what felt like frustration. She flinched away from it. Well, that would end that, it seemed. He was upset at what she'd said. Upset that she was putting a final distance between them.

"I see you are angry," she whispered. "I'll go back to the ball."

She moved toward the door, but he sidestepped into her path. "Yes, I am angry," he said through clenched teeth. "But not at you. I'm angry you were put in that position by someone who used your sweet nature so he could obtain what he wanted. I've known men like him all my life. They are the worst...well, to take a word often used to describe me...libertines. And if the man were not already in the ground, I would find him and exact a little revenge on your behalf."

She ducked her head. "Th-thank you."

She expected that to end the conversation, but he didn't move

145

away from her. Instead his finger slid beneath her chin and he tilted her face up toward his. He felt very close in the warmth of the parlor. Very close and big and all-consuming.

"I'm also upset that you see desire in such a poor light," he continued. "Because as I said earlier, there is nothing wrong with wanting. With pleasure. Using them to hurt someone else is wicked, but giving in to them isn't. That man...that bastard who hurt you, he should have seen what you gave him as the gift it was. He should have taken care of it and you. He should have made certain there was pleasure for you and not just for him, so you wouldn't cringe away from any hint of it. So you wouldn't conflate the stir in your belly when you feel attraction with the pain in your heart at what he did to you."

She could hardly breathe, because his finger was now tracing her jawline, her cheekbone, her ear, the side of her throat. And there was a tingle of awareness that seemed to crackle from his finger, as if he had electricity in his veins and she fire in her own.

Add to that the things he was saying, the forgiveness he demanded she give to herself. The forgiveness she could see perhaps for the first time in years. She found herself lifting toward him, saw his eyes widen with surprise. But he didn't pull away as she wound her arms around his neck and pressed her lips to his.

He froze for a moment. She felt his uncertainty and hesitance, but then he made a soft sound of desire and returned the kiss. It was tender, slow. His arms came around her and he cradled her against his broad chest, careful and gentle. She knew she should pull away. They'd made an agreement not to do this again, but whenever he touched her, whenever his mouth met hers, she could almost forget it wasn't the first time she'd been kissed.

She could almost do exactly what he said and let the desire and the pleasure be a positive, not a negative. She lifted on her tiptoes, pressing a hand to his chest, her fingers clenching against the fabric of his jacket as she sighed and he finally let his tongue dart out to taste her.

She expected him to take it further. To drown her in all the sensation until there was nothing left but it and him. But he didn't. To her surprise, he stepped back and stared at her with wild eyes full of question and something darker. Something deeper.

She smoothed her skirts, trying to find purchase in a world he seemed to so easily turn on its head. "Why are you looking at me like that?" she whispered.

He didn't say anything for a beat, and then he took her hand. "I know we agreed we couldn't do this anymore. I know we both have reasons why whatever attraction exists between us cannot be explored. It has no good end."

She moved to tug her hand away, but he held firm. "Wait, please wait," he pressed. "What that man did to you is a crime. What he took from you is a crime. Not your virginity, though that was needlessly cruel and manipulative."

"He didn't take anything else," she insisted. "It was Hugh's money, not mine."

"Not the money, Elizabeth," he said sharply. "I'm talking about making you think that what you feel is wrong. That what you want is wrong. That when you feel that ache low in your belly, the one that makes you dream of being touched, the one that wakes you sweating, the place between your legs throbbing…that you are wicked for feeling that."

Her breath came short and hard. It was as if he could see into her soul in that moment. More than any other time he had pushed past her defenses and seen everything.

"But I can't go back," she whispered. "You seem to think what I experienced that first time wasn't how it should have been."

"It wasn't," he said, his jaw setting. "If it had been me, I would have made it so good for you."

Her sex pulsed at that thought. *If it had been him.* "Are you offering to make it good for me now?" she whispered. "Out of some kind of pity?"

"Not out of pity." His voice was rough. "And if you asked me to, I could most definitely make it good for you now."

She stared at him, unable to blink, unable to move in shock. "You —you're talking about taking me?" She shook her head. "No. No I can't. I can't make that mistake again."

"Not everything is about taking you. Though God knows I will only think of that for the rest of the night." He squeezed his eyes shut. "I shouldn't have said anything. No matter how unfair what he did to you is, I shouldn't have said anything. I'm sorry."

She watched his mouth move and her head spun. When he touched her, it was everything. When he kissed her it was earth-shaking. But what he was suggesting was something...more. Would it erase the past? No. She wasn't fool enough to believe it could. But she still felt a longing for what he could give. A need that she hated herself for, but couldn't deny. Didn't want to deny when she was so close to him in this small parlor.

She was shaking like a leaf ready to fall from a tree in an autumn breeze. "Y-You said not everything is about taking me. So how would you make it good for me if you...if you didn't?"

His eyes went wide. "Are you asking me to?"

"Tell me how," she repeated. "Sh-show me how."

Now he swallowed, and there was an almost pained expression on his face. A war he was battling. A war she saw him lose as he bent his head, shook it slowly and then sighed. "I would...lock the door."

She watched as he backed toward the door, his gaze never leaving her. He reached back and turned the key in the lock with a quiet click. Her breath hitched, but she didn't tell him to stop.

"Then I'd come back to you," he whispered, and he moved toward her. "And I'd kiss you again. Because I know you like it when I kiss you. Don't you?"

She nodded, unable to speak. What were words when his mouth was coming toward hers? He did deepen the kiss then, as he hadn't earlier, and she wrapped her arms around his neck with a shuddering sigh of pleasure.

He pulled away from her mouth just as she was lost, but he didn't release her from his embrace this time. He backed her toward the settee in front of the fire and lowered her back across it gently. Then he knelt before her, his mouth seeking hers once more.

"Then," he said against her lips. "I would touch you. Not take you, Elizabeth. Touch you." He drew away and met her gaze. "But only if you want it. I'm not like him. I won't be angry if you say no. I'll stop if you've changed your mind."

Her lips parted. This was her chance to refuse him. Her chance to forget this had happened, walk away from it and from him and from all the confusing, maddening, terrifying things this exchange made her feel and want.

Instead she whispered, "Where would you touch me?"

He didn't speak again. He just rested a hand on her right breast. Gently, with almost no pressure, but it was there and she flashed briefly to a night long ago with a very different man. His fingers had dragged against her skin. Almost rough. She'd been too embarrassed to enjoy that touch. But this…this was different. Morgan kissed her as he stroked his fingertips so gently against her breast, plucking at her nipple beneath her gown. It hardened beneath his attention, rising against the fabric, and causing a friction that made her sigh with the echo of pleasure she felt deep inside of her.

His mouth broke from hers and she heard the desperate rasp of his breath. He kept his gaze locked on hers as he slid his hand lower. She braced as his fingers glided over her stomach, across her hip, and then he placed his hand between her legs.

"Then I'd touch you here," he whispered. "First through your dress to let you grow accustomed to it." As he spoke, he moved his fingers lightly, grinding between her thighs, gentle but insistent on her sex.

Aaron hadn't touched her here. Not with his hand. He'd kissed her, stripped her, squeezed and plucked her breasts a bit, and then he'd just…taken. Pain and humiliation had been her strongest emotions that night.

She didn't feel either now. She felt waves of sensation, tingling and heated and oh, so very pleasurable, that seemed to spiral out from wherever his hands touched her. Right now she throbbed between her legs and he added just the right amount of pressure with his touch to make that throb all the better.

"Please," she whispered, uncertain what it was she was asking for, but needing it more than she'd ever needed anything. Oh, she knew what she was doing was imprudent. She should step away and step back and tell him to leave.

But she didn't want him to leave. She wanted him to erase the past, or at least dull it a fraction with his touch. So prudence be damned.

He licked his lips and she shivered at the heated focus of his stare. "I'm going to lift your skirts, Elizabeth," he whispered. "It will be better if you're...bared to me. I can make it so much better."

She swallowed. This felt like another point of no return. And yet she nodded and he seemed relieved as he caught the hem of her pretty dress and pushed it up gently. His hands stroked her calves through her stitched stockings, her knee, her thigh. She writhed beneath those gentle touches, shocked by how much they moved her. He moved her.

At last he bunched her dress against her stomach. She was wearing drawers, so he untied the little ribbon at her waist and tugged them away. She was bared to him. Shockingly naked to his gaze.

And gaze he did, those dark eyes trailing over her in a way no other man's ever had. Probably ever would, considering her criteria for a future marriage was one that didn't include these pleasures.

"Good God, Elizabeth." His voice shook. "You are so gorgeous."

She blinked at the raw tone of his voice, how rough it was. Almost as if he were trying to keep himself under control, in check. But that couldn't be, could it? Men didn't lose themselves around her, especially men with an untamed past like Morgan Banfield.

And yet as he leaned in and brushed his fingers inside her inner thighs, he looked restrained, his expression taut. Like a coiled spring ready to pop free. She wanted to know what would happen if that occurred.

But she couldn't ponder it long, because her mind emptied of all thought when his fingers brushed the apex of her thighs. It was gentle, hardly more than a graze, but the stroke of it had her catching her breath, arching her back, as heat arced through her.

"Morgan," she murmured.

He nodded, as if she'd asked a question. As if he had the answer. Perhaps both were true. In this unspoken language of desire, he was the master, she the student, even if that had never been her intention this night.

He touched her again, this time settling the palm of his hand flush against her. He was warm, his touch firm. She felt a strong urge to move against him, but no ability to know how. He didn't make her find out. He moved instead, grinding up against her with the heel of his palm.

She dipped her head back. What was that sensation? Great God, but it was intense. Like someone had jolted all the nerves between her legs to life at once and now they crackled with pleasure. He pushed against her again, murmuring encouragement as she gripped her hands into the settee cushion.

"Just a little more," he whispered as he leaned in to kiss her.

She wrapped a hand around the back of his neck, deepening the kiss. His fingers stroked along her entrance, tracing her, then he was parting her folds and sliding inside her trembling sheath as if he were taking her.

Her eyes flew open, and she gasped out pleasure and surprise mixed. He remained still a moment, letting her grow accustomed to the feel of his thick finger inside of her, stretching her. When she squeezed around him, testing what it would feel like, he groaned and thrust gently. She arched at the thrilling increase of pleasure, rising to meet him as her head dipped back against the pillows.

He kept thrusting, gently taking, exploring, drowning her in sensation she'd never felt before. It was like what she'd experienced all those years ago, but different. More focused. More powerful. Less frightening and wrong.

This was not wrong. Or at least she couldn't see it as wrong in that charged moment where every movement gave her such intense pleasure. She gripped hard against him, gasping out his name in the quiet.

She couldn't believe anything could ever be better than this. Until she felt the sweep of his tongue against her. She jerked her head from the pillow and gazed down at him. His dark head was between her legs now, his soft beard stroking her sensitive thighs as his tongue traced her entrance.

Was this what people did? This magical, wicked thing? Or was this just special sorcery that Morgan knew and chose to share with her? She didn't know.

To be honest, she didn't care. She just wanted this. Her fingers dug into his hair and she clung to him, rising to meet him as his licks grew more forceful and focused on just one area of her sex, a hidden little nub of pleasure. His finger thrust in time to the licking, building her higher and higher, dragging her toward something she couldn't name. Couldn't express. Couldn't understand.

But she wanted more. She reached for it ceaselessly, crying out softly in the dim parlor until at last the dam he'd built between her legs burst. Sensation jerked through her and she trembled helplessly against it. Her hips thrust, she had to cover her mouth to muffle her screams. The pleasure went on and on and on, seemingly endless as he licked her through it all.

Only when she panted, spent and weightless on the settee pillows, did he press one chaste kiss between her legs, withdraw his fingers and smooth her skirts back down over her. And she knew nothing in her world could ever be the same again.

CHAPTER 14

Lizzie's world was still spinning when Morgan leaned up her body and nuzzled her neck with his mouth. His beard tickled, and she smiled as she lifted her heavy head, pulling him in to kiss her. She tasted herself on his slick lips. Sweet and heady. The taste of pleasure, and her body rippled with renewed need.

He was going to take her now. She knew that had to be next. Men didn't give unless they were going to receive. That was based both on rumor and her own experience.

Except he withdrew from her. He smiled down at her and then helped her to her feet. She stared at him, wobbling a little as he stepped away. She blinked at him in surprise.

"Did I—did I do something wrong?" she asked.

He shook his head and appeared genuinely confused by the question. "Great God, no. That was quite something. I enjoyed every moment of that, I assure you."

She shifted. Perhaps she should just leave this alone, but her mind raced with questions. "But, er, you aren't trying to…that is, you haven't…I mean, you must be…"

"Hard as steel?" he said with a bright smile. "Oh yes. But just because I want something doesn't mean I don't have the ability not to take it. I didn't put my hands and my mouth on you so that I could have my own pleasure, Elizabeth. I did it because I wanted you to see and feel what you should have experienced before. What a man should have done when he touched you."

"Oh," she whispered.

He leaned in and kissed her once again. Gently. Briefly. "You deserve all the pleasure in the world and more. Don't tell yourself that it isn't something you need. It's something you were made for."

She blinked again, trying to let that selfless offering sink in. What was this man about? She had judged him as so much and yet he was...different. Not exactly the rake he pretended to be.

"Well, I...thank you for it. And for not expecting anything else in return." Though when she said the words, they felt hollow. She rather wanted something more.

But he was being stronger than she could be, it seemed. And she should thank him for that, as well, though she didn't.

He glanced over his shoulder. "We've been missing from the ball for a while now," he said. "We probably ought to return, though not together."

She stepped up to the mirror mounted above the sideboard across the room. It was amazing how she could look so unchanged in the reflection when she felt utterly different from head to toe thanks to the man standing behind her. She smoothed her hair and fought with all her might to regain a little purchase. A little dignity.

"You are probably right," she said, forcing a smile, as if she were as unmoved by what had just transpired as he appeared to be. "I'll go back first."

"Probably best," he said with a chuckle. "I need a few moments to become, er, presentable."

He glanced downward and she followed his gaze. His breeches strained against what appeared to be a sizeable bulge. She knew what that was, what it meant, and her stomach fluttered at the sight of his arousal. Well, he'd said he did want her. There was the proof.

Even if he wouldn't take her.

Her cheeks felt like fire as she backed a step away. "I'll see you back in the ballroom, then," she whispered.

His brow wrinkled, and suddenly he moved toward her in three long steps. He leaned in, pressing her back against the door to kiss her one last time. Although the kiss started as a passionate exploration of her mouth, it changed as she wrapped her arms around him. He gentled his tongue, his lips, he tilted his head for different access. He made love to her mouth as he had with her sex a short time before.

And just as then, she felt lost to him when he did.

But finally he broke away and leaned around her to unlock the parlor door. They didn't move, although she could leave now.

"Why—why did you do that?" she asked.

He caught her hand as he stepped away, allowing her space. As he kept eye contact with her, he lifted her hand and kissed her knuckles. "Because I know it might be the last time," he admitted. "And I wanted it to be memorable."

She smiled even though the idea that tonight was the last time they would allow this connection between them to take over was painful. "You have succeeded in that, Morgan, in spades. I will be thinking of tonight for a long time to come. Now, goodnight."

She forced herself to slide her hand from his, forced herself to turn and exit the room. But as she walked away, his gaze hot on her back, her entire body began to shake. She'd spent years telling herself that the pleasure her friends seemed to take in physical intimacy was not something she would ever want or find.

And in a few short moments, this man had torn away her expectations and changed everything in her world. Now she had to decide what to do with that knowledge.

~

A s Elizabeth disappeared around the corner back toward the ballroom, Morgan shut the parlor door and relocked it. He sagged against the surface of the door, the full ramifications of what had happened tonight hitting him in a great wave.

He'd lost control. That was the only way to put it. Hearing Elizabeth talk about her past, about the bastard who had hurt and used her, had stoked a fire in him unlike any that had ever burned before. He'd wanted to ride across the country, her flag flying above him, and strike a deathblow to her enemy.

And when it had become clear that wasn't possible, the other thing he'd wanted to do had become stronger, more undeniable. Touching her, giving her pleasure the other man had denied in his cruelty...it was all Morgan had been able to think about.

"Oh, yes," he muttered out loud as he flopped down in a chair before the fire. His still-hard cock throbbed, and he shifted. "You're so fucking noble."

It was easy to pretend all that had been for her. But that wasn't it, was it? He'd *wanted* to kiss her, even though they'd said they'd never do that again. He'd *wanted* to touch her. He'd *wanted* to lift her skirts and scent her desire and make her shake around him as she moaned his name.

He'd done it for himself as much as for her. And the more he thought about it, the harder he got.

"Bloody hell," he gasped out, and flicked the placard of his trousers down. His cock, hard as steel, bobbed away from the confines and to full attention.

He didn't deserve the pleasure he was about to give himself, but it didn't matter. He spit on his palm and stroked himself from base to head. Pleasure ricocheted through his entire body, bordering on pain, and he let his breath slide out in a long groan.

He thought of many things when he pleasured himself. Scenarios, mostly, situations where he could take what he wanted. It was rarely a specific person who stoked the fire of his pleasure.

But tonight there was only one thing that entered his mind. Elizabeth spread out before him, her sex glistening as he leaned in to taste her remarkable essence. Elizabeth as she arched under his mouth and fingers. Elizabeth as she writhed and pleaded for more and less and everything while she came and came and came.

He stroked himself harder, faster, reaching for the pleasure he would have found if he'd leaned up over her and slid home deep in her tight channel. If he'd thrust into her while her fingers dug into his hair and her mouth collided with his so he could swallow her moans.

He came so hard and so fast that stars exploded before his vision. He jerked against his fingers, murmuring her name as the world swirled down to this primal need she stoked in him. For a few minutes he slouched against the cushion, panting as his heart rate slowly returned to normal.

He was slaked, but strangely unsatisfied. Visions of Elizabeth still danced across his mind. He pushed them aside and got up, reaching into his pocket to find a handkerchief to clean himself up. But his mind kept spinning as he did it, always back to her. Touching her, fucking her…talking to her.

He tucked himself in place and fastened his trousers. He couldn't go back to the ballroom in his present state. *That* was obvious.

His best course of action was to go take a long walk in the cool night and allow everything to calm down a little. Elizabeth would get to regain her footing without having to look at the man who had ravished her. He could try to get himself together before he was forced to smile at her like they were nothing more than acquaintances.

He strolled down the hall away from the ball, into the breakfast room. It led to the terrace and was closer to the set of stairs that went to the garden. He slipped out, watching carefully to make sure any of the attendees of the ball who were farther down on the terrace didn't see him.

Once he reached the garden below, he sucked in a deep breath.

He'd spent so much time lately amongst these flowers and shrubs that it felt like a strangely calming homecoming as he made his way down the path. Who would have thought it? That a garden could become so interesting to him.

"Or perhaps it's the woman," he muttered.

Oh yes, Elizabeth was more than interesting to him. Tonight had proven that in spades. She was so gentle, so kind. So intelligent and amusing. But she was also a bubbling cauldron of hidden passion. Remove that lid and beneath was lava ready to overflow.

He hadn't been ready for that, even if he'd sensed it somehow. Felt it in her touch and her kiss. How many times had a woman's orgasm moved him so deeply? He didn't think anyone else ever had. Yes, he wanted his lovers to have pleasure. He had trained himself to be proficient at finding all the ways to make a lady moan and quake.

But when Elizabeth had lost control beneath his touch, that had felt...different. New. Powerful. He'd couched it as a gift he gave, to make up for the terrible thing that had happened to her. But the gift was his, not hers. And it had...changed him. He felt it now in his soul. And that was terrifying.

He was a rake, wasn't he? Not built to be changed by a woman. Not intending to be swept away by a fine pair of blue eyes and the hesitant smile that went with them. It could never happen. He shouldn't want it to happen—that was a setup for disaster.

And yet this little ache in him grew every time he saw her across a room or this very garden. An ache that whispered he wanted more than her kiss or her pleasure. He wanted her. All of her, body and soul and heart.

That realization hit him like a ton of bricks in the chest, and he pivoted to look back at the house in shock. As he did so, there was a sharp, heavy pain at the back of his skull and then a wave of darkness washed over him. His last conscious thought was that someone was beating him and that he might never see Elizabeth again.

~

L izzie lifted on her tiptoes and peered across the ballroom for what felt like the tenth time in a half an hour. Morgan was still not back after their encounter. What did that mean?

"You look nervous," Katherine said as she slipped up beside Lizzie and slid a friendly arm around her waist. "Is the party very terrible for you?"

"No," Lizzie said, trying to find focus amidst her distraction. "It has been a—a surprising night to say the least."

Katherine's brow wrinkled. "How so?"

Lizzie almost snorted out a laugh. As if she could explain to Morgan's sister-in-law that he had brought color to her drab world with his fingers and tongue in a parlor. There was a casual conversation starter.

So she struggled to find something else to say. "Just so many new friends to meet, I suppose," she said. "But I do wonder where Mr. Banfield is."

Katherine held her gaze a moment, but then she looked around. "You know, now that you say it, I haven't seen him for a while, myself."

Lizzie shifted. "I passed him in the hall not very long ago and he claimed he was going to ask me to dance the next, but two songs have played and he has not materialized."

"And you wish to dance with him," Katherine said softly.

Lizzie froze. She was revealing too much without meaning to do so, especially to someone as observant as Katherine. "Not...necessarily, but I did accept out of, er, politeness. And I only hope he is well."

Katherine frowned and a flash of concern came over her lovely features. "I did see Morgan out on the terrace a short time ago. He was walking into the garden."

Lizzie caught her breath. "Perhaps we should look for him. Just to make certain nothing has happened to him. There are a great many tools and things piled around in the dark. He might have hurt himself."

She didn't believe that, of course. Morgan was well aware of the dangers in certain parts of the garden at present. At his order, those areas had been carefully closed off by the servants so no guest would wander in. But there was a prick of concern that was growing in her with each passing moment, and she would have said almost anything to get Katherine to help her with the search.

"Then let's seek him out," Katherine said, and they linked arms and headed toward the terrace doors.

Lizzie was all but dragging Katherine as they stepped out into the cool night air. She looked around the terrace, but Morgan was not there. She stepped up to the terrace wall. She leaned on it with both hands and peered into the night. The moon was full, so it cast a glow across the grounds that would help their search.

But there was nothing to be found. She looked up and down the paths and corners of the garden below. But then, in the distance, over by where the new gazebo was almost complete, she saw something. A flash of movement.

Her heart raced and she pointed. "There!"

She didn't wait for a response, though she heard Katherine say, "Where?" as she rushed down the stairs. She weaved through the garden, wishing the paths hadn't been made so intricate. And as she came around the last corner, she saw him.

Morgan lay on his back, arms sprawled at his sides. He was unconscious, both his eyes were bruised and there was blood trickling from the corner of his lip.

"Morgan!" she screamed and dropped down beside him.

Katherine skidded to a stop and clamped a hand over her mouth. "Great God! I'll get the others!"

She pivoted and ran away, leaving Lizzie with Morgan. She reached out, hesitating because she feared harming him more. "Morgan," she said, this time softer. "Oh please, you must open your eyes. Please look at me."

He made a soft moan, a pained sound, and her heart leapt as his dark eyes came open. "Elizabeth," he whispered.

She shifted and lifted his head into her lap so he would no longer have to rest it on the cold, hard ground. "What happened?" she whispered. "Stay awake now, love, and tell me what happened."

He blinked hard and the pain of that action fluttered across his handsome face. "Struck...from behind. Dangerous."

"Yes," she soothed, smoothing a lock of hair from his forehead and looking at the bruise at his temple. He was struck from more than just behind. "Whoever did this is certainly dangerous."

"I'm dangerous," he corrected, and his gaze got a bit wild. "*I'm* dangerous, Elizabeth."

She didn't get a chance to respond to that statement. The crowd began to stream from the ballroom, people shouting and racing toward them. Robert, Hugh and Ewan burst into the small area first with their wives at their heels. All the color went out of Robert's face as he looked down at his brother.

Morgan's gaze was starting to clear and he forced a tight smile. "Not so pretty now, am I?"

"Do shut up," Katherine snapped. "Can you stand?"

Morgan glanced at Elizabeth. She shifted, gripping his arm to help him as he struggled first to his knees and then slowly tried to get up further. He staggered, and before she had to catch him, Ewan stepped forward and caught him beneath the armpits. The Duke of Donburrow was a massive man and he held Morgan upright like he weighed nothing. Morgan leaned heavily on him and Lizzie squeezed his arm before she released him.

"My head is spinning," Morgan muttered.

"What happened?" Hugh asked as he looked over his shoulder. All along the terrace, the guests were lined up, watching the drama below unfold. Lizzie could hear them on the paths, too. Curious onlookers, gossips and those with true concern over the injury of a guest. It didn't matter their intent—the outcome of their observations would be the same.

Rumors.

Lizzie swallowed past the lump in her throat. "He's injured," she said as she found her voice. "We can talk about the particulars once we get him inside, can't we?"

The question seemed to snap the others from their shock. Robert lunged forward and slung Morgan's arm around his neck. Together he and Ewan began helping Morgan up the path, the other women circling around the three, clearing the crowd and calling out comfort to those they saw along the way.

Lizzie pivoted on Hugh. "He was attacked," she said.

His eyes widened. "He told you that?"

"Yes, and not much more. So when you are sending for the doctor, may I also recommend you send for the guard?"

Hugh stared down at her, eyes slightly wide. "Anything else, my lady?" he asked.

Her cheeks heated at the pointed question, but she ignored the embarrassment when she thought of Morgan's statement that he was dangerous. He believed it. Believed he had somehow earned the attack on his life.

She waved her brother up the path. "Go then!" she said.

He was shaking his head as he rushed up to the join the others. She followed close behind, and at the entrance back onto the path, she turned. The grass was flattened where the struggle between Morgan and his attacker or attackers had occurred. She saw the boot scrapes and the divots, and she shivered.

She was about to catch up with the others on the path when the moonlight from above glinted on something in the dust. She stepped closer, and there was a cufflink smashed into the dirt. She picked it up and turned it over. It was a flat disk of gold, impressed with the initials *G.C.* Not Morgan's then. Perhaps the man who had attacked him.

It was a fine piece. Not the attire of a common criminal. Though she supposed a thief might have simply dropped his wares gathered from some other unsuspecting mark.

She closed her hand around the item, gripping it tightly as she made her way up the path back toward the house. She needed to get to Morgan's chamber with the rest, to ensure he was well, and then she'd certainly find a chance to ask him about the item. Perhaps together they could determine from the item who had attacked him.

She climbed the stairs to the terrace. There was a crowd there, buzzing and gossiping and staring. All her life, she had hated those eyes. She'd shrunk from her name being whispered across the room. But today she barely paid attention. Morgan was all she could think about, all she could focus on.

But the crowd wouldn't let her through without comment. Her arm was suddenly grasped by Lady Jocelyn, who had spoken to her earlier in the ball. The woman's gaze was lit up with interest, a desire to get at the heart of what had happened so she could spread it and embellish it.

"Your brother's man is quite a bit of trouble," she cooed. "I hope he isn't badly injured. Was he drunk and fell?"

Lizzie yanked her arm away. "You needn't trouble yourself, my lady. Now excuse me. I must return to my duties. You ought to go back into the ball. I'm sure Amelia and Hugh will be back soon enough."

Jocelyn arched one of those fine brows just as Lizzie turned away. "Oh, Lizzie, dear?"

Lizzie clenched her hands at her sides and forced a smile as she looked over her shoulder. "Yes?"

"You've that bastard's blood all over your skirt," she sneered. "You might want to wash it out before it stains."

Lizzie glared at her. She'd wondered when women of this ilk would bring up the subject of Morgan's birth. She, herself, had mentioned he was one of Robert's brothers and the world knew of his famous bastard siblings. Jocelyn wouldn't be stopped from bringing that up if it would sting.

She moved a long step back toward Jocelyn. She had spent years ducking her head to this woman, including as recently as an hour before. She'd feared her, cowed to her, hidden from her because Jocelyn had power in their circles and Lizzie just prayed not to be seen.

But in that moment she didn't give a damn.

"I told you earlier, Jocelyn, we are lucky to have a man of Morgan Banfield's quality to serve at my brother's side. And if you wish to be invited to this house again, you will think before you speak about him again."

Jocelyn's eyes widened. "You—you think you matter to me, little mouse?" she stammered.

Lizzie shrugged. "I matter to very few. But I think everyone knows that the wives of my brother's friends matter very much in Society. Three of them are here now. It would take me half an hour to write to the rest. I choose not to destroy you because it isn't in my nature. But speak on him, and I will speak on you. Do I make myself perfectly clear?"

To her surprise, Jocelyn actually looked...frightened. She backed away and nodded. "You misunderstood me, I assure you. I was only asking after the gentleman's well-being and making certain you knew about the blood."

"Very good," Lizzie said, and then left without so much as a farewell. Her hands shook as she hustled into the house and through the ballroom. She had never set another person down like that in her life, despite the fact that her shyness sometimes brought out the worst in those around her.

And yet protecting Morgan had caused her to do for him what she hadn't ever done for herself. Stand up. Protect.

Why? Well, the answer was clear now. She had fallen in love with him. And she had no idea what to do about it, because if she knew one thing and one thing only, it was that when she fell, it didn't end well. And it couldn't end well this time, either.

CHAPTER 15

Morgan shifted as Robert and Ewan helped him onto the narrow bed in his chamber. Robert stepped away immediately, running a hand through his thick hair as he said, "What happened?"

Ewan sent Morgan a look, and Morgan forced a painful smile as he signed, *"Thank you."*

Ewan's eyes widened and he inclined his head and signed back, *"Any time."*

"Are you going to answer me?" Robert snapped.

Morgan finally met his brother's eyes and saw, to his surprise, not the anger his harsh tone might have implied, but fear. Terror, on Morgan's behalf. His hands shook and Katherine took his arm, but it seemed to make no difference.

"Please," his brother said, a little softer.

It was in that moment that Brighthollow entered the room. "I've sent for a doctor and the guard. I think we all deserve an answer to your brother's question, Morgan. Was this some random act of violence committed in my garden? Do I need to protect my house? And if so, is it from some chance encounter or from something you brought upon it?"

As he asked the question, Elizabeth slipped into the room. She met his eyes as she quietly closed his door. He could see the flutter of her hand as she stared at him. As if she wanted to touch him. To make sure he was unharmed. He didn't deserve that, of course. He hadn't *deserved* anything he'd taken this night.

The attack was just a reminder.

"You know I have a past," he said, breaking his gaze from Elizabeth and shifting it to Robert. "You knew I had a past when you came and fetched me from gaol."

His brother's shoulders rolled forward and all the air left his lungs in a long, hissing sigh. "Morgan," he said softly.

"I...I received a note a few days ago," Morgan said, and his gaze darted to Elizabeth once more. "A threat."

She stepped forward, her lips parting and her hands clenching before her. "The—the note you received just before we were walking through the garden that day? When you showed me my corner?"

The rest of the room shifted their attention and all the heads seemed to swivel between Elizabeth to Morgan and back again. Except for the Duke of Brighthollow. His gaze stayed firmly locked on Morgan, his eyes narrowed.

"Yes," Morgan said softly.

Her breath caught. "But you—you said nothing to me, Morgan. Not that afternoon or later, even though we—" She cut herself off as if she had only just realized the room was full of people analyzing her every word and tone. "I wish you had told me."

Brighthollow was still staring evenly at Morgan, and he sat up straighter on the bed just in case he was about to be punched by the second person that night.

"Yes, *Morgan*. I wish you'd told me, too," Brighthollow said, low and dangerous. "Why are you being threatened?"

Morgan sighed. How he loved airing his dirty linens in this very public manner. But perhaps it was best. He and Elizabeth had gone too far tonight. His mere existence threatened hers. And yet again, he had to try to find a way to distance himself.

This was as good as any.

"In London, I was out of control," he said. "Drinking too much, gambling too much, not caring about boundaries of honor or decency. I took the money of many a man in cards. I fought with them, I—" He cut himself off and watched Elizabeth carefully from the corner of his eye. "I slept with a few of their wives."

Brighthollow flinched. "Lizzie, perhaps you should step out if we're going to discuss—"

She pushed off the door and stared at her brother. "You must be in jest, Hugh." She held his gaze. "You must be forgetting both yourself and what I am."

Brighthollow glanced once more at Morgan and then shook his head. "I apologize. I should not have treated you like a child. If you wish to stay and hear this, I won't object."

Robert stepped up. "So you think it's one of those men, come all the way to Brighthollow to punish you for your misdeeds?"

"I don't know," Morgan admitted. "But the attack and the note cannot be unrelated. It would be too much of a coincidence. Still, I can't say who for certain. The person who struck me did it from behind. I couldn't see his face and I lost consciousness too quickly to make any mental notes on him."

"Blast it all," Robert said, pivoting away and pacing the small room, now extra cramped because of the overload of inhabitants. "Then we cannot know the true nature of the threat or how to thwart it."

Elizabeth cleared her throat and stepped up. "I found this in the garden, ground into the soil where Morgan and his attacker struggled." She opened her hand and there was a cufflink. She'd been holding it so tightly, it had dug a groove into her delicate skin. "Do you recognize it or the initials?"

Morgan reached out and took the golden item from her palm,

resisting the urge to brush his fingertips along her skin just to comfort himself and her. He turned the item over. "G.C." He squeezed his eyes shut and pictured the man that item very likely belonged to. And he didn't want to say it out loud. He didn't want to explain how depraved he'd been. Not to her. Not to them. It was just as he'd feared. His behavior had truly brought this hell down upon Brighthollow's house.

There was a knock on the door and Brighthollow's butler stepped in from the hall. "Dr. West, Your Grace."

As the doctor edged his way into the crowd, Hugh shook his head. "I think we should all step out. Let the man do his job." He motioned for the others to go. "Amelia, you and I need to return to the ball and try to move everyone along with as much tact as is possible. You know I cannot do that alone."

They all began to move, nodding to the doctor, talking softly as they exited into the hall. Elizabeth stood aside as they left, watching him. It was only when just Brighthollow and the doctor remained that she slipped out.

Brighthollow glanced toward him. "This conversation is not over. Dr. West, do take good care of him."

The doctor nodded as the door closed, and Morgan let out his breath. He didn't need a doctor. Now that his mind was clearing, he knew nothing was broken except the trust of his employer. The trust of his brother. And perhaps, the trust of a woman who had allowed him such liberties tonight that he could still taste her on his tongue.

But surely that was all over now. It had to be.

The house was quiet but for the light tick of the clock as Lizzie slipped from her bedchamber and into the hallway. The time was after two, and at last all in the house had gone to their beds. It had been a raucous night. The ball, what she and Morgan had done during it, the attack, having to clear the ballroom. Having Amelia,

Katherine and Charlotte all watch her so closely after they left Morgan. Like they knew, like they could see.

Perhaps they could. Perhaps when she had allowed him to touch her so intimately, it had permanently marked her in some way that good women could identify. Mark. She certainly felt marked.

But she wasn't shamed by it.

She knew Morgan was fine, or would be. He was bruised—she'd heard the doctor say so when she eavesdropped on his evaluation to Hugh and Robert. Morgan needed a few days rest and then he would be right as rain. And that had been that.

But she hadn't been able to stop thinking about him since she'd slipped from his bedchamber hours before. Images of him unmoving on the grass had jumped into her mind over and over, lifting her heart into her throat and making clear the truth.

She *did* love this man. It hadn't been a mere reaction when she saw him lying there, when she thought he might be gone forever. She did love him, and the feeling wasn't fading, but offering her more proof as she tried to force herself not to overthink or over-plan or over-anything.

And here she was, slipping from the family quarters, past the guest quarters, up the stairs into the servant quarters where she'd left Morgan hours before. She needed to see him. To finish the conversation that hadn't been able to be private after his attack. To make sure he was whole and safe. Because she needed that to be true more than she needed breath or food or water. She needed to touch him and feel his warmth that proved he still existed in her world.

She stepped up to his door, and the nerve she'd somehow found after years of being passive faltered. What if she knocked and he didn't answer? Or worse, turned her away? What then?

"Then you'll know your heart is a fool," she muttered as she raised a fist, drew a breath and knocked.

There was a pause and then a rustling from behind the door. Then Morgan's voice called out, "Enter." As she opened the door, he continued from the bed, "You may tell Brighthollow that he needn't keep sending up compresses. I appreciate the doting from the staff, but I am..."

He trailed off as she slipped inside the room and shut the door. "...fine."

He wasn't wearing a shirt, though the blankets were tucked around his waist. Still, there was a lot of very toned flesh on display, and she boggled for a moment at how beautiful he was. How could he be so beautiful?

But then her gaze lifted, and she flinched as the firelight and candlelight danced off the angles of his handsome face. Both his eyes were black, as was his temple.

"Your bruises," she whispered, blinking at tears that leapt to her eyes in the face of his pain.

He lifted a hand and touched the purple skin. "They don't hurt...much."

He smiled at the quip. She didn't.

He cleared his throat. "You are here."

"I am," she said, and clenched her hands behind her back. What in the world had she been planning by coming here? She could scarcely recall when he was so close.

"Why are you here, Elizabeth?" he whispered.

She blinked. She'd been telling herself it was just to check on him, but it wasn't. That was just the excuse she'd used. And now she stood there, with him in his bed, and she knew why she'd really come. The answer terrified her.

She glanced down at her feet. "Are you not going to rise, Mr. Banfield?"

He chuckled. "I'm not wearing any clothes, my lady. If I rise, I think that would shock you."

Her eyes went wide and she choked out, "O-oh. Well, then probably best to stay where you are." She worried her lip. So he was naked. Well, that was something. Just a tug of that blanket and...

She shook her head. "We didn't get a chance to speak after your attack," she said.

He nodded slowly. "And you have questions."

"I suppose we all have questions," she said. "Perhaps I'm not owed answers."

"You are owed answers more than anyone else," he said, and his gaze held hers steadily. "You know why."

She swallowed hard. He was talking about what had happened between them earlier that night. He was talking about the connection that bound them. He might not know that she loved him. He might never know that if she chose to keep it secret, but that they were attracted and connected was obvious to them both.

"Before the doctor came, it was evident you recognized the cufflinks your attacker left behind," she said softly. "Who was he? Why would he do this?"

He let out his breath in a shaky sigh and she saw shame cross his face. It was a funny thing to see it. Morgan so often wore a mask before others. A face that deceived and tricked and played a game. But now it had slipped and she saw the truth. Dark and deep.

"What did you do?" she asked.

He dropped his chin. "*That* is the better question. I do know who the cufflinks belong to. Gareth Covington."

She inched a little closer. "And who is Gareth Covington?" she pressed.

His mouth twisted. He struggled with the answer and her heart hurt for him. Feared for him.

She drew a short breath. "Earlier tonight you promised me no judgment. No reprisals. And I offer you the same thing now."

He shook his head slightly. "Oh, sweet, you can't promise me that. Not once you know. But you need to know. So there's no avoiding it now." He scrubbed a hand through his beard, and then he said, "We were friends in school. Close friends. We snuck out of school grounds together, we gamed together, raced our phaetons together."

"Sounds like a sobering influence," Lizzie said with an arch of her brow.

"I wasn't looking for sobering influences, my dear," he said with a brief chuckle. "And Gareth and I brought out the worst in each other. He started talking about this woman about a year ago. I didn't pay much attention. I was rather annoyed, truth be told, when he rambled about her. I wish now I had paid more attention."

Her brow wrinkled. "Why? What happened?"

He shifted. "I had spent the night with a...a...er...a willing lady."

Lizzie fought not to flinch. She knew what kind of life Morgan had lived before. She had no cause to be jealous of his past.

"I woke to banging on my chamber door. Wild banging and loud yelling. My servants were trying to keep the intruder back but he managed to get past them. It was Gareth. The woman I was still naked in bed with was—"

Lizzie clamped her hand over her mouth. "The woman he'd fallen in love with."

He nodded. "Yes."

"And you didn't know it was her?" Lizzie asked. "Was she disguised?"

"No, I just was a terrible friend. Gareth had asked me to meet her a few times, but I always found some excuse to get out of it. I wasn't interested in his happily ever after because I was an ass more interested in my own pleasure and fun. So when this woman approached me, I had no idea who she was."

Lizzie tried to wrap her head around it. "Did she know who you were?"

"Oh yes." His voice got bitter. "She made that very clear as Gareth tore my chamber apart. She'd seen me from afar."

"Why would she do that?" Lizzie gasped. "Why would she be so cruel?"

He shrugged. "Some people just...are. She and Gareth had had a quarrel, it seems. She was angry and wanted to hurt him. She took her revenge by bedding me…and making certain my friend found out about it so he could catch us."

"She destroyed your friendship," Lizzie whispered.

Morgan nodded. "And a great deal more. Gareth called me out. That was how Robert got involved in my life initially. He heard about the planned duel, raced back from the continent where he and Katherine were touring around and stepped in to try to right the situation. But Gareth has been angry with me ever since."

"That was why you spiraled out of control this last year," Lizzie whispered. "You were mourning what you'd done. What you'd been a puppet in creating."

"Yes," he whispered. "The night I went to gaol, Gareth joined our table in a hell for cards. I kept letting him win. I let him win and win and I drank and drank to keep from seeing the hate on his face. I woke up in Newgate. But whatever else happened that night, it must have renewed his hatred in me. Hearing that I'd taken a respectable job, that I was starting over…"

"It must have triggered his need for a revenge he doesn't feel he has truly taken."

"Because he didn't get his duel. He never evened the score."

Lizzie shook her head. "Oh, Morgan. I'm sorry."

"Why are you sorry?" His brow wrinkled. "I'm the one who did this."

"This woman, she's the one who did it. Would you have bedded your friend's lover if you'd known her identity?"

"Of course not. I'm a libertine, but I have a code," he said immediately.

She almost sagged in relief at his reaction. He was the man she thought him to be. He was the man she loved, indeed. "But she knew *your* identity and pursued you in order to hurt Gareth. That is on her."

He sighed. "Perhaps, but it doesn't matter. My friend is clearly not finished with his punishment. My actions have created danger for your family. For you. Embarrassment for you all, thanks to his attack coming at your ball. I'm certain your brother will wish to discuss it with me further later today. And he'll likely sack me."

She flinched. That was possible. Hugh was an honorable man—he might see Morgan's actions as dishonorable, no matter the explanation. And to protect those he loved, he might, indeed, let Morgan go. He would leave and she would possibly never see him again.

"Morgan, I did come here to ask you about the attack," she whispered. "But it was more than that. I came here because I want…I need…"

"Elizabeth," he whispered, cutting her off. "You can't say it."

"But I must," she said. "If you might be gone tomorrow, then I must say it tonight. I have to ask for it tonight or I'll never have another chance."

She moved forward then, as if magnetized by his presence. "Morgan," she whispered as she sank onto the edge of his bed, cupped his cheeks as gently as she could muster, and brought her lips to his.

"Lizzie," he said, slipping into her nickname as he turned his face slightly away from hers. "My past."

She turned him back to her. "You told me earlier tonight that I had to move beyond my past. Are you sorry for what you did?"

He held her gaze. "Infinitely."

She nodded. "Then you need to let it go, just as you say I do. Now please."

She kissed him again, and this time he didn't pull away. This time his arms came around her, dragging her partly across him on the bed. His mouth opened and their tongues tangled in desperate desire, and she knew with all her heart that tonight she would be his.

And despite all her fears associated with this act, all her questions about prudence, she wanted this more than she'd ever wanted anything.

CHAPTER 16

L izzie shivered as Morgan expertly reversed their positions on the narrow bed, sliding her beneath him. The sheets were trapped between them, but she could still feel the hard length of him pressed against her thigh. He wanted her. She wanted him.

And this was a dance as old as time itself.

His weight pushed her deep within the soft mattress, and she wound her arms around his neck with a sigh. He captured that sound with his mouth, slowing his tongue as he stroked along hers, savoring, just as she savored this moment.

His hands glided along her sides, fingers bunching against her nightrail and robe, pressing into her flesh beneath until she turned her face against his neck with a garbled sound of pleasure.

His breath was short, hot against her skin as he stopping moving, stopped kissing. "I shouldn't do this," he whispered.

She looked up at him outlined in the firelight, and memorized every taut line of his face, his lips, his jaw. "I want you to," she said, and meant it. "Until earlier tonight, I thought that I would never feel pleasure when it came to a man's touch. I thought that was something for everyone else. But what you gave me in the parlor, with your hands and your mouth...it thrilled me. And I know what was supposed to come after. It's all I can think about."

"Elizabeth," he murmured. "You do test me and all my resolve not to be the kind of man everyone thinks me to be."

"If you were the kind of man everyone thinks you to be, you would have claimed me earlier and not given a damn about my pleasure," she retorted. "And you didn't. I know who you are, Morgan. I know what you are and how much you are capable of. And I want that. I want you. I'm asking you for tonight. Won't you please give that to me?"

He stared at her, seeming to ponder that. "Your innocence was already taken, so I won't ruin you."

"You can't," she agreed.

"And if I'm careful, there don't have to be...consequences."

She shut her eyes, trying not to picture a child she could make with this man. She had always loved children and reveled in the babies of her brother's friends. But he was right that creating a child from a liaison was a mistake. It would trap him, and she didn't want him that way.

"The only consequence of this night should be pleasure," she said, to herself as much as him. "I'm not asking for anything else."

His lips thinned, almost as if he didn't like that answer, but then his dark head came down and he claimed her mouth again. Words were forgotten, thoughts forgotten, fears forgotten. All that was left was him and the heated sensation of his mouth molding to hers, exploring hers, his whiskers brushing her skin. His hands began their movement again, his body grinding against hers as she shivered with pleasure.

He kicked at the covers that separated them and she looked down at him as he did so. Her eyes widened. She'd seen a man's cock before. That was the word Aaron had used to describe it that long-ago night. She had remembered it very differently, for it had become, in her mind, an instrument of destruction.

Morgan's cock was not as fearful as those memories. It was hard, of course, curled toward his stomach because he wanted to claim her. But the head wasn't so cruelly red, the length didn't seem punishing or mocking.

"You look afraid," he whispered. "Are you sure you want this?"

"I do," she said. "But last time it wasn't very...nice. I can't help but be nervous."

"Did he force you?" he asked.

She flinched. "No."

"You said you gave yourself to him," he whispered. "Did you do it willingly?"

"Yes," she said after what felt like an eternity of struggle to find the words. "He was many things, but he didn't rape me."

He let out his breath gently. "None of it was your fault."

"So you said. Still, he wasn't like you were earlier. He didn't seem to care about my pleasure. He wasn't trying to cause me more pain, but there was no mitigating it, either."

He frowned. "The pain comes with the first time. And you'll be tight this time because it's been so long. But, Elizabeth, I want you to understand. There won't be pain tonight. This—" He motioned to his cock. "—is here to pleasure you, not hurt you. I'd never, *ever* hurt you."

She believed him in that moment and her love for him swelled even higher. She nodded because she could find no words, and then she looked at him again. "May I...touch it? I was too afraid to ask that night."

He smiled. "Of course."

He rolled on his back and laced his fingers behind his head to support him. She eased to her side, looking him up and down. "You look like a very casual Hades in this pose."

"Well, Persephone, I link my hands behind my head so casually because I'm afraid I won't be able to control myself. And I need to do that. For you."

She blinked down at him, her god of the underworld, and then she smiled. It was time to give in to the darkness. To live in the seductive pleasure he would give. Just one time to surrender to him and his world.

She reached out and touched him, but not his cock. She started at the winged ridges of his collarbone, tracing there, feeling how hot his skin was. She dragged her fingers lower, her nails brushing the flat pectoral, the hard nub of his nipple. He hissed out a breath as she did so, and his muscles tightened like he was struggling for control.

She continued lower, tracing all the ridges of his abdomen, cupping the swell of his hip, and only then did she brush the back of her hand across his thigh and cup the length of him.

He gasped out her name and he sat partially up, his wide eyes focusing as her fingers folded around him, gripping the shaft gently. His skin was soft around that steely erection and she rubbed her thumb across it.

"Elizabeth," he said in a garbled, almost pained tone. "Christ. Stroke it, please."

The *please* was drawn out, begging her. And she met his eyes as she did what she'd been asked. She stroked him from base to tip, smoothing the drop of liquid that had wept from the opening, lubricating him a fraction.

"What do you think of it now that you've touched it?" he gasped out, lifting against her as she stroked him a second time.

"I'm not afraid of it anymore," she admitted. "And I want to see what happens next."

"Good," he grunted, and then he flipped her on her back a second time. His hands pressed into her shoulders, holding her in place as he dropped his mouth to her throat. He sucked there, hard, scraping his teeth across her skin as he ducked his head into the notch where her shoulder and neck met. She drove her fingers into his hair, whispering his name as electric pleasure ricocheted through her.

He smiled against her flesh, nipping lower, lower until he

nuzzled her nipple through the fabric of her dressing gown and nightrail.

"Too many clothes," he muttered, and leaned away to flick open her robe tie with little effort. He parted the fabric, flattening his hand against her belly. She felt the warmth of him through the silk and found herself arching against him, seeking more. "I'm taking them off," he said.

She nodded and pushed at her robe herself, yanking it down her arms, pushing it away as he chuckled at her ardor. Once she was free of it, he leaned in and caught the strap of her nightgown with his teeth. He looked up at her as he dragged it down her shoulder, licking a path until the strap drooped at her shoulder. He kissed his way back up, sliding his hand beneath the fabric, brushing her breast, and then it was bared to the warm air in the room.

She froze and looked down her body. Her breast was naked, cupped in his hand, his thumb stroking over her exquisitely sensitive nipple. He watched her as he touched her, slow and steady, like they had all night, all week, all the rest of their lives to do this.

But that wasn't true. And she needed what he would offer before it disappeared forever. She moaned in frustration-laced pleasure and lifted to him, demanding what she couldn't name. Didn't fully understand. Already he had done more to prepare her than Aaron had all those years ago.

Already she wanted more.

He dropped his head to her and brushed his bearded cheek against her. She hissed, arching, and he smiled before he turned his head and his tongue darted out to trace the exposed nipple. She cried out as sensation threaded through her veins. He lifted his head.

"Hush now or we won't get to finish," he admonished in that dark, seductive voice that dragged her further into his underworld. The only place she wanted to be.

She clamped a hand over her mouth as he sucked her, this time harder, and it felt like every part of her shattered with unexpected, powerful pleasure. She was riding the ocean now, just as she had been when he touched her, licked her between her legs. She knew what would happen when she hit the right wave. She knew what intense pleasure she would find there.

She reached for it, lifting to him, digging her hands into his bare shoulders as he licked his way between her breasts and lowered the opposite strap. Now she was naked from the waist up, and he laved one nipple then the other, always back and forth, always relentless until she was almost incoherent with pleasure and need like no other.

Only then did he trace down her body with his tongue, pulling her nightgown along her stomach, her hips, and finally low enough that she could kick it away. She was naked now, and she blushed as he looked at her.

"So beautiful," he all but purred as he touched her, his rough hands stroking her skin. He caressed her thighs, massaging gently before he pushed her wide and exposed her sex. His gaze lifted, meeting hers, holding it.

Then he bent his head and licked her. She arched up against his tongue, gripping the coverlet with both hands and squeezing her eyes shut as wicked pleasure pulsed through her, at first gently and then more insistently. He was talented with that tongue, swirling around her clitoris, sucking and teasing until she was gasping for breath and she felt the edge of release waiting for her.

But he didn't gift her with that pleasure. Not yet. He lifted his head, his mouth glistening from her body, and smiled. Even with his face bruised and battered from the earlier attack, he was still the most handsome man she'd ever known. When he smiled at her like that, not a charming mask he wore for the world, but a real smile, her heart fluttered.

And she never wanted to lose that. Never wanted it to end. Even though she knew it must. And that made her desperate.

She reached for him and he surged toward her, his mouth finding hers as he settled between her legs. She tasted her essence on his tongue as he kissed her, salty-sweet, and she shivered with renewed pleasure.

He was shifting now, moving over her, his hand sliding between them as he positioned the head of his cock at her entrance. She waited for him to thrust, to take, to claim, and braced herself for the moment.

Instead he withdrew from her kiss and looked down at her. "Are you sure you want this?"

She blinked. Here he was on the cusp of claiming and still he asked her for permission.

She reached up to cup his cheeks, smoothing her thumbs across his skin as she stared up into those beautiful brown eyes. "I want *you*," she corrected softly. "And I've never been more certain of anything in my entire life."

He stared at her, his lips parting slightly, as if he was surprised by that answer. Then he nodded slowly and tipped his hips forward.

She expected resistance as he took her. Past experience said there would be. But there was none. His cock slid past her outer lips, into her wet body without a fraction of opposition. And though she felt herself being stretched, slowly and gently, the resulting experience of that was not pain.

It was something...magical. He fitted himself into her all the way to the hilt and then rested there, unmoving as she grew accustomed to his invasion. She flexed around him gently and he made a pained little sound in his throat.

"You do know how to test a man's control," he whispered before he leaned in to kiss her. She relaxed beneath him a fraction more, losing herself in that gentle kiss. And it was only then that he moved.

One long thrust, almost all the way out of her clinging body, then back in until she took him completely. She gripped his arms as he did so because the sensation was electric and alive and oh, so very good. She realized in this moment that *this* was what she hadn't

JESS MICHAELS

understood about all those happy marriages that surrounded her. This was what this act was all about.

Because it felt intimate and warm. Connected and powerful. It didn't change her love for this man, but it did magnify it, place it in purely physical terms that meant so much. This was...everything. And as he thrust again, she lifted to meet him and accept the beautiful gift he offered. The beautiful one she could give in return.

He took and took, gently and slowly, grinding his hips against hers with every thrust and stimulating the same tingling clitoris he had been licking a few moments before. She rose to meet him, seeking the pleasure, finding it over and over again. It increased in volume and intensity as he increased his own speed. She gasped out against it, trying to find breath and purchase, losing control as she watched the same thing happen to him.

And then it was there. The soaring sensation that hit her in intense, powerful waves. She jolted against him and he caught her keening cries with his mouth so no one would hear them and interrupt this beautiful moment.

Only when she collapsed in exhausted satisfaction beneath him did he grip her hips, pulling her tight as he increased his pace even further. His neck strained, his face turned red, and then he grunted out her name and pulled away from her. She watched, fascinated, as ropes of release spurted from his cock while he stroked himself to completion.

He collapsed over her then, kissing her damp neck and her mouth, whispering incoherent sounds of pleasure. She folded her arms around him, tracing little patterns on his back. And all of them were *I love you*, written over and over again on his skin until she slipped into sleep in his arms.

∽

It had been almost an hour since Elizabeth slipped into his chamber, into his arms, into his bed. Since she'd given herself to him with sweet abandon. And Morgan held her, balancing them both precariously on the narrow bed as she dozed.

He had seen something in her eyes as he made love to her. He'd seen something he welcomed and feared all at once. It was that connection he knew was there, but had tried to ignore since his arrival here in Brighthollow. It was...well, perhaps some people called it love.

He'd seen it there, and he'd known he shouldn't do what he did next. Which was take her. Take that connection. But how could he resist? How could he when she was tempting and overwhelming and...everything. Elizabeth was everything.

He wanted to give her a garden and make her smile. He wanted to make her come until her body quaked and she begged for more and less all at once. He wanted to catch those moments when her strength was on the surface and she was braver than she believed herself to be. He wanted to hold her and have it be for more than just one night.

He wanted to...

No, he had to stop these thoughts. This was foolishness brought on by powerful pleasure. That had to be all it was. Anything more was folly.

In that moment, she rolled over into him, onto his chest. Their legs tangled as she placed her folded hands onto his sternum and then rested her chin on them. She looked up at him with a sleepy, satisfied gaze.

"*You* are punishing yourself," she said softly. A statement, not a question. Because she could see through him.

He considered denying the truth. Trying to put a wall up. But he didn't want a wall. "How could I not?" he asked as he pushed a tangled lock of hair from her forehead.

She smiled softly and leaned up to kiss him. Just a soft brush of her lips on his that soothed every hurt he'd ever felt for a flash of a moment.

"Because," she said as she drew back, "I'm not sorry, Morgan. But I do think I should go."

She pushed from the bed, dropping the sheets as she did so. His body did a little pulse of longing as he watched her pick up her nightrail and tug it over her glorious body. She looked around for her dressing gown and smiled as she found it bunched in a pile halfway under his bed.

She didn't speak as she swirled it over her shoulders and tied the knot back in place. She padded to the door, and there she turned and blew him a kiss.

"Thank you," she whispered.

And then she was gone, without further comment or question or demand. He tugged the covers up over his head with a curse.

Tonight had proven to him many things. That he could be dangerous. That he didn't belong here. That he shouldn't do the very thing he had just done. It was a tangled mess. And he feared it was going to get a great deal worse before it got better.

Worse, he feared that once he was forced to walk away from her, it would never be better again.

CHAPTER 17

L izzie sat at the pianoforte, letting her fingers dance over the keys. Haydn's *Sonata in C minor* filled the room around her, and she shut her eyes as she let her hands guide her. Her mind was so distracted, but she poured her passion into the music and allowed herself to think of Morgan.

Their night together had been magical. She had lain in her bed afterward, reliving the pleasure, yes. But also recounting the deep connection that pleasure had created. Deeper than ever before. She had no idea how he felt, but in some ways it didn't matter. She knew her own heart. She refused to regret how she had allowed it to beat. She had punished herself for that very thing for too long.

And Morgan had reminded her that loving was worth the risk.

It *was* a risk, of course. All of it was a risk. She had no idea what would happen next. At breakfast, Hugh had declared he would speak to Morgan later about the events of the ball the previous night. Once he did...

Well, Morgan might be torn from her.

Even if he wasn't, Morgan had made no promises to her. She had told him she demanded none. It was very possible he would be alarmed by the connection they shared. That he would push her away because he didn't want to risk more. Or didn't feel more at all.

She opened her eyes and looked toward the door. She was surprised to find the Duke of Roseford standing there, watching her. Her fingers fell away from the keys and she pushed to her feet. "Roseford, I did not see you there."

He inclined his head. "Forgive me, Lizzie, I heard you playing from down the hall and had to come and listen. That particular sonata was one of my late mother's favorites. You play it beautifully."

She wrinkled her brow. She had known Robert for so long, though she'd never been as close to him as some of Hugh's friends. Robert had seemed too big and too bold and too...well, too much. She had feared him because of his reputation, especially after her experience with Aaron. She'd seen him as a libertine, though he'd never been anything but kind to her.

In this moment, she saw pain on his face. Loss. And he reminded her of Morgan when he was at his most vulnerable. How could she not like him then? How could she not offer the little bit of comfort he seemed to require?

She retook her seat and smiled at him. "If that is true, then I shall begin again and play it for you in full."

"Thank you," he said, and entered the room. He settled into a seat and she began to play again from the beginning.

It was a long piece. As the music filled the room again, Robert shut his eyes and leaned back, seeming to soak in every note. And again, she saw the hints of how he and his brother were similar. She knew their relationship was strained and yet they were both trying.

So she poured all her hopes for their relationship into every note, as if she could will their friendship, their bond into deeper existence. They both needed it. And she wanted Morgan to have everything he needed in this world and more.

When she finished at last, Roseford opened his eyes and smiled at her. "Thank you, Lizzie. That was wonderful."

She nodded and then shifted on the bench to more fully face her companion. "Have you seen Morgan..." She caught herself and shook her head. "...Mr. Banfield this morning?"

Robert arched a brow at the slip in propriety, but then he smiled. Something knowing. "Morgan. Should we talk about *Morgan*?"

She sucked in a breath. She had entered dangerous waters without truly meaning to do so. And yet here she was. "Why would I not wish to speak about him?"

"Do I need to answer that? Are we playing that game with each other? After all these years of acquaintance?"

She pursed her lips. He would push her, it seemed. "He—he works for my brother," she said, and could hear how false that dismissal was. "We've become...*friends* since we started working together on the garden."

"Well, that is true if nothing else," Robert muttered beneath his breath.

She ignored the gentle jab. "I'm interested in his well-being."

Robert was quiet a moment. Then he got up and walked to the fireplace, where he watched the flames. "You know our father kept us apart. Some would say that made sense. That his bastard children were only half-blood and didn't...deserve more."

She arched a brow at the disgust that hung heavy in his tone. "What did you believe?" she asked.

He was quiet for what felt like forever, but his voice broke when he said, "Whatever he told me to believe for a very long time. My failing, no one else's. Once I took over the estate, I never handled much but approving the payments to my half-siblings until recently."

"Why did you come to know him only recently?" She thought of Morgan's confession earlier in the night. That Robert had thwarted the duel with Gareth Covington. But Roseford revealed nothing of that as he turned to face her.

"Katherine made me understand the value in connection. And

she was right. Morgan is...challenging." Roseford's smile was soft. "But he's...*good.*"

Lizzie bent her head and relived in a flash every moment she had spent with the topic of their discourse. Including last night. "Yes," she said. "I see that in him. Daily."

Robert stepped toward her. "Lizzie—"

She pivoted away, for she could see he wanted to push her on this topic. That her heart was too revealed. She had to remedy that immediately, else she make things worse for Morgan. "Have you seen him this morning?" she asked. "Is he well after last night's attack?"

There was a long pause, but then Robert said, "Yes. He will be fine, thank God."

"Good," she said, and smoothed her skirts with both hands. "Well, I should probably go. I'm to join Amelia, Katherine and Charlotte for a round of cards before tea."

She edged toward the door, but as she reached it, Robert's voice stopped her. "Lizzie."

She froze. Damn, she had thought to get away. "Yes?" She turned and met his eyes. So similar to Morgan's eyes.

"You deserve to be happy," Robert said softly.

Tears pricked at her unexpectedly and she blinked them away. "Thank you, Your Grace."

"Don't allow the past to destroy you," he continued. "I almost did that myself."

Her hands shook and she clenched them before her. "What about him? Morgan. Do you think...do you think *he* will destroy himself?"

His lips parted and understanding crossed his face. "I—don't know," he said, his voice halting and his concern clear. "I hope not. I hope nothing he did in the past, nothing he will do in the future, will destroy him."

She moved toward him a step. "You love him."

"Yes," Robert replied, this time with none of the hesitation that had been present throughout this awkward conversation. "He might not believe that, but I do."

"Then he's lucky," Lizzie said. "I know the power of the love of an older brother."

His smile widened. "Good day, Lizzie."

"Good day," she repeated, and slipped from the room. When she did, she let out the breath she hadn't realized she'd been holding in a long sigh. She knew Morgan was about to face all the things he'd done, everything he'd admitted to her the night before.

She could only hope he wouldn't lose everything when he did. That she wouldn't either.

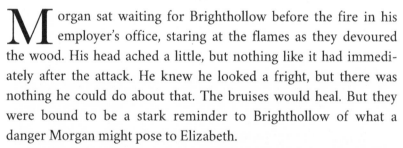

M organ sat waiting for Brighthollow before the fire in his employer's office, staring at the flames as they devoured the wood. His head ached a little, but nothing like it had immediately after the attack. He knew he looked a fright, but there was nothing he could do about that. The bruises would heal. But they were bound to be a stark reminder to Brighthollow of what a danger Morgan might pose to Elizabeth.

Elizabeth. His mind wandered as he waited, but not to the places it should have. He should have been preparing what to say, thinking through his strategy no matter how Brighthollow responded.

Instead, he thought of how lovely Elizabeth was clothed only in firelight. How much warmer and brighter she was than either sun or moon. And how desperately he wanted to repeat what he knew was a one-time gift. He wanted to hold her against him for hours, days, weeks. For as long as it took to make himself forget that he didn't deserve her.

The door across the room opened, and he jolted from those thoughts and rose to his feet as Brighthollow entered. The duke looked stern as his gaze flitted over Morgan. He shut the door and motioned Morgan back to his seat.

"How is your head?" he asked, and crossed to the sideboard where he picked up a sherry bottle and waved it toward Morgan.

Morgan nodded and watched his employer pour two glasses. "Better," he said. "I'm only made slightly more hideous by the experience."

"Lucky for that. Being knocked unconscious is nothing to play about with." Brighthollow handed over Morgan's glass and sat in the chair across from him. He took a sip of his own drink as he took Morgan in more closely. Too closely.

"Thank you for your concern, Your Grace," Morgan said. "But I think you didn't call me here to speak to me about my condition. I know you have questions about the attack."

Brighthollow inclined his head. "I do. My key concern is if my family is in danger. Because it's…changing."

There was something about the way Brighthollow said it that made Morgan sit up a bit straighter. "You are…"

"The duchess is expecting," Hugh said, and there was no denying the joy to his expression. "No one knows, not even Lizzie. We planned to announce to her and all our friends before we return to London."

"Congratulations," Morgan said softly, though his mind went to Elizabeth. She would be happy for her brother, he knew. She was incapable of anything but joy for him. But he also worried about her. She put so much blame on herself for the past. Would she feel she could be part of her family's new future?

"Thank you. But you can see why my worry is increased."

"Yes, Your Grace." Morgan sighed. "I'd like to explain."

He did so, telling Hugh the same sordid story about Gareth Covington as he had done with Elizabeth. About Robert's intervention on his behalf in the thwarted duel. Brighthollow's expression remained impassive through it all. Unreadable. The man seemed an expert at that.

Morgan sighed when he'd told it all. "I'm not proud of what I did. Or how it was handled afterward. It was evident in my recent interaction with Gareth that he didn't feel appeased by a payout. He wanted personal vengeance. And I can hardly blame him."

Brighthollow got up. "You didn't know the woman was his lover, so you do not own all the blame." He ran a hand through his hair. "How can he be dealt with?"

Morgan stood up, as well. "I've thought about that. I know this man. He was once my friend. I owe him what he was denied by my well-meaning brother."

Brighthollow's eyes widened. "A duel? You want to let the man *kill* you?"

Morgan gripped the back of the chair he'd just abandoned. Once he'd not thought much of death. Men died young all the time. But now...now he felt like he had something to lose. Something of great worth.

Even though she wasn't really his.

"I-I don't think Gareth would actually kill me," he choked. "His honor was damaged. If we met on the field and I owned my part, I think he wouldn't shoot. And that would end it."

Brighthollow ran a hand through his hair. "Your brother will be livid at this option."

"And it is not his decision. I never should have allowed him to intervene in the first place." Morgan shook his head. "I'm a man. It was my situation to create and mine to solve."

"Fuck." Brighthollow muttered beneath his breath. "But I know a bit about well-meaning brothers. Could you find this Covington if you tried?"

"I think so," Morgan said slowly. "He came all the way to Brighthollow to manage this. He must be staying close by. A few feelers in the village and I'm certain he could be reached and offered the option to finish what he started."

There was a long silence, and he could see Brighthollow was considering this.

"If Robert will not be your second, I will," the duke said at last.

Morgan stared at him, wide eyed with surprise at the offer. "You do not owe me that," he said. "I wouldn't be offended if you sacked me."

Brighthollow shrugged. "I did consider it. I hired you because of Robert, after all."

"I'm sure my brother would understand your position," Morgan said, straightening and preparing himself for the worst.

"Only the longer you've been here, the more you've proven yourself to be bright and capable. You are a good addition to my household. And one I do not regret making...on the whole."

Morgan swallowed hard. "On the whole?"

"Yes." Brighthollow arched a brow, and discomfort entered his expression. "Lizzie is my only remaining hesitation. I've seen you two interact. More to the point, I've seen how you look at her."

Morgan set his jaw. Every baser instinct inside of him told him to turn to flippancy and distraction to address this issue. Only he wasn't the same man anymore. It was shocking to realize that fact in this uncomfortable moment looking into the face of his lover's brother. He didn't want to dismiss or play or dance around this subject.

"I understand your hesitance. Even if I were to harbor some... attraction toward your sister, I assure you I *know* it would have no good end." He bent his head. "For either of us. I am not good enough for Lady Elizabeth, for a great many reasons."

If he had expected Brighthollow to heartily agree with that sentiment, he was surprised that instead the other man looked troubled. "Well," he said. "I'm glad we're...apparently of a mind."

"Yes," Morgan said as he got up. Brighthollow extended a hand and they shook. "I'll reach out and let you know when I've heard from Covington. In the meantime, may I hire a few men to watch the house? I will pay for it from my own pocket since this is my doing."

"Do hire them," Brighthollow said. "But I'll pay."

The two men held stares for a moment, then Morgan inclined his head. "Thank you."

THE LOVE OF A LIBERTINE

"Good day, Morgan," Brighthollow said softly.

"Good day." He stepped into the hallway and drew in a sharp breath. He knew what he planned to do was right. And he hoped he was also right about his former friend's intention if they faced each other honorably.

But if he was wrong, he would die. An outcome he was not ready for.

CHAPTER 18

I t had been two days since Lizzie had made love to Morgan. Two long days where he seemed to be…avoiding her. She tried to tell herself it was because he was resting. That was true. Hugh had certainly given him time to recover from the attack and didn't seem to be preparing to sack Morgan. So that was at least something.

But she couldn't dismiss all his avoidance as due to his injuries, because she knew he was working. She saw him, certainly, in the halls where he simply nodded in acknowledgment as he went back and forth to her brother's study, papers in hand. And when he joined the party for supper, he sat on the far end of the table and only spoke to her when propriety dictated it.

Because of all that, she had not dared to go to his room again. Not when he seemed to be so willing to end their affiliation. It had been a one-night experience, it seemed. And she was trying to accept that, even though she wanted so much to slip into his bed and experience that wonderful pleasure all over again. She dreamed of it, waking to find her hands clenched between her legs, rocking against her fingers to find some shadow version of the pleasure he always gave.

She often found it, but it wasn't enough.

She frowned, pushing away those thoughts as she entered the breakfast room. The rest of the party was already there, talking and laughing as they broke bread. Among them was Morgan.

Heat filled her cheeks as she slipped in and took a place at the table. She managed to say good morning to all those around her, but her gaze kept flitting to him. He was watching her too, over the rim of his coffee cup. She smiled, a wavering expression, she knew. And he hesitated a moment before he returned the smile and gave her just the tiniest peace by doing so.

The talk of the group continued, though Lizzie focused mostly on her food. And eventually, as they all finished their breakfasts, Katherine leaned away from the table and slid her hand into Robert's. "I cannot believe we will all return to London in just a few days," she said. "The time here has flown by."

Ewan signed and Charlotte translated, "It has, as time amongst friends always seems to do. This has been an especially lively little gathering."

The table laughed in unison. Even Lizzie managed a smile at the quip.

"It has been that," Hugh said, and then cast a glance at Amelia. "Perhaps the time has come to tell them."

Amelia blushed and nodded, her smile shy as she edged a little closer to Hugh. Lizzie sat up a bit straighter. "Tell us what?" she asked.

Hugh beamed as he said, "We've been trying to find the right time and place to say this for days. Amelia is expecting."

Lizzie's mouth fell open as she stared at her brother and sister-in-law. They were both smiling as the rest of the table burst into joyful congratulations. Everyone rose to hug the happy couple, and Lizzie managed to get to her feet, as well, though her legs were shaking.

She glanced down the table and found Morgan watching not the others, but her. And he didn't look surprised by this news. Her ears were ringing as she looked again at Hugh and Amelia.

There were so many emotions hitting her, she could scarcely parse them out. She was happy for them, of course she was. They had been married for three years and she knew they'd wanted a family for a long time. She was pleased and excited to welcome a new baby into their family.

But there were other feelings too. Ones that hit her with so much force they nearly knocked her backward. There was fear. Fear for her own future. Fear because the circle would become Hugh and Amelia and their baby and their future babies. Lizzie would have to start to edge outside of the embrace of their family. It was simply mathematics.

And there was something else too. Something she hated herself for. Jealousy. She stared at her brother, who had raised her and taken care of her and been nothing but kind to her...and she was jealous. Jealous of the life he'd claimed for himself out of suffering. Jealous of the future that glowed out before him while hers felt so...dark.

"Lizzie?" Amelia said. "You are staring at us like you've seen a ghost. Have we shocked you?"

Lizzie could hear the nervousness in Amelia's tone and she pushed aside all her tangled thoughts and forced a smile to her face. "I am surprised, but delighted," she said as she stepped around the table and hugged Amelia and then Hugh. "When will the baby come?"

"A little while longer," Amelia said. "In December. There will be no hiding that I am increasing soon enough. But there will be plenty of time to plan. I hope you'll help me with the nursery, here and in London."

"Of course," Lizzie said, but her own voice felt far away. So far away, and like she was underwater.

Luckily Katherine and Charlotte rushed forward, and Amelia and Hugh were distracted by cooing duchesses and suggestions for names, as well as potential future matches amongst the children of their friends. Lizzie was able to step back, toward the chamber door. Away from her family.

She found herself continuing to edge away. Farther and farther. Because she needed a moment. She needed an escape from the powerful feelings she didn't want to feel. She certainly didn't want to show them like a spoiled ninny.

So she turned and slipped from the room as the rest were distracted, racing through the hallway to find a parlor where she could just...breathe. She was three steps away when she heard the footfalls behind her. She knew who it was without looking.

"Please, just let me be," she said softly as she stepped into the parlor.

"Elizabeth," Morgan's voice came, gentle but insistent. She moved to shut the door on him, but he caught it.

She pivoted away. "Please!" she repeated. "Just let me have a moment."

She was going to walk to the fire, but he caught her upper arm gently and tugged her back. Toward his warmth. Toward his gentle support. Toward everything she wanted and was trying to remind herself she couldn't have. And it made all her dark feelings worse, not better.

She stared up into his face and saw the future she wouldn't be allowed. It all hurt more. She almost hated him for it.

"Elizabeth," he whispered, and then he bent his head and his lips brushed hers.

Dark thoughts filtered away, dissipating in the air as she leaned into the thing she wanted and couldn't have. Leaned into his embrace and let herself have his comfort, if only for a moment. And it was only a moment, because he parted from her and moved away a long step.

"Morgan," she whispered. "This is not your burden. Just go back to the celebration and let me have a moment."

"It may not be my burden, but I see it," he said. "I see what you feel, Elizabeth. As plain as if your heart were mine."

She flinched at his choice of words. As if his heart were hers? He wouldn't let it be. "You don't know," she snapped, a little harsher than she had intended as she walked away from him.

He sighed. "Your closest friend and companion has been your brother for as long as you can recall," he said softly. His words were gentle but still pointed blades against her heart. "When he married Amelia, you thought things might change. They did, but you adore her like a sister and you settled into your new life. But now...a baby is coming. Their family will change. There won't be as much space in it, you know that. Where will your place be?"

She was taken off guard by how succinctly he had laid out her feelings. Hearing them out loud made them feel even worse. "I know how much they want this. I've wanted it for them. I'm horrible to feel even an inkling of something that isn't joy."

His brow wrinkled. "You aren't. You're just...changing. You want to find a place in this world and this makes you realize that it isn't in these walls, not forever. How could you not feel conflicted about that?"

She stared at him, loving him and wanting him to love her back. "If my place isn't here, then where is it, Morgan?"

"Elizabeth." His expression shifted, turned pained as he glanced away from her. And her heart broke.

"Not with you," she whispered. "You are too cowardly to say it. You hide from me so you won't have to say it, but you want me to understand that my future could never be with you."

His lips parted. "You already know it can't. I don't have to tell you, do I?"

She folded her arms, trying to raise a shield even though he'd already vaulted over her walls and pillaged everything of value inside of her. "How long have you known about Amelia?"

His jaw set and he shrugged one shoulder. "Since Brighthollow took me aside the afternoon after the attack. A couple of days."

She shook her head. "You didn't even think to tell me. To warn me so I wouldn't be surprised."

"It…it wasn't my place," he insisted. "We aren't—"

"We aren't what?" she interrupted, moving toward him, her chin lifted in defiance she wished she felt in her heart. "Say to me what we aren't."

He shook his head slowly. "I'm—I'm going to fight a duel, Elizabeth."

She caught her breath and staggered backward, her hand coming up to cover her mouth as his words sank in. "What are you saying? What do you mean?"

"I know I did the wrong thing when it came to Gareth," he said softly. "He wanted to settle it in one way a year ago, but he was denied that. It's made him dangerous. So, I've reached out to him and he has agreed to meet me on the field…tomorrow at dawn."

Lizzie blinked up at him, willing this to be a dream. A nightmare. A fuzzy, nasty hallucination brought on by something she ate. But it wasn't. Morgan was standing in front of her. And he was saying he would die for honor, that he refused to live for himself. For her.

She wanted to find the words to stop this. To fight him. But before she could put them together, Robert's voice came from the doorway behind them.

"What the hell are you saying, Morgan? What the hell do you mean that you will meet someone on the field at dawn?"

~

Morgan turned away from Lizzie's pale and horrified face and found himself staring at Robert's equally sick expression. His brother was red as a tomato, his hands shaking at his sides as he plowed into the room.

"Explain yourself!" Robert shouted as he caught Morgan's arm and shook it.

Morgan yanked it away as he glared at him. "Why are you here?"

Robert's eyes went wide. "Because I watched you sneak out of the room, following Lizzie, and I'm trying to keep you out of trouble. It seems like a foolish occupation, though, considering that you keep finding it over and over again. You keep digging yourself into holes like you enjoy being buried. Well, I *don't* enjoy finding a way to get you out of them, Morgan!"

"I'm not asking you to!" Morgan snapped. He shook his head because now the door was crowded with faces. The others in their party had come to the shouting, it seemed. Because all of this had to be played out for all to see.

It was inevitable, in a way.

"I'm not asking you to save me," he said, this time more gently. He glanced at Brighthollow, who looked sick at the exchange. At Donburrow, who looked confused as he clearly tried to discern what was happening.

Katherine stepped up, setting her hand on Robert's chest, gently backing him away. "Morgan, what is going on? Why are you shouting? What is Robert saving you from?"

He shook his head. "I did something, I wronged someone last year. That's why I was attacked a few days ago." He sighed. "Robert meant well—I know you mean well. I know you...I know you care for me. I know you want to make up for...for our father. For the years all of us bastard siblings were left to fend for ourselves."

Robert turned his face, but the truth of what Morgan said was plain across his features. "Yes," he said softly.

"You intervened when Covington wanted a duel the first time," Morgan said. "You stepped in to save me. But paying him off didn't end this. It never could because it offers no satisfaction to the injured party, and the injured party isn't me. Not this time. So yes, I intend to meet Gareth at dawn tomorrow."

The ladies in the room gasped, all but Elizabeth. She just stood there, her eyes filled with tears, her cheeks pale. She never looked away from him, and her eyes were filled with pain and accusation and fear all stirred into one beautiful, stormy blue sea. He hated himself for causing her this agony, even though he'd always known that was what he would do. He would hurt her. And he had tried not to do so. He'd failed.

"You would die for a mistake?" Robert whispered, and his voice cracked.

Morgan moved toward him and Katherine stepped away, allowing the two brothers the moment Morgan needed. He squeezed Robert's shoulder. "You don't trust me. I know you don't." Robert opened his mouth, but Morgan shook his head. "Don't lie to me. You don't. I haven't earned it, perhaps. I want to do so someday. But I need you to hear me. I know my friend. I know he won't shoot."

Robert rolled his eyes. "He asked for a duel, you have to assume he will fire upon you."

"He won't," Morgan said softly. "I believe that."

"And if he does?" Amelia interjected.

Morgan cleared his throat and his gaze again shifted to Elizabeth. "Then I'll take the punishment I deserve."

She gasped out a sob at that and then rushed from the room. Amelia glanced at Hugh and whispered, "I'll go after her."

Katherine and the Duchess of Donburrow followed, too, after sending their own husbands silent looks. And so Morgan was left with the men. All three of the dukes watched him, with equal looks of concern on their faces.

"I've never been honorable in my life," Morgan whispered, and couldn't help but think of that beautiful night with Elizabeth. He was happier than ever that he had taken it. Earned or not, it was worth it. "Please let me be honorable in this."

Robert bent his head and acceptance flowed over his face. "Who would you like as your second?" he asked.

Brighthollow stepped forward, his expression serious. "I already offered to do so, but if you would prefer to take that role, I will relinquish it."

Robert jerked his head up. "You knew?"

Morgan could see the two men, the two friends...the two

brothers could easily come to blows in this taut and emotional environment, so he stepped between them. "He knew I was reaching out to Gareth, but we didn't know if he would accept my offer to fulfill the duel you interrupted last year."

"I would have told you once I knew," Brighthollow said softly.

"I wasn't going to keep you in the dark either." Morgan met his gaze and held it there. "And if you would stand at my side as my second, brother, then I would be happy to have you there."

Donburrow stepped forward and pulled out his notebook to write. He scribbled for a moment and then handed the note to Robert.

"He says that both he and Hugh will come as witnesses," Robert said. "And friends to us both."

"We will," Hugh said softly.

Robert turned away from all three men and paced to the window. He stood there for a long time, staring out at the garden. Finally, he turned. "I've only just found you," he said with a shake of his head. "I hope you're right that I won't lose you."

Morgan stepped to him, his heart swelling for this man he had once resented, then tolerated and now...loved. As a true brother and a friend.

"You won't," he promised.

Robert embraced him, and Morgan sagged a little with relief. At least he would have friends with him tomorrow morning. But he couldn't help but think of Lizzie. Her face when she left the room had been...harrowing. And he hated himself for hurting her more than he hated himself for any selfish act he'd ever committed, including the one that would take him to the dueling field at dawn.

CHAPTER 19

L izzie sat on the cushioned window seat in her bedroom, staring out at the moonlit garden below. Once upon a time the garden comforted her. But now it only reminded her of what she might lose. Morgan would go to the dueling field tomorrow.

And every time she thought of it, she collapsed in on herself again. She rested her head on her knees and let the tears fall for what felt like the hundredth time that horrible day.

There was a light knock at her door, and she shook her head against her legs before she called out, "Yes?"

The door opened and Amelia stepped inside. Her sister-in-law's face was lined with concern as she moved toward Lizzie. "I know you told us earlier that you didn't wish to discuss what happened today, but Lizzie, I cannot leave it be any longer. We must talk."

Lizzie had known Amelia would come. And perhaps it was best to have it over now. "I suppose you want to speak to me about my running out of the room when you and Hugh told everyone about the baby."

Amelia wrinkled her brow as she sank onto the window seat beside Lizzie. "Yes, I assume we'll do that at some point. I know you're happy for us. But it is also a trying subject. There will be mixed emotions for you. I never expected otherwise."

Lizzie leaned back in surprise. "You didn't?"

"Gracious, you are not emotionless, I know that." Amelia caught her hand and squeezed gently. "You don't owe me perfect, absolute joy, my dearest sister. Never, ever. But *that* isn't why I want to talk to you."

Lizzie sighed. "No?"

"Are you in love with Morgan Banfield?" Amelia whispered.

Lizzie jolted at the pointed question. She'd expected a great many things, but not that. And perhaps it was because she was taken so off guard that she found herself nodding.

"I am," she said. "I'm in love with him."

She tensed as she waited for Amelia to scold her or tell her what a terrible idea it all was or to argue with her. But she didn't. She just reached out and caught Lizzie's hand, drawing it into her lap as she patted the top gently. "I always hoped you would let yourself love again," she whispered. "After what you went through with Aaron—"

"What we both went through," Lizzie corrected softly.

"Yes," Amelia said. "Both of us. But I found my happy ending. The happiest. And you deserve the same. You deserve to love someone…and to have them love you in return."

"Well," Lizzie said, and withdrew her hand slowly. "That may not be possible, I fear."

"You don't think he loves you?" Amelia asked, and seemed genuinely surprised. "I admit I've watched you two together since his arrival. He isn't immune to you, that much is very clear. He cares for you, I believe that with all my heart."

"And yet seems determined that there can be nothing between us," Lizzie said as she got to her feet. "And so I'm left with…this. This limbo. And he's going to duel tomorrow. He might die, regardless of his perhaps foolhardy belief that this former friend of his won't fire a gun on him."

Amelia worried her lip. "I'm sorry."

"I am too." She glanced at Amelia from the corner of her eye. "I am going to the duel."

"What?" Amelia drew back. "Lizzie—"

"I adore you," Lizzie whispered. "But it's not a question."

Amelia was silent for a moment, but then she smiled softly. "Katherine wants to go too. She's worried sick about Robert and what this will mean for him. That settles it, I suppose. We'll all go. There's a hill above the agreed upon dueling ground. The men don't need to know our plans. We'll ride there after they leave. At least then we'll know what has happened. We won't have to sit and wait for the news."

"Yes." A shudder wracked Lizzie from head to toe. "At least we'll know."

Amelia got up and crossed to Lizzie. She hugged her gently, and before she pulled away, she whispered, "Don't leave something unsaid, my dear. You'll regret it." She drew back and squeezed her hand. "I'll see you at dawn."

"Dawn," Lizzie agreed, and waved as her sister-in-law left her chamber.

Amelia's parting advice rang in the room around her. There were so few times in life that one knew the next time one saw the person they loved that it could truly be the last. And yet it was always true. Tomorrow Morgan could be wrong—he could be shot and that would be the end. What she felt would always hang in the air around her.

She couldn't let it. She hurried to the door to her chamber and was about to rush into the hall, when there was a second knock. She tensed as she flung it open, ready to find Amelia returned to offer more advice, but to her shock it was Morgan standing there, staring at her.

"Morgan," she breathed, and sucked in a great gulp of air to say the rest, all of it, but he didn't let her.

He caught her cheeks in his hands, crushing his mouth down on hers. "Don't say anything," he murmured as he kicked her door shut, reached behind himself to lock it. "Please don't say it. Just...let me. Let me."

She nodded against his seeking mouth, and desperation took over. She clawed at his jacket, he pulled at the buttons along the back of her gown. They stripped each other down in a few moments, their mouths never parting. He pushed her toward the bed, lifting her on the edge. She wrapped her legs around his waist, driving her tongue into his mouth as he lifted his cock into her waiting sex.

They both shuddered, and at last their mouths parted. His face was just millimeters from hers and she stared into his dark eyes as he thrust a second time. Over and over, their gazes locked, he took and took, she gave and gave. He didn't want to hear the words she had to say and so she told him how much she loved him with her body. That same body sang with sensation as a result.

But after immeasurable time had gone by, he pulled away from her, leaving her empty and bereft. But it wasn't for long. He urged her back on the bed and joined her there. She expected him to settle between her legs, but instead he propped her pillows up against the carved headboard and sat there. He motioned to her.

She stared because she realized what he wanted. Her astride him. She hadn't thought there were more...ways to do this than the way they'd first done it. But the idea of riding him, well, that was certainly titillating.

She crawled up his body. He caught her hips. Wordlessly he positioned her above him, then reached between them. His fingers swept across her entrance, teasing her clitoris, and she shivered with powerful pleasure. He rubbed the head of his cock back and forth against her, stimulating her, until she whispered his name and ground down.

He slipped inside of her with no resistance, and she gripped her thighs against his as she rose up and crashed back down. Waves of the ocean over him, reaching and reaching. He cupped the back of her neck and their mouths tangled again. His kiss was gentler now and she ground a bit softer in response, drawing out the need, the desire, the sensation, for as long as she could.

But soon it wasn't enough. Her body refused to go slow, she ground harder and faster, feeling the sharp edge of ultimate pleasure build on the horizon. She had to catch it. He gripped her hips, his neck straining as she fought for what she wanted, dragging him toward it.

When she caught it, it was more powerful than anything she'd ever felt before. She dipped her head back, jolting over him as she opened her mouth for a silent scream.

He lifted into her, his mouth finding her throat, his hands cupping her backside and continuing to grind her over him as he extended her pleasure for moments, hours, days, years. None of it mattered anymore. All there was was the man beneath her and their hearts and bodies tangled.

She felt him edging toward his own release. His thrusts grew harder and faster, his fingers dug deeper into her flesh. At last he rolled her onto her back, pounded a few times and pulled out, moaning her name into her neck as he came between them and then gathered her closer, kissing her with the same desperation they'd started with.

And how could he not? After all, he might have made love to her again. He might have poured some piece of himself into her and she back into him. But dawn would still come.

And the future was still a desperate, dark, painful question.

❧

Elizabeth was sleeping. Curled partly into his body, her hand gripped into a loose fist against his chest, her body only half-covered by the sheets, she slept. She'd earned the sleep, after all, after the night they'd shared.

It was wrong of him to take it. In a few hours, he might be dead. And that was why he'd done it. To burn this one good thing into his mind and heart and soul, even if he didn't deserve it. So that he could hold it as the last thing just in case he'd vastly misread the situation he'd find with Gareth.

He traced the lines of her shoulder with his fingertips, the curve of her breast, the smooth skin of her sides. She smiled in her sleep and cuddled a little closer.

She'd wanted to talk to him about the duel. About...about her heart, he thought. He'd seen that in her eyes. But he'd distracted her, making love to her over and over and over again until she collapsed, weak against him, and slept.

Was that a cruel trick or a kind one? Perhaps both. He'd thwarted one need but fulfilled another. Now it was almost dawn and he had to leave her. Perhaps for a few hours. Perhaps forever. And he didn't want to.

He loved her. He knew it even if he'd been too afraid to name it until now. Too afraid to claim it. But he could no longer argue against it, so it sat there, an undeniable truth rather than a question. He loved this woman, and the very idea that he might never see her beautiful face again was painful beyond measure.

He leaned down and kissed her. She lifted into him, whispering, "Morgan."

"Shhh," he soothed as he moved her arm from his body, tucked the covers around her and left her bed. "Sleep now."

Her smile faded and her expression grew troubled, even in slumber, but she didn't fully wake. Good. Because if she did, if she pressed and questioned and confessed—and he feared she might— walking away might be impossible. And it was the only way now. The only right thing to do after a lifetime of doing the wrong thing.

Like taking her.

But no, he wouldn't consider that wrong. It *wasn't* wrong. He wouldn't sully it by telling himself it was. She needed what he'd given. He'd never taken more than she had to give in return.

He dressed swiftly and then crept to her door. He had an hour at most before he had to be ready to face Gareth Covington. He needed to change and filter away the many fears and regrets that clouded his mind.

He needed to ready himself. And so he turned at her door and gave Elizabeth a long look. And knew it might be the last one. So he held that image close as he returned to his own chamber and the preparations he had to make within.

CHAPTER 20

Light filtered from the east as Morgan finished preparing his horse. Dawn would fully break in a quarter of an hour, perhaps less, and they needed to get on the road to meet with Gareth at the arranged spot on Brighthollow's property.

He turned to urge his brother, Brighthollow and Donburrow to get on their mounts—and froze. The duchesses were standing on the step, saying their goodbyes to their husbands.

And Elizabeth. She had her hands clasped before her, her shoulders back and one would have never known that she'd had no sleep the night before. She was so utterly, perfectly beautiful.

He wished she hadn't come down. He bent his head and murmured, "Thank you all. I hope I'll see you shortly."

"Good luck," Katherine whispered, and came down to squeeze his hand. "And know how much you are loved."

He blinked at the stinging in his eyes as he lifted his sister-in-law's hand to his lips and kissed her knuckles. "Thank you, Katherine."

She stepped away, eyes glittering with the same tears as were in the eyes of the other ladies. Morgan could bear the looks no longer and swung up on his horse. "Let's go," he grumbled, his voice rough.

He rode away, desperate not to look back. Within seconds, he was flanked by Brighthollow on one side, Robert on the other, and Donburrow was behind him. He waited for them to speak, to lighten the mood, but no one said a word and the silence was gentle and supportive as they rode the short way through Brighthollow's estate.

It was a beautiful place, one he had come to know and love in the time he'd been here. Morgan tried to take it all in as he rode. Their path at present went through a leafy, forested patch that meandered toward a hill in the distance. They crested it and down in the valley below, Morgan saw three riders waiting for them beneath a lone tree and a stream.

"Gareth and his second, along with the doctor, I suppose," he murmured.

Robert pulled up beside him, his mouth a grim line as he stared down. "Shall we review the plan?"

"You'll ride out to meet his second and tell him I would like to offer my apology. Just as I suggested in my letter." Morgan shook his head. "I hope he'll hear me out and that will put an end to it."

"If he doesn't?" Brighthollow asked.

Morgan swallowed hard past the sudden lump in his throat. "Then I suppose I owe him his satisfaction."

Robert pivoted. "His lover betrayed him, but you didn't know who she was. You didn't wrong him on purpose. It was never your intent."

Morgan patted his brother's arm. "Intent is not the same as result, though. I was imprudent, as I often am. It resulted in harm to a friend. That is the end of the conversation. Now let's ride down. It's time to settle this."

He could tell Robert had more to say, but Donburrow wedged his mount between them and his gentle hand on Robert's silenced him. He twisted toward Morgan and signed, *"We're with you."*

Morgan carefully signed out, *"Thank you."* Then he rode down the hill in front of the rest.

Gareth was watching him. Morgan had been drunk the last time they met face to face, as he didn't count the attack in the garden. Now he was sober and he could see the lines of emotion on his old friend's face. The pain, the loss, the betrayal. Gareth had been stewing on this, probably since the last duel was thwarted. And suddenly Morgan wasn't so certain he wouldn't fire if the opportunity arose.

Fear gripped him, but he pushed it aside and swung off his mount. One of the three men came forward, sweating and nervous as he extended a hand. "Are you Mr. Banfield?" he asked.

Morgan nodded. "I am."

"Dr. Shirley," the man said. "And now I shall go over to this lovely stream and see if I can spot some fish. You'll fetch me if I'm needed." He inclined his head to the dukes in attendance and hustled off, leather medical bag in shaking hand.

Brighthollow and Donburrow stepped away, as well, and Robert turned toward Morgan. "I wish I could talk you out of this. The brother in me wants to save you again. To stop you like I did before. But...I am proud of who you are, Morgan. Of the responsibility you're trying to take."

"Thank you," Morgan whispered.

His brother's breath was shaky as he left Morgan and headed for the middle of the field. Gareth's second joined him there, and the two men talked. Morgan didn't recognize the second. It might have been a new friend. He hoped it was. It seemed that Gareth needed that.

After a few moments, Robert returned and his mouth was grim. "The second, a man named Barton, says he isn't certain Covington will hear your apology, but he is relaying the message regardless."

Morgan pursed his lips. He'd been so sure he understood the situation. So perfectly certain of himself. And that was the problem, wasn't it? He'd spent his life cocksure and proud, never doubting his ability to seduce or convince or even deceive if it served his purposes.

Now his chickens had come to roost. He couldn't say he didn't deserve them. And whatever would happen next.

Gareth looked across the expanse at him and then headed forward, shoulders back. Morgan's heart leapt, and he glanced briefly at Robert before he moved to join his former friend in the center of the empty space.

As they met, he held out a hand, but Gareth folded his arms and simply glared instead of taking it. "What do you have to say?" he grunted.

Morgan drew a long breath. He'd prepared for this moment. His statement had been crafted to be eloquent, emotional, pleasing. But now that he stared at this man who he'd called friend, as he thought about all he had to lose if he failed today...he threw away the prepared speech.

"Gareth," he said softly. "I know I wronged you."

"Do you now?" Gareth grunted, clearly unmoved by the beginning.

"I do," he said. "And not just by bedding Violet, but by refusing to take any responsibility for the pain it caused you. I acted rashly and without thought. You were harmed. Beyond that, you were then denied your chance to settle the harm when my brother bullied his way into our previously scheduled duel."

Gareth nudged his head toward Robert in the distance. "That him?"

Morgan nodded. "It is."

"Seems a decent enough sort, according to my second."

"He's the best of men," Morgan agreed. "Though don't tell him I said so."

He hoped that would encourage his old friend to smile, but Gareth remained tight-jawed and focused.

Morgan cleared his throat. "I didn't understand how you felt back when this terrible mistake was made. I couldn't fathom how, if I didn't know the identity of the woman I bedded, you could be angry at me for taking her. But...but you loved her. You loved her, no matter the circumstances. And I love someone now. If a friend interfered, it wouldn't matter that he did it knowingly or not. I would be...*broken*. I'd be destroyed. But back then, I handled it badly, from beginning to end. And I am truly, deeply...sorry."

Gareth held his gaze a long moment. Morgan held his breath as he waited and hoped that what he said, what he meant, would be accepted. But instead of shaking his hand, Gareth pivoted and returned to his second.

Morgan stared after him, blinking in disbelief. The cold, cruel veil of reality settled over him and suddenly his entire body felt numb. The duel was going to happen. It was real. Gareth was a good shot. If he fired first, he would strike Morgan down for sure.

He staggered back to Robert, who was as pale and shaking as he was. "He didn't accept?" Robert whispered.

"He—he said nothing," Morgan admitted. "You—you should go inspect the pistols."

"Morgan—" Robert said, his voice sharp. "What do you intend to do?"

"Go inspect the pistols," Morgan choked. "Please."

Robert's lips shook, but he didn't refuse and went to Gareth's second to examine the pistols that had been produced from the fine cherrywood box attached to the second's mount.

Robert had asked Morgan what he would do. And he had no idea about the answer. No idea what step to take next. And no idea how to catalogue his life if it only had a few moments remaining in it.

～

Lizzie's knees buckled as she watched Morgan and Gareth Covington speak in the middle of the field below. Up on the hill, she couldn't hear them, but she was an expert in Morgan's body language by now. She could tell he was pouring his heart out.

She couldn't breathe, couldn't think as she waited, frozen in fear, for them to shake hands and end this. But they didn't. After a few moments that lasted a lifetime, Covington turned away and went back to his second, who fetched the pistols.

"No!" she gasped, spinning to face Amelia, Katherine and Charlotte, who had all joined her in this spying expedition. All three were as pale and sick-looking as she was, herself.

"They're getting the guns," Lizzie choked. "They're going to fire. I must...I must go down. I must stop them."

She pivoted to run down the hill, but Amelia lunged for one arm and Katherine caught the other. As she struggled against them, Charlotte swept around and cupped Lizzie's cheeks gently. "You mustn't."

"Stop!" Lizzie sobbed. "Let me go!"

Charlotte's eyes were full of tears. "I can't imagine what you are feeling, but you mustn't, love. I'm so sorry. You would never make it in time and even if you did, you could be the one who ended up shot and that would solve nothing."

Lizzie collapsed to her knees, and Charlotte and the others joined her there. Their arms around her in a circle of love as they all stared at the drama playing out below.

"They could still fire their pistols in the air," Amelia assured her. "They could still end in honorable acceptance rather than blood."

"If he didn't accept Morgan's apology, why wouldn't he shoot?" she whispered as reality sank in. Someone would die this morning. It could be Morgan. She wouldn't see him again, wouldn't touch him again, wouldn't get to whisper in the dark to him or smell that spot on his neck that made her shiver.

He would be gone, and she would never be the same.

The men put their backs to each other and then began to pace forward. Morgan was coming toward the group on the hill, though she knew he couldn't see them up here, where the steepness masked the top. Probably better, for he would be distracted if he knew she was here in this place he surely didn't want her.

All she could hope was that he would feel her love for him. She stared at him and sent him those loving thoughts with all her might.

They reached ten paces and turned. She watched in what felt like slow motion as Morgan raised his pistol and pointed it to the sky. Of course he would. He wouldn't kill this man. Not even to save himself.

Her gaze shifted to Covington. Unlike Morgan, he had pointed his pistol directly at the chest of the man she loved. She lifted both her hands to her mouth, her breath coming short and hard as tears flowed down her cheeks. And then, just as she thought it was over, just as the world itself seemed to be at the cusp of ending, Covington lifted the muzzle of his gun to the sky and fired his shot above him.

She collapsed against the ground, gripping the long grass with both hands as the duchesses all gasped and cried out with joy. She felt their arms come around her, felt their happy tears merge with her own.

It was over. Or at least this part was. Morgan wouldn't be in danger anymore. He could go on and live his life in whatever way he pleased. She had no idea if he would let that include her, but she did know that she had to try. Because almost losing him today made her fully aware that she never wanted to live another day without him.

And she would just have to be bold enough to pursue that desire, without fear of rejection or consequence. That was what he'd taught her in the past few weeks. That life was worth living. And she was going to live it.

Morgan's hands shook as he headed back to the middle of the field where Covington stood waiting for him. Robert, Brighthollow and Donburrow rushed to join them. The guns were taken, hands were shaken all around and then the rest backed away to leave the two once-friends to have their final talk.

"You...didn't kill me," Morgan said softly.

Covington glanced him up and down, his lips pursed. "I thought about it. The thought of killing you has tormented my mind for a year. But your words today rang in my head when the moment came. They made me see a bit clearer. I know it wasn't just you. Violet was the one who did the most. She knew you were my friend and she pursued you to hurt me."

"I'm sorry." Morgan held out a hand and, after a brief hesitation, Gareth shook it. "Where is she now?"

"Married to some officer," Gareth said with a shake of his head. "Who she cheats on regularly, if rumor is true. Perhaps she did me a favor, in the end. What about you? This woman you spoke of, do you have a future?"

Morgan glanced toward Brighthollow. He was talking to the doctor, a grim frown on his face. The duke wouldn't sack him, not for this. But he still knew that Hugh expected more for Lizzie. Wanted more.

But did that matter? Would it keep him from her? Could he somehow earn the pleasure of her hand and her life and her love?

"I don't know," he admitted. "I suppose I ought to find out."

"If you don't, you're a coward," Gareth said. "Goodbye, Banfield."

Morgan drew his attention back to his former friend. Their feud was over, it seemed. But the friendship was gone too, proof that sometimes the past couldn't be overcome.

"Goodbye, Gareth. Good luck."

Gareth grunted and turned away, motioning to his second and the doctor. As they rode off, each of the dukes moved to Morgan, shaking his hand in turn. The last was Robert.

Morgan extended a hand to him, but Robert surprised him by yanking him into a hug. As his brother pounded his back, he whispered, "Never scare me like that again. I don't want a world where you aren't there to pester me."

He pulled away and Morgan smiled. "I'll do my best. Now let's ride back, shall we?"

"Yes," Donburrow signed. *"The ladies will be worried."*

Morgan translated for the others and they all agreed. They

217

swung up on their mounts and rode back toward the house. And Morgan knew he was riding into a different kind of confrontation than the one he'd just left.

He was riding not to his death, but to his future. And it was currently cloudy as could be.

CHAPTER 21

Morgan swung off his horse and handed the reins to the waiting footman.

"Glad to have you back, Mr. Banfield," the young man said before he ducked away.

"Thank you," Morgan said. He was surprised to find each servant he passed nodding in greeting, their relief palpable. It was an odd thing. He'd come here to appease his brother. To find some way to stay out of trouble for a while.

But he'd found...a place here. A position he was good at. A woman he loved. He'd found home. This place was home, and his heart swelled as he entered the foyer and found the women gathered in a semi-circle waiting for him.

Katherine rushed forward first, bussing his cheek. The rest followed, but all Morgan could do was look at Elizabeth. She was pale as paper, her eyes red with tears as she approached him. Her hands shook as she reached out and took both of his.

"I-I'm glad you're here," she whispered, and then cast a quick glance at her brother.

Brighthollow stepped forward and she pulled away, ducking her head as color filled her cheeks. "It's been a trying morning for us

JESS MICHAELS

all," he announced. "Why don't we let Morgan have a moment and all gather ourselves? We can meet in the breakfast room in half an hour."

That seemed to please the group. They parted in couples, and Elizabeth was drawn along by her brother as he spoke quietly to her. Morgan shook his head as he followed them all up the stairs. They needed to talk. That much was clear. But it wasn't going to happen right now in the midst of the uproar the duel had created. His heart ached as he turned toward the stairs to the third floor and left the others to go to the guest and family quarters. He wanted so much to speak to her now.

He entered his bedroom and moved to the basin across the room. He was about to splash water on his face when the door behind him opened. He turned to find Elizabeth there, and the world stopped turning immediately.

"Morgan," she said. Then she was racing across the room to him.

His arms came around her and he held her as tightly as he could, feeling her tremble and quake as her tears fell and joined with his own, which were suddenly streaming down his face.

"I'm sorry," he whispered. "I'm sorry I caused you even a moment of fear."

She lifted her face to his and drew him down. His mouth found hers and he kissed her, murmuring her name against her lips. She lifted against him, clinging to him as his hand came into her hair and he angled her head for better access.

He had words to say. Confessions to make if he was brave enough to make them. But right now all he could do was cradle her against his body and try to forget that there was a moment when he'd known he'd die without ever doing this again. And he'd mourned the loss of something he never should have taken in the first place.

Something that ought not be his, and yet here she was, sliding her hands beneath his jacket, unfastening this buttons to push the heavier fabric away. Her fingers bunched on his waistcoat and she deepened the kiss.

God, how he wanted her. He'd wanted her last night because it might be the last time. And today he wanted her because it wasn't. There was hope now, dangerous, daring hope that he feared and embraced all at once. As precious to him as the woman who had sparked it.

He drew away and stared down at her. Drinking in her beauty, her sweetness, her charm. Drinking in all she was and all she meant to him. He traced the track of one tear with his thumb and then took her mouth again as his hands came around to the back of her dress.

He was ready to unfasten her. To just have this moment before he decided how to proceed. But he hadn't loosened but one button when the door to his room opened a second time.

And the Duke of Brighthollow entered, head down as he said, "Sorry to disturb, Banfield, but I was wondering if you might want more time to—"

He cut himself off as he looked up and found Elizabeth not only in Morgan's room with the door shut, but with Morgan's jacket in a pile at their feet and the back of her dress gaping slightly. She pivoted with a gasp, but she didn't step away. Of course she didn't.

She threw her arms back as if to shield Morgan. And it was a good instinct, because Brighthollow charged forward a long step.

"What the hell do you think you're doing?" he shouted. Loud enough that it felt like he could bring the house down around them.

"Stop!" she called out, reaching a hand toward her brother either in entreaty or to ward him off. Perhaps both. "Hugh, look at me. Look at me."

Brighthollow's dark gaze flashed down at her and she flinched when she got what she required. "Lizzie," he said, a warning, a disappointment, a shocked admonishment. And Morgan saw how it buckled her a little.

The shouting, though, had brought the others. Robert appeared first in the door to the narrow chamber and his mouth dropped open. "Christ, Morgan," he muttered as he edged his way in. Katherine and Amelia followed, while the Duke and Duchess of Donburrow stayed in the doorway, exchanging a look that said a million words.

"Oh God," Lizzie moaned, and reached up behind her, trying to button her gown. She kept missing the buttonhole, her hands were shaking so much, and at last Morgan stepped forward and fastened it quickly.

"Take your damned hands off of her," Brighthollow growled as he held out a hand to her. "Lizzie, come here."

There was a moment when Morgan thought Elizabeth might obey. This man had raised her, after all. He loved her. She loved and adored him in return and never wanted to disappoint him.

But then she straightened her spine, pushed her shoulders back and shook her head. "No."

Brighthollow blinked at her. "No? Lizzie, you must be in jest. I know today was trying. The past few days have been difficult, and it is easy to be confused—"

"I'm not confused," Lizzie whispered. "I know what I want. And who." She looked back over her shoulder and her eyes found his. "I know exactly who I want."

Morgan's heart leapt in that moment. Because he hadn't imagined these feelings. She did share them. This wasn't mere passion gone mad or a mistake she would regret. She cared for him, as he cared for her.

Only he still feared if this was the right choice. Love could fade over time, after all. Leaving regret in its wake. He'd seen it before. He didn't want to cause it or feel the sting of it.

He had to be sure she was sure.

"Elizabeth," he said, taking her hand. "That you...want this, want me, means everything. But your brother's concerns are valid, you must know that in your heart. He wants to protect you."

"Protect me from you?" she said.

"Yes," Brighthollow said through clenched teeth. "You must see why I'd be concerned. Banfield's history, his reputation—"

"Watch yourself," Robert growled.

The two men were distracted by each other, and the others in the room all began talking at once as they faced each other.

But Morgan ignored them. Their interference actually gave him the privacy he'd been seeking, at least for a moment. "He's not wrong. I am not worthy, Elizabeth," he insisted. "I just fought a bloody duel, for God's sake, over my wicked behavior."

"I know! I watched you," she cried out.

Everyone in the room stopped, and suddenly all the eyes shifted back to Elizabeth. Morgan saw the discomfort that caused her—he knew how she hated it. But she lifted her chin, her lower lip trembling with indignant anger and passion.

"What are you talking about?" he asked, his voice barely carrying.

She folded her arms. "I followed you," she whispered. "We all did."

"Amelia," Brighthollow said with a shake of his head as he glared at his wife.

The Duchess of Brighthollow arched a brow. "Don't *Amelia* me, my love. I wasn't about to let you all go dueling like children fighting over a toy and not keep an eye on you. Now hush. Lizzie has something to say and you *will* listen."

Brighthollow huffed out a breath, but to Morgan's surprise, he didn't interrupt again.

Lizzie was shaking from head to toe, her gaze never leaving Morgan's. "I stood on a hill and watched you, knowing that if you were wrong about your friend, that I would never get to tell you that I...I love you."

A ripple moved through the room and Morgan felt it zip up his spine. Love. Loved *him*.

"And when it turned out you were all right, that you would live..." She caught her breath on a shaky gasp. "I knew that I couldn't let another day, another hour, another moment go by without telling you how I felt. I wanted to do it privately, but now I have to do it in front of my friends and my family while you and my brother argue over how little you are worth compared to me."

"It's not an argument," Morgan said, casting a quick glance toward Brighthollow. "You are worth far more than I am."

"That is bollocks!" she all but shouted, clenching her fists at her sides. When the room gasped in surprise at her language, she glared around at them. "It is. I am not a princess in a tower."

"You should be protected like a princess," Brighthollow said, but he no longer sounded so certain. "Taken care of and—"

"Can you not see how you diminish me, both of you, by seeing me this way?" she asked.

Morgan drew back, shaking his head. "Diminish?"

"Yes." She bent her head and her breath exhaled shakily. "I am *not* a princess. I am *not* an icon. I am *not* a delicate flower. I am a woman, with a woman's heart. No different than Charlotte or Katherine or Amelia. I have desires."

Brighthollow turned his face, his cheeks red, but he didn't interrupt her again. Morgan didn't either. No matter what he wanted to say, how he wanted to react, he folded his arms and forced himself not to.

She was owed it.

"I have made mistakes," she continued. "Everyone knows what they were. I own those mistakes. They were never anyone else's. And I have walked a road that led me here. I say again that I know what I want: you, Morgan Banfield. I want..." Her face brightened, as if saying these things had freed her. "I want you."

L izzie felt a weight come off her chest even though nothing had been resolved. Even though she had to share this moment with a roomful of people, including her angry brother who still looked as though he could kill.

Even though Morgan was just standing there, staring at her, as if he had been caught in a trap and now had no idea how to escape or what to do.

"Please say something," she said softly.

Before he could, Hugh stepped forward. "Lizzie, emotions are running high. And you and Mr. Banfield have become close thanks to the garden. I can see how you might mistake your feelings."

"My feelings are not mistaken," she said with a glare for him. "I'm not a child, Hugh. Not anymore. This isn't like the last time."

"It feels the same," Hugh retorted.

That brought Roseford forward, his hands gripped at his sides. "I would request you do not compare my brother to a man who used your sister ill and then nearly killed your wife."

Hugh glared at Roseford, and it looked for a moment that they, too, might come to blows. But before they could, the Duke of Donburrow stepped into the room and put a hand on each man's chest. He shook his head slowly, sliding his glance back and forth.

"Well said, my dear," Charlotte said as she entered the room. "Forgive me, but you two are being idiots."

"I agree," Katherine chimed in. "This is between Lizzie and Morgan. It doesn't involve any of us."

"Doesn't involve us?" Hugh sputtered. "She is my sister and this is—"

"The man she loves," Amelia interrupted with a quick, kind and supportive glance toward Lizzie. She took Hugh's hand. "I know you're protective. I love that you are. But in this, you are being heavy-handed."

"I...am not," Hugh muttered, but he no longer sounded so certain. Lizzie saw her opening.

She swallowed hard. "You are," she whispered. "With Morgan I am...I am happy. I'm free. I'm not afraid. When he enters a room, there's...sunshine for me. I would hope that is what you'd want for me. Nothing less than the feelings you've found for yourself."

"Of course," Hugh admitted. He glared at Morgan again. "But what does he think? He has not declared his feelings, despite you spilling out your own in this public manner."

"Public because you made it so," Morgan said softly.

Hugh's jaw set, but he didn't retort.

Lizzie turned toward Morgan. "Then pretend it is just you and me. Like it should be. I have told you I love you, Morgan. If you don't love me in return, then please just tell me quickly. I can't..." She dropped her chin. "I can suffer the truth, but not this uncertainty."

Morgan slid a finger beneath her chin and lifted her gaze to his again. "I've spent a lifetime pretending so that I didn't have to feel what was in my heart. Whether that was fear or sorrow or love, I didn't want any of it. It was dangerous. But since I met you, Elizabeth, I can't pretend anymore. You strip away my masks, you challenge me to be brave without them. You make me want to be better."

Her breath caught as he stepped closer. He didn't seem to care that they were surrounded, that her watchful brother still stood close enough that he might punch Morgan in the face for making the wrong move.

"I do love you, Elizabeth. And I still fear I don't deserve the beautiful heart you have offered, but I can't deny that it's all I want. All I need. That I would sacrifice all I am and all I ever could be in order to never walk away from you again."

Her knees shook at his admission, finally made. It felt like it was just the two of them. And she smiled up at him as the world felt like it got warmer and happier and easier because he was with her.

She lifted on her tiptoes and then she kissed him. And it was only when she heard Charlotte behind them say, "Brava, Lizzie" that she even recalled anyone else was there.

She blushed as she caught Morgan's hand in both of hers and then turned back. They stood together, two against the world if need be, and she looked at Hugh. He was staring at them, his expression unreadable.

"Please don't make me choose between my brother and my heart," she whispered. "If you send him away, I will follow, no matter what happens next."

Ewan signed a few things, and Charlotte smiled. "He says that if Hugh cannot abide your decision, he would hire Morgan for his own man of affairs and settle you both with a lovely home on our estate."

Lizzie nodded in thanks at the kindness, but she didn't want that. She wanted her brother to accept this. And when Hugh let out his breath in a long sigh, it was as if the world came to half time as she waited.

"You cannot steal my man of affairs, Donburrow," he said at last. "So you should not try."

She smiled as Hugh smiled, relief pulsing through her. He stepped forward and kissed her forehead. Then he shook Morgan's hand.

"You'll endeavor to deserve her," Hugh said softly, a statement not a question.

Morgan nodded. "Every day if she'll allow it. And I realize that everyone wants to hug us and congratulate us and celebrate this outrageous and wonderful day. But I have not yet gotten to ask the lady a question. And I think *it* must be asked in private." Lizzie lifted her face to his, tears filling her happy eyes. He smiled back at her. "May I take you to the garden?"

She nodded, not waiting for anyone else to answer. He took her hand and led her through the crowd of their friends, their family and down the long hallway to the stairs.

Lizzie heard Amelia say to Hugh, "Come, you'll help me tell the servants to prepare a breakfast to celebrate that he didn't die, and for their engagement. And you'll stop frowning, because you know you're happy if she is happy."

She didn't have to hear the rest, all that mattered was the man at her side as he took her through the house and out to the terrace. They followed the path they'd taken a hundred times since his arrival, weaving through this beautiful sanctuary they had created together, and at last they came to the corner where they'd first met to discuss the garden what felt like a lifetime ago.

Persephone stood in her place, her gaze knowing and flirtatious, and at last Lizzie understood it in a way she hadn't ever before. Morgan led her to the bench there in front of the statue and took both her hands. She stared into his face, loving that it would be the face she looked into for the rest of her days. The face that would look upon their children, that would see her age, that would meet her eyes as they shared their twilight years.

"I'm sorry that situation deteriorated so terribly," Morgan said as he swept a lock of hair from her cheek.

She smiled. "I don't think it would be us if there weren't some kind of chaos involved."

"I suppose not," he said, but his tone was troubled. "I brought that into your life, I fear. The chaos."

"No, you didn't," she whispered. "I've felt uncertain and out of sorts and unclear about my life and my future for years. *That* was chaos. You were…a north star. You always will be."

He did chuckle then. "Funny, for I feel the same way about you. Elizabeth, today at the duel, all I could think about was how I might not see you again. And how I would regret that I told you I wanted you, that I showed you that. But that I was too cowardly to tell you that I love you."

He had said it before, but she loved hearing it again. Loved knowing that it was true, that he was true. And hers. Always hers now.

"But you are here, and you have told me."

"I have. Your brother says he'll allow me to stay on, probably because he doesn't want to lose you. But I can't promise it will be an easy life. I have very little to offer."

"Except your strength," she said, touching his cheek. "And your faith in me that no one else has ever truly had. And your love."

"Those are all yours," he promised. "If you take me as your husband, you will have them and anything else I can give to you to ensure your happiness for the rest of my days."

He dropped from the bench to one knee. She was weeping as he did so, though she didn't recall the moment she had begun to cry. Happy tears. The happiest she had ever wept. He wiped them away before he took her hand.

"*Lady* Elizabeth Margolis, will you do me the great honor of being my wife?"

She cupped his cheeks, laughing and crying at once as she kissed him. "Yes," she murmured against his mouth. "Yes, yes, yes, yes..."

She continued to whisper that word as she kissed him. Continued to whisper it as she held him close to her. And she knew it would be what she said to him every day, every night, for the rest of her life.

EPILOGUE

A few weeks later

The party to celebrate of the sudden elopement of Morgan and Elizabeth Banfield was held in London immediately upon the return of the entire family and their friends. Elizabeth had invited only her closest friends, as well as the dukes who had formed Morgan's brother's friend circle. He liked the men, despite his once jealous feelings toward them. They were a good lot.

And they all adored his wife, those dukes and duchesses. Which made Morgan all the more disposed to appreciating them. He stood back from the crowd, watching as Elizabeth danced with the Duke of Kingsacre. She glanced at Morgan from time to time, blushing and smiling any time she caught his eye.

And the love he felt for her swelled with each passing moment.

"Dear God, you truly are smitten."

He turned to find his sister, Selina, coming toward him, a glass of wine perched in her hand. She stepped up and followed his gaze a moment. "Does she truly make you happy, my once-wild brother?"

"She does," he said without hesitation. "My wild days are over."

"Drat and damn," Selina sighed. "I shall have to find trouble all by myself now." She smiled at him. "Though I suppose it is worth it to see you smile like that. Many felicitations."

"Thank you."

"I like her," Selina continued. "I was nervous she would be stand-offish since I am only your half-blood. But she is very kind."

"She is," he said. "No one has ever been kinder."

Selina made a face, but quickly smiled. "And have you taken her to meet Nicholas yet?"

"No," Morgan said with a slight frown. "I know he is still recovering or I would have invited him tonight. I'll take her soon. I know she'd like him. They're both of a studious bent."

His sister bussed his cheek as the song ended, and Elizabeth left the floor with her partner and then started Morgan's way. "We'll talk soon. I can see you wish to be alone with your wife."

Morgan said thank you. Or he thought he did. It was hard to focus when his wife stopped in front of him and slipped her arm through his.

"Your sister is very nice," Elizabeth said as she squeezed his bicep. "I can't wait to know her better."

"Yes. Very much."

She laughed. "Are you even attending? I wonder at that response to what I said."

"I'm not," he admitted. "I'm standing here staring at my wife and wondering how long I must wait to take her upstairs and prove how much I love her."

Elizabeth's expression shifted. The light of wanting entered her eyes. And then she glanced at the door. "We could creep away now."

He grinned at her ardor. He loved her for that and so much more. "Then lead the way, fair lady. For the rest of my life."

THE END

AUTHOR NOTE

I hope you enjoyed the first book in The Duke's By-Blows series! If you want to know more about the dukes and duchesses featured in this story, check out their books in the 1797 Club series!

And now, turn the page for an excerpt from the second in The Duke's By-Blows, The Heart of a Hellion (Selina's book).

THE DUKE'S BY-BLOWS

ENJOY AND EXCERPT OF BOOK 2, THE HEART OF A
HELLION

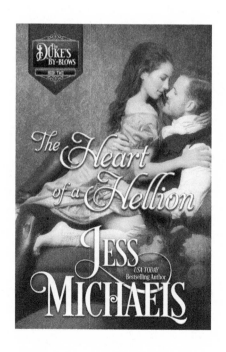

EXCERPT OF THE HEART OF A HELLION

THE DUKE'S BY-BLOWS BOOK 2

D errick stood in the middle of the Duke of Roseford's vast library, looking up around him at the beautiful bookcases that vaulted high into the room above his head. Hundreds of books, all waiting to be read.

He'd always appreciated a library. When he was taken to visit his grandfather as a lad, he'd loved nothing more than to go to his library. First to escape, for there had always been yelling during those visits. But escape had turned to pleasure as he lost himself in stories and history and learning.

Now he rested his fingers against the woven spines of the books, dragging the tips across their uneven rows and breathing in the scent of pages and words and adventures yet to be had. Before he could choose one of these future friends to pluck from the shelf, he felt a fissure of awareness up his spine. He was being watched.

He turned, guarded but trying to keep that from being obvious before he knew who was staring at his back. When he turned his heart thudded.

Selina Oliver was standing in the doorway. She wore a red dress with a deep v-neckline, one that only skirted the limits of modesty because of a silk rose that rested between what appeared to be lovely breasts. Her hair had been curled and piled artfully on the crown of her head, with a silk ribbon laced within that matched the scarlet gown to perfection.

She was stunning, just as she had been on the drive. With her bright blue eyes that flitted over him and dusky pink lips curled into a cocksure smile, the kind most women were forced by Society to hide.

But this woman hid nothing. And that artless seduction in her every look and move woke something...dark in him. Stirred his interest and his cock in equal measure.

"Mr. Huntington," she said, her rough, breathless voice breaking the silence that had stretched between them since he saw her in the doorway.

"Miss Oliver," he managed to choke out. His throat was suddenly very dry. "I have your brother's permission to explore the library."

Her brow wrinkled and then her smile widened. "Why wouldn't you? You're a guest, after all."

He frowned. He'd been so stymied by her appearance he'd almost forgotten his role of invited guest and friend, rather than outsider. Strange that she could so easily sweep his duties out of the way. Dangerous.

"Of course. I suppose I'm just not accustomed to roaming freely through a duke's home," he said. "Friend of his brother or not."

Her stare wavered at that and she stepped into the room. Now that they were closer, he could scent the faint hint of vanilla from her hair. He suddenly wanted to pull that ribbon from her locks and let the cascade of her sleek, dark hair fall around her like a waterfall.

What the hell was wrong with him? This was a distraction he could not afford. And if she knew his thoughts, she surely wouldn't welcome them, knowing smile or not.

"Are you a great reader, Mr. Huntington?" she asked, gliding past him close enough that the air between them stirred with warmth.

He cleared his throat and resisted the urge to loosen his

suddenly tight cravat. "I don't know if I would say a great reader, but a passionate one."

She pivoted at that word. "A passionate reader. Is reading the passion in itself, or do you specifically seek out passionate subjects?"

He shifted. "Perhaps both, depending on the mood."

A smile twitched at the corners of her lips again. "Hmmm, yes, a great deal depends on the mood."

She held his gaze a moment and then pivoted away again. She lifted up on her tiptoes to see a shelf just above her sightline and her dress shifted against her backside. A very shapely backside at that.

He glanced at the fire. Why was it so blasted hot in here? That could not be good for the books. It certainly wasn't good for his constitution.

"And what about you?" he asked, hearing how low and rough his voice was in the quiet of the room.

She shrugged one shoulder. "Reading is a favorite pastime for me, as well. Perhaps that means we'll encounter each other here often during the party. We can...compare books."

He drew in a long breath and tried to find a modicum of decorum and calm in the face of the hurricane that was this woman. He was an investigator, sent here to do just that. He couldn't forget it just because a wildly attractive woman batted her exquisitely long eyelashes at him and gave him a come-hither look.

So what could he deduce about Selina Oliver? Beyond her beauty, beyond her intoxicating charm. She was bold, that was one thing. Brash, he supposed some would say and they wouldn't be wrong. It was a playful boldness, at least on its surface. But as he gazed deeper into those lovely eyes, he also saw something...else. Something deeper and more purposeful.

As if this dance she was dancing had meaning beyond flirtation. And suddenly his interest became not just about her scent or the warmth of her or the directness of her attraction, but about what it was exactly she was trying to achieve by approaching him.

He thought of the disappearing blue gown earlier in the parlor.

Hers, he was more and more certain. And that made him wonder about those motives all the more.

He cleared his throat and straightened up. "Any time you'd like to compare books, Miss Oliver, I am at your service."

She arched a brow. "Then I look forward to it."

ALSO BY JESS MICHAELS

~

The Duke's By-Blows

The Love of a Libertine

The Heart of a Hellion

The Matter of a Marquess

The Shelley Sisters

A Reluctant Bride

A Reckless Runaway

A Counterfeit Courtesan

The Scandal Sheet

The Return of Lady Jane

Stealing the Duke

Lady No Says Yes

My Fair Viscount

Guarding the Countess

The House of Pleasure

The 1797 Club

The Daring Duke

Her Favorite Duke

The Broken Duke

The Silent Duke

The Duke of Nothing

The Undercover Duke

The Duke of Hearts

The Duke Who Lied

The Duke of Desire

The Last Duke

Seasons

An Affair in Winter

A Spring Deception

One Summer of Surrender

Adored in Autumn

The Wicked Woodleys

Forbidden

Deceived

Tempted

Ruined

Seduced

Fascinated

The Notorious Flynns

The Other Duke

The Scoundrel's Lover

The Widow Wager

No Gentleman for Georgina

A Marquis for Mary

To see a complete listing of Jess Michaels' titles, please visit:

http://www.authorjessmichaels.com/books

ABOUT THE AUTHOR

USA Today Bestselling author Jess Michaels likes geeky stuff, Vanilla Coke Zero, anything coconut, cheese, fluffy cats, smooth cats, any cats, many dogs and people who care about the welfare of their fellow humans. She is lucky enough to be married to her favorite person in the world and lives in the heart of Dallas, TX where she's trying to eat all the amazing food in the city.

When she's not obsessively checking her steps on Fitbit or trying out new flavors of Greek yogurt, she writes historical romances with smoking hot alpha males and sassy ladies who do anything but wait to get what they want. She has written for numerous publishers and is now fully indie and loving every moment of it (well, almost every moment).

Jess loves to hear from fans! So please feel free to contact her in any of the following ways (or carrier pigeon):

www.AuthorJessMichaels.com
Email: Jess@AuthorJessMichaels.com

Jess Michaels raffles a gift certificate EVERY month to members of her newsletter, so sign up on her website:
http://www.AuthorJessMichaels.com/

facebook.com/JessMichaelsBks
twitter.com/JessMichaelsBks
instagram.com/JessMichaelsBks
bookbub.com/authors/jess-michaels

Made in the USA
Coppell, TX
23 January 2021